A PARROT IN THE C

MURDER PICKS A ROSE

BOOK ONE

SANDRA K. SULLIVAN

Ramirez & Clark
PUBLISHERS

Murder Picks a Rose
Copyright © Sandra K Sullivan

Ramirez and Clark Publishers LLC
PO BOX 551420
Jacksonville, FL 32255
904.945.6202

ISBN: 978-1-955171-39-7 (ebook)
ISBN: 978-1-955171-40-3 (paperback)

Cover design by PhillipsCovers.com
Edited by Kirk Colvin

DEDICATION

To Rose lovers and Parrot lovers everywhere.

1

Veronica sat on the antique porch swing, sipped her coffee, and gazed out over the acres of gardens where roses reigned supreme, but her thoughts distracted her from the beauty that was before her. Even her recent accomplishment of earning her degrees in both horticulture and business administration from UC Davis, was pushed into a shadowed corner of her mind.

While her dream of being able to take over care of Serenity Valley Gardens and the business of breeding and selling her grandfather's roses could now be realized someday, she couldn't pull her thoughts away from the conversation she'd had with her seven-year-old son, Salvador, as she took him to his homeschool program earlier that morning.

He was quieter than usual. Veronica had glanced behind the passenger seat where he was buckled into his booster seat and asked, "Are you okay, *Mijo?*"

"That girl came into my room again last night." Salvador's quiet voice had a slight whine to it.

"What girl? And what do you mean again?" Veronica had a feeling she knew where the conversation was going.

"The girl who used to live in the house a long time ago. She said her name was Maggie."

"You've seen her before? How come you haven't told me?" *A long time ago. How long ago? Maggie … Could that have been Margaret Mason? She died over a hundred years ago.*

"She always says not to tell anyone."

"How long have you been seeing her, and what happened last night that you want to tell me?"

"She said something bad is going to happen, Mom."

Veronica pulled over to the side of the road so she could turn around and talk to her son more directly. "Did you tell you what the bad thing was?"

"No, she just said something bad."

Veronica reached back to hold his hand. "I'm sorry if she scared you, *Mijo*. I'll ask Papa Al about her. I'm sure he knows who she is. Are you going to be okay to go to school?"

"*Si Mama.*"

Even after dropping Salvador off at school and returning home, Veronica couldn't let go of the image of her son gazing at her with tears in his eyes.

The door of the grand front entrance opened, pulling Veronica back into the present.

Her same age cousin, Lee Mason, came out and sat down beside her. "Are you okay? Gramps asked where you were, on his way out to the greenhouse." Lee, a typical Mason was tall and blond, with striking green eyes. When he wasn't pounding nails or wielding a variety of power tools, while assisting in the restoration of the Historic Mason House, he was at the gym lifting weights.

As cousins they both had the slender Mason build, but they were very different in appearance. Veronica carried her beauty in a mix of her Latino father and her mother's Irish heritage. She had her father's skin tone and jet-black hair, and her mother's heart shaped face with soft brown eyes.

"I'm fine. I just needed some "me" time," said Veronica.

"Girl, as hard as you work, you should take all the "me" time you need."

Veronica gave her cousin a lopsided smile. "There aren't enough hours in the day. So, what are you up to today?"

"Tyler and I are going to finish setting the tile in the basement bathroom, then we're going to install the water heater.

If we have time, we're going to hang the wallpaper you picked out for the lounge."

"The work you two have been doing is so awesome. I'd better go help Papa Al."

They both stood to go back inside. Lee stepped past her and held the door open for her.

On her way through the kitchen to go out into the backyard, to get to the greenhouse, there was a sharp knock from inside the narrow closet next to the refrigerator. A loud voice called out, "Hello."

Veronica made a detour to the closet, returned the tap on the door with her fingernail and offered her own greeting, "Hello?"

The closet door opened a crack. A large, ivory colored hook beak appeared. A round yellow eye with a large black pupil looked up at her. The following request was clearly spoken. "Cracker?"

Veronica opened the door the rest of the way and reached out with her hand. "Up, up. What are you doing back in your closet, Bee Bop?"

The brilliant rainbow of scarlet, green, and blue of a large Greenwing macaw stepped up onto her hand and said, "Give me kiss."

Veronica raised Bee Bop to face level and kissed her beak. Bee Bop responded with a touch of her tongue to Veronica's nose, made loud kissing sounds, then said, "Cracker," again.

Concerned about why the Bee Bop was back in her closet, she set the macaw in her cage through the open door and offered her a whole walnut which the bird would open as easily as a person can open a peanut. "What's wrong, Pretty Girl? Why are you back in your closet with the door shut? Did Maggie come visit you too?"

2

In the expansive greenhouse that was the heart of Albert Mason's rose breeding business, Veronica found her grandfather leaning over the table checking each of the rose stems, stuck into pots, from that winter's pruning in hopes that with proper care and God's will, they would grow roots and become beautiful rose bushes. Veronica carefully stepped around Brandy, her grandfather's golden retriever laying of the rubberized paving bricks next to him. She stood next to her Papa Al without touching him. "How can I help you, Papa?"

Albert looked at Veronica from under his bushy eyebrows and nodded toward the potting bench where a bottle of special root growth enhancing fertilizer sat next to a watering can. Over the past ten years, from the time she was thirteen, she and her grandfather had developed a language of unspoken communication.

When she was young, she hadn't understood her mother and uncle's comments about her grandfather's lack of social skills, she only knew he was more comfortable not talking to people unless it was about his roses or his work in genetics.

Disregarding his hesitancy for spoken communication, Veronica felt a gratitude toward her grandfather that she wanted to repay so deeply it was often on her mind. In addition to being her mentor and encouraging her love of gardening, he'd offered her a home and a place to raise her son when her mother kicked her out of the house because she'd gotten pregnant at the age of sixteen. The gift she didn't know if she'd ever be able to requite, was that he'd paid for her entire college education.

At the work bench, she mixed the proper amount of fertilizer with water. She held out the watering can to him and asked, "Papa, do you know of the girl, Maggie, is who used to live here a long time ago?"

"Hmm. That would be Margaret Mason." Albert took the watering can and began pouring a small amount into each pot. "She died shortly after she came out west with her mother and brother Elijah, once their father finished building the Mason House. She's buried up on the hill in the family plot with the rest of the Masons, except Eli, my great grandfather. He lived here and ran the inn until he disappeared, or so the story goes. From what I've read about our family history, Maggie was the first Mason buried there. A cute little thing."

"You've seen her?"

"Mmm. She's one of our regular apparitions, along with old Eli. She used to follow me around when I was younger. Did you see her?"

"No. On the way to school this morning, Sal told me he talked to a girl named Maggie last night and that he's seen her before."

"Sal's a very sensitive kid. With his ability to talk to animals, I'm not surprised he's able to see apparitions, as well as talk to them. Maggie's never caused any trouble. She's just a visitor."

With Brandy at his side, Albert unlocked the security door to the small greenhouse within the larger greenhouse. His focus seemed to go inward for a moment, before he said, "Let's check the blues. They're all in bud."

Because seeing ghosts wasn't an unusual occurrence at the historic Mason House, Veronica was able to focus her attention on the roses. "When do you think we'll see color, Papa?"

Albert ran a finger along several of the buds. "We should see color in the next few days. The first blooms always seem to take longer for the engineered roses. With the amount of rain we've been getting and as cloudy as it's been, the bloom cycle for all the roses have slowed."

"Should we put them under lights? Sort of give them a little boost?"

"No, the sun's out today. Natural sunlight is always best."

"But another storm is predicted to come in this evening."

"That's part of nature, Sprout. We just need to be patient." He had called her Sprout from the time she was six and showed an intense interest in his roses. "We need to let things unfold as they are meant to happen. It's supposed to be a short storm, so the university should have nice weather for their picnic day tomorrow. You and Sal will have fun.

"When we're finished here, I want to mark which plants are ready to go out to the sales yard for the Garden's opening day."

"We have a lot of roses ready for sale this year," said Veronica. She looked out across the tops of the two-year-old cuttings, all of them in bud. "I can't believe how many of the cuttings grew last year. We only lost like, three percent. With what doesn't sell this year, we'll have twice as many roses ready for sale next year."

"I think we have to thank your studies for our success." Albert put his hand on her shoulder in a rare display of affection. "I'm proud of you, Sprout. The Gardens will be in good hands when I'm gone."

A pang of anxiety hit Veronica so hard she felt as if someone slapped her. "Is everything alright, Papa?"

3

"Everything is just as it's supposed to be." He motioned toward the small rose. "Just like my success in creating a blue rose."

Veronica crowded next to him, eager to check for color. To her disappointment, all the buds were still closed tight. She noticed a very slight mar on one of the buds. "What happened here?"

"Mmm, good eye, Sprout. I feel like a kid at Christmas, peeking at presents. I had to check, so I took a small tissue sample."

Veronica whirled around to face her grandfather. She didn't try to contain her excitement. "Could you tell?"

"The DNA for blue was there." Albert pursed his lips for a moment. His eyes brightened. "I think I did it this time, Sprout. I think I've got the world's first true, blue rose. Do you know what that means?"

"It means your dream has come true." Veronica gasped a breath. "It also means you'll be rich and famous."

"Probably. But the downside is that we'll have to be very, very careful until it sells."

"Are you going to name it and apply for a patent before you sell it?"

"Yes. I decided to name it Blue Moon. As my grandfather used to say, "Something this special only happens once in a Blue Moon." I've already started the patent paperwork, but we need a photo of the bloom to finish the application. The patent will make it all the more valuable."

"Have you thought about who you're going to sell it to?"

"I already contacted my friends at Weeks, Jackson and Perkins, Lighthouse Roses, and Meilland Roses in France, to let them know what I think I have. The word is getting out because I've gotten calls from other growers, from all around the world, wanting to see it. You and I will need to discuss how to handle private showings. I don't want sales reps here going after each other or us, so I'm going to hire security for the viewing and sale, and until that plant is safely on its way with whoever buys it."

"As in security guards?" Veronica's back tightened at the thought that they may be in danger. "Why?"

"With something like a true, blue rose, you never know what people will do. In my experience it's best to be prepared."

"Have you been in danger before, Papa? Because of the work you did or a plant you created?"

Albert looked away for a moment, then nodded his head. "Yes, there have been a few times my team and I have been in danger."

"What happened?" Veronica's words squeaked out.

"Working in genetics the way we did, had always been fraught with danger. There was a time in El Salvador when our team was attacked in order to steal the corn seeds we'd created. It was discovered that a rival genetics firm was behind the attempted theft, even though they tried to make the attack look like a drug cartel." Albert took the moisture sensor off the shelf behind him and began checking the water level in the soil of each of the pots.

"There were also three separate times when anti-genetic engineering groups tried to sabotage our lab. Inman Labs had just announced the rice plant I'd developed which was immune to a common fungus that often destroyed entire crops.

"What those groups didn't want to see was that I'd spent years traveling around the world looking for plants that had a natural immunity to the fungus. Once I found that one plant, I isolated the gene that created the immunity, and began adding it to ordinary seeds. While I have created some genetically altered plants, just like I added the gene for the color blue to create a blue rose, I didn't genetically alter anything with the rice, I just added what was already there naturally."

"So the Blue Moon creates a danger just by existing."

"We'll have to prepare for that possibility."

"From what I've read, it seems like just about every genetics company in the world has tried to create a true blue rose, but failed." Veronica caressed a leaf of one of the color engineered roses. "Once the word gets out that the Blue Moon is real, not a photo-shopped fake, it will be like the government offering proof that aliens from outer space are real."

4

Albert chuckled, "Aliens would probably get more attention, but you pretty much nailed it on the head, Sprout."

Veronica pulled her phone out of her pocket when it beeped to alert her that someone was coming down the drive. She gave it a quick glance. "Jessica's here."

"I sure like that girl. That husband of hers, Jesus and his father are good people too." Albert nodded as he put the moisture sensor back on the shelf. "It's a comfort to know the care of the house and Gardens are in such good hands."

"I need to go talk to Arturo and Jesus," said Veronica. "I noticed some gopher mounds. It's time to put out the live traps again."

Papa Al, with Brandy at his side, walked with Veronica to the greenhouse door. "They know where the traps are in the shop, but we might have to buy more bait this year."

"I'll let them know. Thanks, Papa." As Veronica walked through the back yard and around to the front yard, she took a deep breath to counteract her urge to join the roses in holding their breath until every bud broke open in celebration of the world's most beloved flower.

The beautifully landscaped yard with its wide lawn and flowerbeds bursting with new growth and spring colors was the exact antithesis of the inside of the house where everything was threadbare and seemed to hold together only by the grace of God.

Following the path of large, slate steppingstones, bordered by primroses along the edge, backed by miniature roses of all colors, and columbines behind them, she entered the first public garden through the side gate where most of the species or wild roses were, along with many of the old garden or Historic roses and modern English shrub roses. Planted in an informal English garden style, rambler roses of every color formed tall, weeping willow-like shapes where they grew up and over what Veronica called mushroom towers. This garden was dotted with small fountains and an abundance of garden art objects, many of them hand made by local artists.

Derelict furniture, such as wooden chairs with pots nestled in the seat where cushions used to be, and antique farm equipment, had been repurposed as planters and garden art. Miniature roses and annuals such as asters, dianthus, pansies, and geraniums, brightened the rusted metal and aged wood with brilliant color all summer long.

She entered the next garden, the Victorian themed garden, through an arched gate draped in a climbing Don Juan rose, covered in deep red buds on the brink of opening.

The summer before, after several requests from locals to use the gardens for their weddings, Albert and Lydia, his wife of ten years, had decided to set up part of the Victorian garden for weddings. The wide lawn area where chairs and tables would be set up, faced a gazebo graced with a white, climbing Swan Lake rose.

Once the wedding area was designed, Lee began working with Tyler Arnold, the one-time contractor, who lived in the servant's quarters in the basement, which he rebuilt into a modern apartment. The two of them were building a bridal lounge in a part of the basement that had been used as storage for nearly two hundred years.

This garden, complete with glass gazing balls, garden art, and elegant park benches, included a beautiful reflecting pool with a few comet goldfish to keep the mosquito population in check. Perfectly groomed paths led guests around the garden to explore mesmerizing art pieces that moved and changed shape with the slightest breeze. Even in this Victorian garden, modern tea roses, floribunda roses, as well as some old garden roses such as Cecile Brunner, also known as Sweetheart Rose stood out as show pieces of color and beauty.

Veronica paused before entering the front garden. Designed in the style of an Old-World formal garden, tea, grandiflora, floribunda, miniature, and even tree roses grew in organized beds next to smooth decomposed granite walkways, dotted with comfortable benches. An antique French fountain graced the center of the garden with a soothing splash when the water was turned on. Her gazed lingered on the fountain. Second only to the roses, it was the showpiece of the gardens. Imported in the late nineteenth century, when it was already over a hundred years old, it drew visitors from all over the country.

That's where she found the gardeners, Arturo and his son Jesus. Their white straw cowboy hats shading their faces. With the water turned off and drained, the two men were carefully applying a coat of conditioner to preserve and protect the historic marble.

"*Hola*," she called out. Neighbors when she was growing up, Arturo and his wife Maria, were like a second family to her. They taught her Spanish, often only speaking to her in that language, and were now offering the same favor to Salvador. Jesus, only two years older than Veronica, was like a big brother to her.

Both Arturo and Jesus tipped their battered cowboy hats as she approached. Arturo put his arm around her shoulder for a hug and said, "*Buenos dais, Chiquita.*"

Speaking in Spanish, they discussed the plan to put out humane, live gopher traps, and reviewed what needed to be done before the Garden's opening day in two weeks, on Mother's Day weekend. Everything was in place and ready, but Veronica's thoughts kept going back to Salvador's comment about the girl who came into his room and told him something bad was going to happen.

5

The next morning, Saturday, Veronica went out to the greenhouse to say goodbye to her grandfather. "We're leaving for Davis now, Papa." She took a deep breath. The scent of roses saturated the air.

"You two have fun." Albert Mason looked up from mixing food for the tropical plants in the sunroom section of the greenhouse with its entrance from the greatroom in the House. In the rarest show of affection, he gave Veronica a quick peck on the cheek. "Take care of yourself, Sprout."

UC Davis Picnic Day was everything Veronica hoped for. Expanded to include the entire city of Davis, since it began in 1909, there was a parade, activities for children, special events in the gardens and livestock portion of the school, and the ever-popular Dachshund races. Veronica was sure she never stopped smiling and Salvador never slowed down.

On top of meeting with several of her professors she'd grown close to, she spent the day with classmates, including Gustavo.

An *emigre* from Colombia as an infant with his mother, he grew up as American as any kid raised in Northern California. His and Veronica's relationship had become closer than just classmates while they worked together on horticulture projects in their classes.

At the end of the day, Veronica buckled Salvador into his booster seat, shut the back door of her truck, then turned to face Gustavo. His large, dark eyes held the warmth of the late afternoon sun. He had walked with her to her truck where they planned to say their goodbyes. They spent most of the day together, but being with other classmates they hadn't had time for any private conversations.

Beyond the parking lot, the UC Davis buildings rose above the trees. Veronica gazed over Gustavo's shoulder and soaked in the atmosphere of the university, probably for the last time–at least until next year's Picnic Day. She smiled to herself. In some ways she knew she'd miss being here but her feelings of achievement were complete. After earning her AA at the local junior college, she had transferred to UC Davis.

She felt pride at having worked so hard to realize her dreams. While one of her Christian friends commented that being prideful was a sin, Veronica felt there was no sin in feeling joy and happiness at being successful at something she worked so hard to accomplish. She also felt there was nothing wrong with making the self-comment of, "I did it." She felt a warm glow when she thought of her Papa Al's praise that he was proud of her for how hard she worked and that she had achieved her goal.

"I'd like to see you again," said Gustavo. He sighed and his shoulders drooped ever so slightly. "I know, I said that when we finished school last month, but with job hunting and interviews, I've barely had time to stop at home to see my mom and do laundry."

"I can only imagine how hard it must be to think about leaving family and friends, but it has to be exciting, too. You've been to some of the most beautiful gardens in the country."

Gustavo exhaled a short laugh, "Yesterday the country. Tomorrow the world. I do have to admit that my mother is so proud of me. I'm the first person in the family who has gone to college. I just hope I can live up to her expectations."

"You've applied to some of the nation's most beautiful botanical gardens. As a horticulturalist, even if you have to start at the bottom, you have a solid career ahead of you. I've seen your work. You're good and you know your plants."

Gustavo smiled. His dark brown eyes seemed to light up as he reached out and took Veronica's hand. "Thanks for the confidence booster. That's why I'd like to see you again. In the last three years I don't think I've ever heard you say anything negative to or about anyone. You're so beautiful, kind, smart, and responsible, it's almost scary."

Veronica glanced at Salvador nodding off in his booster seat. "Speaking of responsibility. I have a very tired seven-year-old I'd better get home before he wakes up and the grumpies get loose."

Gustavo burst out with a full, open laugh. "Salvador is like the coolest kid I've ever met. And you, Miss Vallejo, are the coolest mom I've ever met." He pulled her to him, ever so gently. "I'd like to give you a kiss goodbye."

Veronica pushed herself back a step. "Maybe another time." The attention from Gustavo was thrilling and frightening at the same time. They'd worked well as a team, she just wasn't sure she wanted to take their relationship any further. It was as much discomfort as it was fear. She had matured and worked through most of the trauma she'd experienced as a young girl, but she realized that, because of that trauma, she avoided relationships.

Before she could say more, he leaned forward and gave her a quick peck on the cheek then backed away. *"Adios, Hermosa Mujer.* Maybe someday." Gustavo pulled his keys out of his pocket and walked away.

Veronica watched him for a moment then went around her twenty-year-old F150 and slid into the driver's seat. She glanced back at Salvador. Exhausted, he was sound asleep and probably wouldn't wake up until they got home. Typical of an energetic seven-year-old, he hadn't stopped all day long. He'd dragged her to every dairy cow, goat, and horse presentation, took on every kid-sized ropes course challenge, and sampled every treat she allowed, even the chocolate covered crickets.

The drive home to Placerville had become so routine she quickly shelved her thoughts about Gustavo and divided her attention between driving and planning marketing and advertising for the Gardens.

A little over an hour later she felt a sense of relief as she turned down the familiar gravel drive to the Historic Inn that had been her home for the past seven years. Parking in her usual spot, next to the newer garage, attached to the end of the main structure of the inn, Veronica reached back and rubbed Salvador's arm. *"Despierta, Mijo."* She went around and opened the back door, knowing he wouldn't be fully awake until Brandy greeted them and begged for Salvador's attention.

Once in the backyard, Veronica felt Salvador's grip on her hand tighten. "Where's Brandy?"

"She must be in the house with Papa Al." With Salvador still holding her hand, Veronica went through the back door into the kitchen, and tried to ignore the apprehension skittering around her mind at the edge of her awareness. The quiet felt thick. She dropped her day pack on the small kitchen table.

Salvador raced into the greatroom calling for his great grandfather and Brandy. After circling the large area he returned to his mother. "Where's Papa and Brandy?"

Salvador's question brought Veronica's mind to a halt like a dog hitting the end of its leash. "I don't know."

6

As she spoke, Bee Bop burst out of the tall narrow cupboard next to the refrigerator and waddled across the floor toward them. "Hello? Hello? Cracker?"

Salvador dropped to his knees and held out his hands. "Hello, Bee Bop. Up up."

"Hello Bee Bop. Up up. Cracker." The large macaw offered her own greeting as she stepped up onto Salvador's hand. Once Salvador raised her up to his eye level and stroked the feathers of her head. She made kissing sounds and said, "Give me kiss."

Salvador kissed her large upper hook beak and offered his nose for her to give him her dry tongue kiss. "Mom, can I give Bee Bop a cracker?" he asked.

Bee Bop's version of a cracker was any kind of treat, from an almond or walnut, a banana chip, dried apple chips, and a real cracker, to almost anything her humans were eating.

"Of course." Veronica reached into the glass bowl on the counter and handed an almond to him.

Salvador set Bee Bop on the floor and gave her the treat. "Where's Papa and Brandy, Bee Bop?"

The same question flew into Veronica mind. She also wondered what kind of communication might be going on between her son and the macaw. From the time he could talk, he said animals spoke to him. "I wonder if Bee Bop has seen them," she said. At this time of day her grandfather and Lydia, were usually relaxed in the greatroom watching TV with Brandy at Papa Al's side.

"She doesn't know where they are," said Salvador. "They went outside."

That jittery, apprehensive feeling crawled up Veronica's arms to her back and chest like a swarm of termites, tunneling into her heart and stomach. That fact that Brandy hadn't greeted them meant something was wrong. "If they came in through the front door, the garage or the greenhouse, Bee Bop might not have seen them. I'll check the library and the greenhouse. Why don't you check the office and Papa Al and Lydia's rooms, then go through the game room into the garage to see if the car is there?"

Salvador took off down the hall to the north wing of the building. He peeked in through the open door of the office and her grandfather's and Lydia's rooms, then into the one-time bar with the door into the garage.

Veronica went the opposite direction through the great room. She stopped at the library. The door was closed as usual. Veronica looked inside. Her gaze swept across its polished wood shelves full of books and the large antique table in the center of the room. No one was there.

She shut the door and took her keys out of her pocket to open the security door into the greenhouse. The first section, a miniature conservatory/sunroom, with a low glass table and comfortable chairs, showed no sign of anyone being there. She went through into the main greenhouse, the heart of her grandfather's rose breeding business. She called for Brandy, and walked all the way to the end, then around the center table and back through the sunroom. He wasn't there.

Veronica had just relocked the doors back into the greatroom when Salvador came around the corner. His brows were knit tight. "No one's here. Lydia's car isn't in the garage and all the doors are locked."

All the doors locked, meant the door to the lab, the inside door from the house, and the door to the yard were all locked. The door to the lab would be open if Papa Al was down there and Brandy would be waiting patiently at the door as she wasn't allowed in the lab.

Veronica had to believe Papa Al and Lydia were gone. It wasn't unusual for the elderly couple to go somewhere for the evening. It was Saturday and many of the restaurants and wineries had live music on the weekends. They often took Brandy as many of the venues were outside and dog friendly. Veronica pulled her phone out of her back pocket and called her Papa. There was no answer. Next, she called Lydia. Again, no answer. Her apprehension notched up a level to worry.

"Where's Lee?" asked Salvador.

"If he's downstairs working, maybe Papa and Brandy are with him," Veronica replied. "Let's go check. Tyler's truck is gone, but Lee's car is here, so he could be down there."

She turned away from the ancient, stone stairs that led down to the basement from the kitchen because that area sort of creeped her out with its strange noises and ghostly sightings. Veronica often felt a 'presence' in the area, so she tended to avoid it.

"Let's go out front." She led Salvador out the grand front door, down the stairs, and along the sidewalk to the basement entrance at ground level. Opening the locked door, she looked inside and called out. No one answered.

Salvador dashed into the basement that took up nearly the entire area under the one-time inn. He returned breathing as if he'd run a race. "They're not here. What if they're out in the gardens?"

"They might be, let's go check. You can call for Brandy. She'll come if she hears you." If her grandfather had fallen in the yard somewhere, Brandy wouldn't have left his side, but she would bark if she heard Salvador call for her.

Salvador called for Brandy while darting between bushes, around trees, and checking all the hidden spots he knew from hours of play. Veronica called her grandfather's and Lydia's numbers again and texted Lee as she walked along the fence and looked down into Hangtown Creek, the stream at the edge of the property. It had rained hard overnight, and the water was still running high. There was no answer to any of her attempts to contact anyone. Veronica began to wonder. Could Papa Al have gone down to the creek for some reason, then lost his balance and fallen?

At the front gate, after going through all three gardens, Veronica called for Salvador to come to her. She took his hand and they walked down near the part of the creek she couldn't see from the Gardens. They walked up stream past the new picnic area just below the gift shop. When the wild blackberries prevented them from going any farther, they turned around. At that point Veronica began calling the neighbors. Had they seen her grandfather or Brandy? No one had.

7

By the time they got back to the picnic area Salvador was in tears. "Maggie said something bad was going to happen."

Veronica knew there was nothing she could say to make things better, but a thought did occur. "Maybe Papa Al and Lydia went somewhere and took Brandy with them. Maybe they left a note and I missed it. Let's go check."

They had just walked up the front steps when Veronica saw Lydia's newer, luxury sedan come down the drive. Even from that distance she could see Lydia was alone. The garage door opened and Lydia drove right in, the door shutting behind her.

When Veronica and Salvador went inside, Bee Bop began to scream. Salvador put hands over his ears. "Too loud, Bee Bop!"

Veronica and Salvador rushed into the kitchen. Bee Bop was on top of her cage. She screamed again, wings raised and spread in agitation. Lydia came into the kitchen from the garage. "What is Bee Bop screaming about?"

"I don't know. She just started screaming when we came inside," said Veronica.

"Where's Al. He's usually able to calm her," said Lydia.

"I don't know. He wasn't here when Sal and I came home. I was hoping he was with you."

"No, Al said he had work to do in the greenhouse. That's where he was when I left. How long have you been home?"

Veronica told Lydia they'd been home for about an hour. After the three of them did another search of the expansive Mason House Inn, including the part of the attic they could get into, Lydia said, "Somethings wrong. I'm going to make a missing person report to the police."

Thirty minutes later a county sheriff came. In the greatroom, Veronica and Lydia shared when they last saw Albert and where they had looked for him. When the deputy asked them to tell him about Albert, Lydia took the officer to her and Papa's rooms and shut the door behind them.

Eventually the deputy came out and asked Veronica again about where she was all day, and about her search. Because of her Papa's age, he wondered if he'd just wandered away from the house and said that he would put out a BOL, Be On the Lookout, for him.

The evening was quiet with stress as the undertone. It was just as unusual that Lydia stayed in her rooms. Veronica knocked on the bedroom door several times to ask how the older woman was doing.

Each time, Lydia was on her computer in the sitting room. "I'm just so worried about Al. I'm researching police procedures for missing persons and studying the satellite area maps that are in real time. I've checked the camera feed but most of them don't come on until dark, and there's nothing on the door and greenhouse cameras."

Veronica did what she could to comfort Lydia when she broke into tears, but there were few words of comfort she could offer other than, "We're going to do what we can Lydia. He's got to be somewhere."

"Thank you for your concern, Ronnie, but I just want to be left alone right now."

Veronica spent the rest of the evening consoling Salvador and answering his questions the best she could. When she tucked him into bed, she said, "How about you and I going out and doing our own search in the morning? If Papa Al did just wander away, Brandy would be with him, maybe she'll hear us calling her and will bark, leading us to Papa."

"But tomorrow is Sunday, what about church?"

"I'm sure God will understand why we didn't go. He knows how important Papa is to us."

The next morning Veronica bagged up some dog food and treats. She packed her Papa's morning medicine, a few snacks and bottles of water for themselves. Lee hadn't come back, but he did call saying he had spent the night with a friend and hadn't checked his phone until a moment ago.

Lydia came out of her rooms long enough to eat breakfast and announce she was going to drive around to the neighbors to see if anyone had seen Al.

After breakfast, Salvador sat on the floor in the kitchen with Bee Bop. He was quiet until Veronica announced she was ready to go. He stood with Bee Bop on his arm. "We need to take Bee Bop. She can call out louder than we can. If Brandy hears her, she'll come."

Veronica couldn't fault his logic. "Let me put her harness and flight leash on her. We'll set up her perch in the back seat so she can sit next to you."

The route she chose, took them to as many places along Hangtown Creek as possible. They pulled over next to the road and into parking lots to see the areas along the stream bed and called out in hopes Brandy would hear them. The circular route took them into Downtown Placerville, then down Placerville Drive and to Mallard Lane.

As they crossed over the creek at the bottom of the hill the sound of an explosion from under the truck ripped through Veronica's disquieted thoughts.

8

Veronica inhaled a gasp that, if exhaled, would have come out as a scream when her truck lurched toward the edge of the road. Her grip on the steering wheel was a conscious effort for control when they swerved toward the drop-off into Hangtown Creek. The "F" bomb that burst from the back seat was exactly want Veronica wanted to scream out as she stomped on the breaks in a panic reaction.

Struggling as much to maintain control of her fear as her truck, they finally came to a halt just beyond the culvert where the creek ran under the road. As a series of ear-splitting screams erupted from behind her, a small, brilliant scarlet feather drifted over Veronica's shoulder to land in her lap. Through the screams, she heard her seven-year-old son's voice yell, "Too loud, Bee Bop. Too loud!" A quick glance in the rear-view mirror showed Salvador with his hands over his ears. Unbidden, the common question among macaw owners popped into her mind. "Which is louder, a macaw screaming or a fighter jet engine starting up?" The answer was always – a macaw.

Veronica set the parking brake and did a quick mental check of herself. Her hands shook and her heart pounded, but they were safe.

She looked up into the bright afternoon spring sky, through the windshield, and spoke in her mind. I don't need this. What I need is to find Papa Al. And I am going to find you Papa.

Wherever you are and what ever happened, I'm going to find you. She inhaled deeply when she realized she'd been holding her breath. A habit she'd had since she was young, during moments of high anxiety.

The sound of loud crying came from the back seat. Concerned about Salvador, Veronica unfastened her seatbelt and turned around as far as she could. In his booster seat behind the front seat on the passenger side, Salvador gripped the arms rests of his seat with white knuckled intensity. *"Todo esta bien, Mijo."* Veronica reassured her son. It was then that she realized it was Bee Bop who was crying.

"It's okay, pretty bird." Veronica reached back between the two front seats and ran her fingertips across the pure white cheek skin of the macaw sitting on the natural branch perch between the seats.

"Mom, what happened?" Salvador's voice rose to a high-pitched shriek.

"I think we had a blowout." She kept her voice as calm and matter of fact as possible. "No big deal."

"What blew up?" the anxiety level in Salvador's increased.

"Nothing blew up, *Mijo*. A tire went flat. Can you feel how the truck is leaning? It must be the front tire on your side."

"That was just a flat tire?" There was a hint of incredulity in Salvador's tone.

"Yeah, blow outs can be pretty loud." Veronica tried to add a chuckle to her comment to relieve her son's tension.

A second later, Salvador made the kind of sound only a child could make when ratting out a sibling for swearing. "Did you hear what Bee Bop said?"

"Yeah." Veronica forced herself not to laugh and stroked the brilliant red feathers on Bee Bop's head. "I think the blow-out scared her too."

Bee Bop pushed her head into Veronica's hand and gently grasped her thumb with her beak that had the power to open a walnut as if it was a grape. Her next word was still very clear. "Cracker?"

"Okay, if that will help. The blowout was scary. It almost threw you off your perch." Veronica took a piece of dried banana out of a plastic bag in one of the cup holders and held it out to the large macaw. "There you go pretty bird, just don't think you're getting a treat for swearing."

"I never heard her say that word before." Salvador reached over and petted Bee Bop's head, affirming his close relationship with the bird.

"It's probably a word she learned before Papa adopted her from the rescue. I just hope she doesn't get in the habit of saying it." *That's all I need, Bee Bop, is to have you teaching Sal to swear.*

"What are we gonna do about the tire?" asked Salvador.

Veronica slipped her phone out of the hands-free adapter on the dashboard. "I'll call my roadside service to come fix it."

Salvador twisted around in his seat with a sudden jerk, stared at the macaw, and said, "Look at what?"

9

Salvador leaned toward his mother. "Bee Bop says we need to get out and look."

Veronica glanced between Salvador and Bee Bop. She knew not to question the psychic connection between her son and animals, especially her grandfather's macaw. A connection most humans, especially adults, couldn't accept or understand. "Alright, if Bee Bop thinks we need to."

Bee Bop rocked from side to side. "Up-up. Up-up."

Veronica reached for another banana chip. "No, you need to stay here."

A typical warm, California foothills day in late April, Veronica powered down the windows knowing Bee Bop wouldn't get chilled. "I'll leave the windows open so you can hear us. Here, have another cracker."

Bee Bop gladly took it with her beak then transferred it to her foot to hold as she started breaking off small pieces, dropping more than she ate.

As Salvador unstrapped himself from his safety seat Veronica said, "Give me a second to go around and open the door for you." Veronica checked for traffic, waited for a car to go by, then walked around to the other side of the truck.

With Salvador next to her, Veronica squatted down to study the huge gaping hole along the outside edge of the tire tread. "Sh..." She stopped herself from swearing. Her shoulders drooped in frustration. "Really?" With her grandfather missing, a flat tire was the least of her worries, but it was something she didn't need at the moment. "I don't believe it. I just bought these tires."

Veronica pulled her phone out of her back pocket, went into her contacts, and speed dialed her roadside service.

She put her phone on speaker so Salvador could hear the conversation. She wanted him to grow up informed and aware. As young as he was, if he didn't understand something she took the time to explain it to him.

The answer to her call was quick. She gave the requisite information and assured the operator she was safe, and yes, she understood it would be thirty to forty minutes before the service truck got there.

"Are they going to bring us a new tire?" asked Salvador.

"No, we have a good spare tire. They'll use that."

Salvador stepped back and looked at the truck. "Where?"

"Back here. I'll show you." Partially to satisfy herself that the spare was there, Veronica led Salvador to the back of the truck and showed him where the spare tire was nestled up under the truck bed. A pang of anxiety squeezed her chest. She wished it would be that easy to find her grandfather.

Through the open windows the words, "Here Brandy! Come," was followed by a loud whistle.

Veronica nodded in response. That was why Salvador insisted they take Bee Bop to look for Papa Al. His golden retriever was always with him and if she heard Bee Bop calling, she would bark or come when called by the animal companion she loved.

Salvador turned away from the truck and leaned into the low chain link fence that served as a protective barrier along the road over the culvert. He pointed to the dead oak no more than a hundred feet from the road. The tree was visible above the brush and smaller trees. "Mom, look at all the vultures. There must be something dead down near the stream."

Veronica gazed up at the tree. Several of the large black birds flew up from the stream directly under the road. They landed on a bare branches, bleached silver, and as lifeless as the birds' preferred meal. Veronica wrinkled her nose. The tree looked as if someone had inflated a half-dozen black garbage bags and tied them to the branches. *It's probably a deer, the poor thing.* Black tail deer were numerous in the county and collisions between deer and automobiles on the roadways were all too common.

The carrion eaters sat quietly. They could afford to be patient. Whatever they were feeding on wasn't going anywhere.

"It must be in the stream under the bridge." Salvador walked along the fence, looking down into the tangled matt of brush and blackberry vines.

"Sal, stay on the sidewalk and don't go beyond the truck." Veronica glanced both directions along the road. Parked against the curb of the narrow sidewalk, her truck stuck out into the road beyond the meager bike lane. Even though traffic was constant, visibility was good in both directions, so she wasn't worried about Salvador walking next to the truck, as he peered down into the ravine.

Just then another thought flashed to the front of her mind the way the deer had a habit of leaping out of the brush in front of cars. There was something dead down there. What if her grandfather had fallen in the water? The thought of Papa Al falling, being injured, then being washed down stream, ripped at her heart as brutally as the distressing thought of what the vultures might be eating.

Veronica's shoulders tightened and she clenched her fists. At the same time, Salvador moved out of her peripheral vision. Veronica looked over in time to see Salvador start down the steep trail to the stream below. Her heart leaped into her throat as Salvador disappear from sight. It wasn't him seeing a dead deer that bothered her, he was a country boy. He and two of his friends, had studied the deer they'd found dead and partially eaten on the neighbor's property in January. It was that "what if" that worried her.

Fed by street drains and smaller runoff streams for miles up-stream, the water was still high from the rain two nights before. She called out as she started down the trail after him. "Salvador, come back up here."

Salvador stopped and looked up the trail at her. "This is where Bee Bop told me to go look." He spun around and called out, "Papa!" Then raced down the trail.

A new kind of pressure squeezed Veronica's chest. The way Salvador called out, it sounded like he'd seen, or heard his great grandfather call him. Could he be down there? Making her way down the trail, she followed her son. When she heard him cry out, tension clutched at her gut. Visions of him being swept away by the water roared through her brain. "Sal!?"

"Mom!" Salvador scrambled back up the trail to her. Eyes wide with terror. His breaths came in panting gasps. "Papa's down there."

"What?" *Could it be?* "What's he doing?"

"He's not doing anything," cried Salvador. "He's dead."

10

"Oh God … Sal … Papa Al? … It can't be …." Veronica's words and thoughts came in halting gasps. Her mind spun into a whirlpool of anxiety. *No. Please no. NO!* Black spots popped before her eyes. She had to grab the branches of a small oak to keep herself upright.

"Parts of him are all eaten up!" Salvador's normally warm brown complexion was pale, tears streamed down his cheeks. "What're we gonna do?" His voice an octave higher than normal.Veronica pulled her son to her as if to keep herself from flying apart. "You're going to stay right here. I'm going to have to go down there and look, then I'm going to call 911." She pulled her phone out of her back pocket. "Can you stay right here and wait for me? I don't want you going near the road. Do you understand?"

Salvador nodded without saying anything.

"Good. I'll be right back."

Phone in hand, Veronica worked her way carefully around the thicket of blackberries at the stream's edge. She didn't want to call until she knew for sure what Salvador saw. Just in case it was a deer and a pile of clothing washed down from one of the many homeless camps up stream.

The corpse was wedged into the blackberries at the water's edge. The red checkered flannel shirt, khakis pants, and gardening tool belt around his slender waist, left no doubt who it was. Salvador knew as well. Her heart dropped into her stomach. She didn't have to wonder what the face looked like before the vultures commenced their operation as nature's clean-up crew.

"Oh no. No!" Veronica gagged on the taste of bile in her throat as her stomach turned inside out and her vision narrowed to a thin tunnel. She staggered backwards until her legs gave out. She collapsed to her knees and threw up. Tears blurred her vision. She didn't want to look again at the body after the vultures had been at work, but was unable to erase the image from her mind.

The warmth of a light touch slid around her shoulders. For just a moment she felt at peace, comforted. She reached out. Her hand swept through empty space. She turned and looked, expecting to see the anguish wracked face of her son. No one was there. "Sal?" She called out.

Salvador rushed down the trail. Veronica wrapped her arms around him when he got close enough. "That's Papa, huh," whispered Salvador. "He always wears clothes like that."

"Yes ... I think it's Papa." She burst into a new round of tears and leaned into the comfort offered by the small person that was her son. In that moment, accepting the body in the stream as her grandfather, Veronica's mind tried to go into an attempt at full denial. *Maybe it's not him. I can't see his face. A lot of old people garden. Oh what am I thinking, it's my papa.* After a couple of deep, sobbing breaths, with hands shaking, she made the call to 911. "My name is Veronica Vallejo. I live at 100 Serenity Valley Drive. My grandfather was reported missing last night. We just found his body in Hangtown Creek under Mallard Lane." She listened for a moment then said, "Okay. I'll stay on the line until the police get here."

"Mom, no one can see us down here. The police won't know where we are."

Veronica looked into her son's eyes. Eyes that seemed to hold a sage-like knowledge of years, maybe even centuries. She couldn't help but acknowledge the profound wisdom innate in the soul of this little boy. "You're right." She spoke into the phone. "We'll go up to the road."

Veronica guided Salvador in front of her, telling herself she wanted to be there in case he slipped and fell, but there was that voice in her mind that told her she needed to focus on something other than the body in the creek. Her focus turned to her grandfather's words. He often told her that nothing happened by coincidence. *"Everything that happens in this universe happens by design and for a reason."*

She had to believe having a flat tire at this exact spot and Bee Bop telling Salvador to go down to the streams and look, was not a coincidence. The embrace she had just experienced down by the stream flew into her mind. Salvador had called out to his Papa. Could Papa Al or one of the other apparitions inhabiting the Historic Mason House Inn, have touched her? She almost felt a sense that her Papa Al might be dead, but maybe he wasn't gone.

At the top of the steep trail, Veronica sat down on the narrow sidewalk that bordered Mallard Lane and fought with every ounce of strength she had not to cry again as Salvador hugged her side and cried. She had to hold herself together for Salvador's sake. With her son safe beside her, the feeling of sadness engulfed her on a different level. The anguish became all consuming.

Veronica broke into a new round of tears. Grief overwhelmed her. She felt like the life in which she'd found purpose and comfort had become like one of the burritos from that fast food place on Broadway. Just when she started to relax, to enjoy it, the outer shell that was life became a soggy, unstable wrapping. The second she tried to hold on to it, it fell apart, spilling its filling in an unmanageable mess of loss and fear.

11

In the quiet of the rural area, the police siren could be heard from a distance. Veronica stood and watched the road. The Placerville City Police car came into view at the bottom of the steep hill of Mallard Lane. Still on her phone, she said, "An officer is here. Thank you for the quick response." She disconnected the call, stood up, and stuck the phone in her back pocket. Salvador stood with her. Bee Bop went into the barking watch dog routine she'd learned from Brandy, as soon as the car pulled up behind the truck. Veronica held Salvador's hand. "Stay here with me. The officer will come to us, then we'll talk to him. Remember, don't say anything about Bee Bop telling you to look."

"Okay, Mama."

The officer who got out was young and muscular. He had a strong, clean-shaven jaw and a military short haircut. He walked along the sidewalk and looked into the truck. His eyebrows went up when he looked into the passenger side window, then continued to where Veronica was standing with Salvador. "Miss. Vallejo?"

"Yes."

"I'm Officer Gage." The face that went with the voice was strong and angular. His grey eyes held a warmth that told her he was there to help and understand. He glanced down at Salvador. "Who's your friend here?"

"This is my son, Salvador." Veronica could almost see the officer's mind switch gears. At first identifying her as a single young woman, then as a young, single mother as she hadn't corrected him when he called her "Miss Vallejo" not Mrs.

"Are you sure of the identity of the victim?" he asked.

"Yes. He's Albert Mason. My grandfather. He lives…." She burst into tears again.

"You said you found him in the creek?"

"I found him down there," Salvador began to cry and pointed at the dead oak tree. "There were vultures." The vultures had vacated their perches to circle overhead. "I saw them in the tree and some were down there." He pointed in the direction of the culvert. "They all flew away now."

"Did you touch anything or go right up to the–your grandfather?" Officer Gage asked.

Veronica shook her head. "I didn't." She looked at her son. "Sal, did you go all the way down?"

Salvador shook his head. "No. You said not to go near the water."

"The police will need to examine the bod–your grandfather. The detective is on the way. She'll need to ask you some questions."

An ambulance and a firetruck came and parked behind the police car. That got Salvador's attention. He stepped away from Veronica to better view of the big vehicles.

"I'll be right back." Office Gage walked back to talk to the fireman and ambulance driver. An unmarked Jeep parked behind the emergency vehicles. Officer Gage spoke to the driver through the open window, then backed away as the Jeep continued around the emergency vehicles to park in front of Veronica's truck.

A woman got out of the Jeep. She looked young. Her short hair was a natural light blond. Her stride spoke of strength and confidence.

A loud wolf whistle and a, "Hey Baby!" erupted from the truck through the open window.

The woman's head whipped around toward the sound. "Who's in the truck?"

"That's Bee Bop," announced Salvador. "She's a green wing macaw."

"That voice was very clear. May I see her?"

Veronica heard the challenge in the woman's voice. "Of course, but please don't try to pet her. She might be a little stressed. A bite could be very serious." With Salvador at her side, Veronica opened the passenger side door so she could open the back door. Bee Bop bobbed her head and ruffled her feathers. "Hello, hello."

"Hello, Bee Bop," said Salvador.

"Hello," squawked Bee Bop.

"Thank you." The woman's gaze softened.

Officer Gage did the introductions. "Detective Russell, this is Veronica Vallejo and her son Salvador. They found their grandfather."

Detective Russell nodded. "I'm sorry to meet you under such sad circumstances." She turned to Officer Gage. "Ethan, would you mind if Veronica and her son sat down on the back seat of your car? I'm going to go down to the stream."

"I'll secure the scene around the–their grandfather, as soon as you return."

"Thank you, sir," said the detective. She motioned for Veronica to take a seat then started down the trail. Veronica sat on the edge of the seat and pulled Salvador back to sit on her lap. The detective wasn't gone very long. When she returned, she had her phone in her hand. "I'm going to record our conversation. Veronica, your last name is Vallejo?"

"Yes." Veronica noticed the detective didn't ask if there was a Mr. Vallejo.

"Your grandfather is Albert Mason? I have a missing person's report for him from yesterday evening. A Lydia Mason called in the report that her husband was missing. Did he have a history of wandering or getting lost?"

Veronica wiped at the tears flowing down her cheeks and shook her head. "No. His mind was as sharp as it had ever been."

"His address is 100 Serenity Valley Road? Where do you live?"

"We live with him and his wife."

"His wife. Not your grandmother?"

"No, my grandmother died of cancer when I was little. He married Lydia about ten years ago. They used to work together."

"What made you stop here and go down to the stream?"

Veronica motioned toward her truck with a wave of her hand. "I got a flat tire. We got out of the truck to see what happened. Sal noticed the vultures while I was calling my roadside service."

"When's the last time you saw your grandfather?"

"Yesterday morning, right before we left for UC Davis."

"Do you go to school there?"

"I did. I finished last month. I took Sal to their Picnic Day, yesterday. We've gone every year for the past four years." Alarm knotted Veronica's throat when she noticed Officer Gage blocking off the area with crime tape. Her voice came out as a hoarse squeak. "Why is he putting up crime tape?"

"Veronica, we don't know how your grandfather died and ended up in the stream. Even if it was just a tragic accident, we'll treat it like a crime scene until we know for sure."

12

Detective Russell looked at Veronica, her forehead knit. "Do you know why your grandfather would be down by the creek?"

"He wouldn't be. I mean, he owns Serenity Valley Rose Gardens, which is right next to the creek, but after the rain he wouldn't be down by the water. He was always telling me and Sal how dangerous the creek was when the water was high, so he wouldn't go by himself." *He wouldn't be by himself. Brandy would be with him. Brandy! Oh, where are you puppy?*

Veronica almost said something until she looked down at Salvador. Losing his Papa Al *and* the dog he loved would be too much. It was too much for her. She pictured that kind, loving Golden Retriever drowning as she tried to pull her owner from the turbulent water when he fell in.

"Serenity Valley Rose Gardens. That's part of the historic Mason House Inn property. I haven't been there, but I've read about it." Detective Russell tapped her phone screen and looked at something on it, then looked back at Veronica. "The missing person's report I have says that your grandfather was in his late seventies. Do you know if he has a history of falling?"

"No, he didn't, but I do know he'd been taking more care about where he walked, because he said he didn't want to fall. We exercised together almost every day, and he'd been doing balance exercises during our workouts for as long as I remember."

"The report says you were the last one to see your grandfather yesterday afternoon."

"No, I saw him yesterday morning before we left. He wasn't there when we got home. Sal and I looked all over the house and gardens for him. It was Lydia who called the police. That's why we're out driving around today. Brandy, his dog is also missing so we thought she might be with him and if we called for her, she might bark or come if she could hear us."

Russell held her phone out to continue recording their conversation. "Would there have been anyone else at the house that might have seen your grandfather yesterday?"

Veronica almost rolled her eyes. It seemed like half the county was at the Gardens at times. "My cousin Lee was there in the morning when we left yesterday. He's been working with Tyler Arnold, the contractor who is doing restoration work on the place."

"Tyler Arnold," said Officer Gage who had walked up behind Detective Russell. "I know that name."

There was no easy way to talk about Tyler's struggles. Veronica looked down at her hands for a second then looked up to meet Officer Gage's gaze. "Then you know he has been through some very rough times. He used to have his own construction business, but lost it due to his drinking. He's clean and dry now. Papa Al said Tyler does excellent work, so he wanted to give him a chance to stay clean and get back on his feet. The place needs a lot of work done so Papa offered Tyler a place to live and meals in exchange for work with a small salary."

"You said your cousin, Lee, works with Mr. Arnold? Where does Lee live?"

"He still lives with his dad in El Dorado Hills, but they don't get along very well so he's been spending nights at the house. I know he asked Papa Al about moving in with us so he could help Tyler, but I don't what they decided."

"Are there other people working at the Gardens? Does anyone else work with Mr. Arnold other than your cousin?"

"Yes. We have a housekeeper, Jessica, who works Monday through Friday. Her husband, Jesus, and his father, Arturo

Gonzales, are our full-time gardeners. They work weekdays, except some weekends once the Gardens open on Mother's Day. Tyler's son, Tyson, used to come help him, but he doesn't come anymore."

"What can you tell me about Tyson?"

"He's seventeen and lives with his mom somewhere in the area, Camino, I think. He helped Tyler sometimes, and used to stay with him, but when he was caught on camera in the middle of the night, meeting friends in the parking area and smoking something, Papa said he couldn't stay anymore. Then when he took Tyler's truck without permission one afternoon and ran into the front fence around the sales garden, Papa said he couldn't come on the property anymore. That whole thing was pretty ugly."

"Caught on camera. You have security cameras?"

"Yes. At different locations around the property. Security is important to Papa Al. There are cameras on the doors, the drive, the gift shop, and greenhouse. They're all motion sensor cameras, but most of them are only active at night."

While Bee Bop continued doing her watch dog routine of barking at cars. Veronica couldn't help but noticed more cars converging on the road around them. Along with the firetruck and the ambulance, there were county sheriffs and a van marked with the county logo. Veronica heard the throaty roar of a "muscle" car pull up right next to Officer Gage's car then continue on to park in front of Detective Russell's Jeep.

She was surprised that Bee Bop remained quiet when the man who got out of the car walked next to her truck. Bee Bop was an excellent judge of character and there was something about the presence of this man that stilled her. He was older, with thinning grey hair. He walked with a slight hitch in his gait, but he was still powerfully built. Tall with broad shoulders. When he stopped in front of Veronica and Salvador, she was able to see into his eyes. They were eyes that had years of experience seeing everything and missing nothing. Veronica was comforted by his presence.

"Veronica," said Detective Russell, "This is Detective Phil Norton. He's with the county."

Norton greeted Veronica with a simple, "Hello," then smiled when he greeted Salvador. She had the feeling he was a grandfather himself.

"I'm very sorry for your loss, Ms. Vallejo." Norton motioned away from the cars with his chin and spoke to Detective Russell. "Can I have a word with you in private, Detective?"

Veronica watched the two detectives walk away from where she sat in Officer Gage's car. Whatever was being discussed was clearly important.

Detective Russell came back by herself. "Phil is going to the house. I'm sorry Miss Vallejo, I'm going to have to ask you some more questions." She glanced at Officer Gage then at Salvador. "Salvador, would you mind hanging out with Officer Gage for a few minutes while I talk to your mom? Maybe he can show you around the firetruck."

Veronica set Salvador down and almost had to pry his hand from hers. "I'll be right back. You'll be safe with Officer Gage."

"Nooo," Salvador burst into tears. "The police are going to take you away!"

13

Russell knelt next to Veronica where she held Salvador close to her and whispered. "I'm not going to take your mom away, Sal. We're just going to talk for a minute. Can you be brave for your mom and wait for her?" Salvador nodded and sniffed back his tears. Detective Russell put a hand on Salvador's shoulder. "I'm going to keep your mom safe for you. She'll be right back."

The detective led Veronica near the front of her truck. "This truck is yours?"

"Yes. It was Papa Al's. He sold it to me four years ago."

"Do you have any records of your mileage to Davis? When you left the house and when you returned?"

"You mean like written down? No, but the driveway camera should show us leaving and coming home."

"Well, it's not important right now, but it might be in the future so we're going to need that camera feed."

A truck pulled up and stopped next to Veronica's truck. Painted red, white, and blue, the truck had the name of a local towing service as well as her roadside service company, painted on the side. "That's the roadside service I called for. May I get my tire fixed?" asked Veronica.

"Of course." Detective Russell led the way.

Salvador rushed to his mother's side and latched onto her hand. There was no question that he was staying with her.

Veronica went up to the roadside service man. He was older, but trim. His thick, salt and pepper mustache matched his hair which waved just over his ears. He looked around at all the emergency vehicles and scratched his mustache with the end of his pen. "Am I in the right place?"

"Yes. I'm Veronica Vallejo. I'm the one who called you and this is my truck. I had a blowout."

Detective Russell stepped up to him. "I'm Detective Jillian Russell, with City Police. We have an investigation going on here, but please go about doing what you need to do."

"Okay. I'm Derrell Townsend with Placerville Towing. Let's see what we've got." He pointed toward Veronica's truck. "This is your truck?"

"Yes," said Veronica. "It's the right front tire."

Townsend walked over to the truck. A loud, "Hello, baby," blasted through the open window. Townsend's eyebrows shot up and his eyes opened wide when he looked into the truck, through the open window. "Well, hello to you, too, my big, feathered friend." He glanced over at Veronica and said, "That's a big bird."

He continued around the front of the truck and squatted down to run his hand over the tire. He fingered the large hole where the tire gave way "These tires look brand new, but I see the problem."

Veronica stood next to him. "Yeah, we saw that, too."

"Because these tires look fairly new, I'd have to guess there was probably a flaw in this one, and it gave way all of a sudden," said Townsend. "Be thankful you weren't traveling at speed. That could have been scary."

"It was scary!" said Salvador.

Veronica put her arm around Salvador's shoulder. She was thankful for how well he'd gotten himself back together. At the same time, she wondered when the full, major breakdown would happen.

"I bet it was," chuckled Townsend. He walked to the back of the truck and looked under the bed. "Do you have the key to let down your spare?" He turned his attention to Detective

Russell. "I'll need that Jeep moved so I can pull in there to jack up the front and change the tire."

"Mom, can I hold Bee Bop while the tire's being fixed?" asked Salvador.

Veronica studied her son's face. It was tear-streaked, and his eyes were red and puffy from crying. She leaned down and kissed him on the cheek. "Yes, you can. I think Bee Bop could use some cuddle time." She reached in and disconnected the strap from the perch to Bee Bop's harness, then snapped on the nylon leash.

Announcing the usual parrot command of, "Up up" for herself, Bee Bop stepped gently onto Veronica's hand.

Detective Russell took two steps back. "That's a really big bird."

Bee Bop responded by raising her wings to their full height. A defensive pose. She let out a squawk then settled her wings against her sides. She cocked her head to look at the detective with one eye and then gave a wolf whistle, followed by a loud kissing sound, and, "Pretty girl!"

"Does she know what she's saying?" asked Russell.

"Yes. I believe she does. While macaws aren't the talkers the Greys and Amazons are, they're still very intelligent. Papa Al said Bee Bop hovers in the genius range, and I think he was right."

Russell nodded. A slight smile tugged at the corners of her mouth. "Well, thank you, Bee Bop."

Veronica settled Bee Bop on Salvador's small forearm. "Just don't get too close to the people and put the loop of her flight leash around your wrist. You know she's generally good with strangers, but animals can feel their humans' stress." She watched carefully for any signs of agitation or discomfort from the bird. She didn't want Salvador to get hurt.

Salvador sat down on the sidewalk away from everyone but where he could see the tire being changed. Within moments, Bee Bop was leaning against his chest and humming Rock-a-by

Baby as Salvador gently dug his fingertips into her feathers to scritch her head and neck.

Once the tire was changed, Veronica said, "Would it be all right if I left now? I really want to go home."

"Are you okay to drive? You've had a very upsetting experience," said Detective Russell. Veronica could hear the warmth and concern in her voice.

"I'll be fine," Veronica bit her lower lip as she sniffed back a new round of tears pressing against her eyes.

"I'll follow you. I want to know what Detective Norton has learned from questioning anyone there."

14

If they could have followed the stream, the house was only a short distance away, but no roads went that way, so they had to go out to Cold Springs Road, make a right, and another right on Serenity Valley Trail to make a loop back to the creek.

Veronica drove past the sales yard, which bordered the public gardens, and continued to the rambling structure she'd called home for the past seven years. She drove past her mother's car and Lee's small sporty coupe, and parked in her usual spot, under the awning next to the workshop, a new structure detached from the garage. Tyler's truck, washed and waxed to a shine, was parked in front of the shop. Detective Norton's car and a county sheriff car were parked behind it.

Salvador unhooked his seat belt. "The police are here. Are we going to take us away?"

"No *Mijo*. Detective Russell said they were just going to talk to Lee and Tyler. They need to find out how Papa Al died."

"Do you want me to take Bee Bop so you can talk to grandma?"

Veronica turned around to gaze at her son and wondered, *what did I do to deserve such an incredible soul in this child I call my son?* "Thank you, but I want to take Bee Bop. With my mom and Detective Norton inside, she might stress out."

Careful not to rub against the wall with its moss-covered stones and weathered boards with peeling paint, they walked the short distance along the back side of the building to the kitchen door. Inside, the air smelled the same as it always did. No matter how much Jessica cleaned, using a simple recipe of white vinegar and water with a small amount of dish soap so as not to harm Bee Bop, there was always a lingering odor of mustiness from old curtains and horsehair stuffed furniture. Veronica was sure that up close she could smell the nearly two hundred years-worth of pipe and cigar smoke that impregnated the furniture and the walls.

Bee Bop announced their arrival with a loud scream and wing flaps without flight. "We're in here, Ronnie." Lydia's voice, soft with a slight tremor, came from what was called the greatroom, the large open area just beyond the kitchen.

Taking up most of one wall was a fireplace made of natural river rock. An ancient rifle and an English broadsword hung on embedded railroad spikes on either side. Out in the center of the room, around old, threadbare wool rugs, was a variety of chairs and couches. The only modern furnishing were two recliners, a new widescreen TV, and a music system. The antique dining table, large enough to seat a dozen people, was off to one side, closer to the kitchen.

"We need to go see Lydia and your grandma, Sal," said Veronica. With Bee Bop still on her hand, she and Salvador went into the great room. Veronica's mother, Brenda Mason, who had changed back to her maiden name after each divorce, sat in a wingback chair across from Lydia, in her recliner. Both women had tears in their eyes and tissues in their hands.

Veronica felt the tears building behind her eyes. She sniffed and nodded as she bent over and gave Lydia a one arm hug. Bee Bop raised her wings, stretched out her neck, and let out an open beaked growl. Veronica backed away, surprised at Bee Bop's reaction. "I think Bee Bop's stressed with all that's going on right now. Let me put her in her cage."

"I don't blame her." Lydia held out her arms to Sal. "Oh Sal, I could really use a snuggle right now."

Salvador wrapped his arms around her neck. "Are you sad that Papa Al is dead?"

Lydia picked him up as if he was a feather and nestled him into her lap. "I'm more than sad, Sal. I think I'm going to cry every day for a long time."

Veronica put Bee Bop in her cage and returned to her mother. "How are you doing Mom?" She laid a hand on her mother's hand.

Her mother pulled her hand away from under Veronica's and looked out the window.

"It's been a shock."

A twang of pain strummed against Veronica's heart strings. She couldn't understand her mother's reaction. Her rejection. Given the trauma Veronica had been through, she knew she'd struggled in life especially as a teen, but she also wondered if her mother's rejection was because she looked so much like her father. She had been told by many that she had her mother's beautiful Irish facial structure and her Latino father's thick, wavy, black hair, warm brown skin and brown eyes. Carlos Vallejo had been a handsome man, but Veronica only knew him from the pictures her Papa Al had. Carlos had left his wife and two-year-old daughter, taking his five–year-old son with him. Veronica never saw or heard from her father or brother again.

"We couldn't find Brandy." There was utter defeat in Salvador's voice. He had scooted out of Lydia's lap to stand in front of her.

"I'm so sorry you didn't find her," said Lydia. "We might have to accept that she's gone."

Salvador melted into devastation. He collapsed to his knees in front of the nearby couch and buried his face in his folded arms on the edge of the cushions. Veronica quickly knelt next to her son. He threw himself into her arms and cried. Veronica rocked him as she held him. "I know how much you loved Papa Al, and Brandy. We're going to do everything we can to find Brandy, *Mijo*."

"Where is she? She wouldn't run away. I know she wouldn't." Sal sobbed against Veronica's chest. "We have to find her."

"I don't know where she is *amorcito*, but we're not going to give up looking." Once Sal had calmed to sniffles Veronica settled him on the couch nearer to Lydia who was more like a grandmother than her own mother. Needing a break, she went into the kitchen, reached into Bee Bop's cage and asked her to step up. As she had already removed Bee Bop's harness, Veronica set her on the floor with one last head scritch, knowing the macaw would make a beeline for her broom closet in the corner by the refrigerator.

Bee Bop began whistling, *Home on the Range*, opened the door with her beak, then held it with her foot as she stepped into her closet, allowing the door to shut behind her. As she left the kitchen, Veronica could still hear Bee Bop whistling.

Back in the greatroom, Salvador stood by Brenda, his grandmother, holding her hand. Veronica was shocked at her son's comment to his grandmother.

15

"Papa Al was your dad, huh, Grandma," said Salvador. "Now you're like me and Mom. We don't have our dads either, but mom says it's okay not having a dad, because we have each other, and other people who love us." Salvador hugged his grandmother. "I love you Grandma."

A knock at the front door took Veronica's attention away from her mother. She glanced at the small monitor on the wall. It was Detective Russell. She opened the door to greet the Detective. "Come in Detective Russell. Let me introduce you to my mother, Brenda Mason, and my Papa's wife, Lydia."

After introductions to Veronica's mother and Lydia, Detective Russell said, "I noticed Detective Norton's car out by the garage."

"He's downstairs talking to Tyler and Lee," said Lydia.

"I'll take you down there." Veronica felt Salvador's small hand slip into hers and he pressed against her side. She understood his need to be with her. They walked together into the kitchen. Next to the new, double door aluminum refrigerator was a recently added wood door that slid smoothly into the wall when it opened. Veronica pushed the door back to reveal a wide stone step rounded and worn smooth over the nearly two centuries of use. Beyond was a near black emptiness.

Veronica touched a panel next to the refrigerator, turning on a light to expose rough stone walls that had been hidden in the darkness. With Salvador at her side, she stepped down into the emptiness. Detective Russell followed close behind. Even though the stairway was wide, it had a closed in, dungeon sort of feel. What Veronica didn't want to think about was that this stone staircase was one of several places in the Mason House where voices, ghostly forms, and freezing cold spots were often encountered.

"Where does this lead?" There was tension in Russell's voice.

"I guess you'd call it the basement. It takes up the entire underside of the building. It was mostly storage, the servants' quarters, and the wine cellar–back in the day. Sometime along the way a laundry room was added. When we decided to open the Garden for weddings, Papa Al hired Tyler to build a bridal dressing lounge with bathroom and storage for tables and chairs.

"Tyler rebuilt the servants' quarters, so he had somewhere nice to live while he's here. It really is beautiful, and he's almost done with the bridal lounge."

They stopped on a landing that was one large, solid piece of granite. Here, there was a door and the stairs took a ninety degree turn before continuing down.

"What's behind this door?" Russell put her hand against the thick oak planks. Salvador lifted the latch and pushed the ancient wood door inward. He flipped on the light and went inside. Wiring for electricity ran inside a tube tucked neatly against the edge of the ceiling.

"Because this was an inn, it's sort of like a pantry on steroids," said Veronica. "Most of the kitchen is original, so there isn't that much storage space." She pointed to shelves that held everything from boxes of cereal to canned food, and jars of local, organic honey. Other shelves held sealed containers of sugar, flour, corn meal, and different kinds of pasta. Over an open bin of potatoes hung braided strands of garlic and peppers. A large, upright freezer and a refrigerator stood against the back wall. "As you can see, we still use it. The walls are stone so mice can't get in, and it's underground, so it stays cool all year."

The detective took a flashlight out of her coat pocket and trained the light on the walls and corners, free of dust and cobwebs due to Jessica's diligence. "You have all this food for four people?"

"There may only be four people who actually live here, but everyone comes for lunch and dinner during the week. That means Papa Al, Lydia, me, Sal, Tyler, Jesus, and Jessica, and lately Lee and sometimes his younger brother, Marcus are here. Arturo is here for lunch but goes home after work, for dinner." It wasn't until after she said it that Veronica realized she included her papa as if he was still with them.

From where she stood on the landing, Veronica could hear Detective Norton and Tyler's voices downstairs. "Is it normal to have two detectives asking people questions?" she asked.

"The Mason House is outside of the city limits, but your grandfather was found right at the border between city and county jurisdiction. That means that if this becomes an investigation, we'll work together."

At the foot of the stairs Detective Norton stepped into view. Russell continued down to the bottom to talk to him. "I want to ask Mr. Arnold and Lee Mason a few questions. Then you and I can talk."

"I haven't talked to Mr. Mason yet," said Detective Norton. "He's waiting in the lounge. Why don't you interview him while I finish with Mr. Arnold."

Veronica took Salvador by the hand and started back up the stairs. Salvador balked. "But…. What if Tyler or Lee saw Brandy?"

"I'll ask them about Brandy," offered Detective Russell. "You go upstairs with your mom."

Back in the kitchen, Veronica grabbed her purse and led Salvador back into the great room to the grand, curving staircase that went to the second floor where her bedroom, study, and bathroom, and Salvador's bedroom and playroom, along with six other bedrooms and a common bathroom were located.

After seeing Salvador into his room across the hall from hers, Veronica went into her room and stood at the window, staring out at the gardens. A thought, sharp as a knife, cut through her mind. *What's going to happen to the gardens?* When she started college, she and her grandfather had often talked about her taking over the care and management of the gardens someday.

Sometimes Veronica imagined herself watching newly planted trees growing to maturity as she got old. She even dreamed about expanding the gardens to include a vegetable garden, a small orchard of fruit trees, and cultivating the wild blackberries that overran the slope down by the creek. Picking the area's blackberries was a summer passion for many locals. With water and care, the berries were a solid cash crop for any property owner willing to pick them or let people pick their own during berry season.

Now however, reality reared its ugly head. With her Papa gone the Mason House with its gardens would probably go to her mother and her Uncle Jerold.

16

Salvador came into her room, "Mom, can I go into the garden and play with my trucks?"

"Yes, of course. I think I'll go with you." She could use the distraction. "I'd like to spend some time with Papa's roses."

Veronica followed Salvador down the stairs and out the grand front door. From there they could see the entire garden complex that covered nearly five acres, at the bottom of the slope away from the house.

The colors of the roses were just starting to show. Veronica took a deep breath as if she'd be able to wrap herself in the fragrance of the world's most beloved flower from the porch. "Do you need to go get your trucks?"

"No, they're in the garden." Salvador took his mother's hand and led her down the steps and through the front yard. The beautifully landscaped yard with its wide lawn and flower-beds were bursting with new growth and spring colors.

They followed the path of large, slate steppingstones and entered the original garden, planted in 1853, where most of the old species and shrub roses were. Salvador pulled his trucks out from under a bench and began pushing his dump truck along the winding paths. Veronica sat on a bench and watched him pick up small twigs and leaves and place them in his dump truck. She stood when she heard footsteps on the decomposed granite path behind her.

Lee, enveloped wrapped her in his arms for a hug. "Oh God. I am so sorry about what happened. Finding Gramps that way must have been horrible."

Veronica looked up at her cousin. She laid her face against his chest. "I don't think I'll ever get that image out of my head, but I'm trying to be thankful we found him." Veronica stepped away from him and glanced around. "Where's Sal?" The tension built with a tint of worry. "I don't want him to be alone right now."

Lee backed up a step and nodded with his chin for her to look beyond the garden they were in. "Your clean-up crew just moved into the next garden."

Veronica walked with Lee along the path to enter the Victorian garden through an arched gate draped in the climbing Don Juan rose, covered in deep red buds.

She walked a distance behind Salvador as he pushed his truck along the path picking up fallen twigs and leaves brought down during the storm on Friday night. "Were you home anytime yesterday?" Veronica asked her cousin.

"No. I left to go into town right after you left for Davis."

"You were in town all day? What were you doing? Your car was here and you didn't answer when I called and texted you several times Saturday evening."

"You sound like that detective, asking me questions." Lee pursed his lips and ran his fingers through his blond hair. "I'm sorry, Ronnie. I guess that's just kind of a personal question. I was with someone, and I didn't have my phone on me most of the afternoon and evening."

Lee's phone rang. He took it out of his back pocket and glanced at the number. "It's Dad. I'd better take this call." He put the phone to his ear, said, "Yeah," and walked away.

Veronica continued following Salvador along the path toward the front garden. Entering through an elegant arch way, this was the last garden to be planted. When she sat down on a nearby bench Salvador joined her and crawled into her lap. "How are we going to find Brandy?"

She hugged him close. "I don't know, I haven't really thought about it. How about if we put up lost dog posters." Veronica tried organizing her thoughts, but her brain felt as if it was stuck in a blender. Random thoughts spun through her mind so fast she couldn't focus on anything.

Finally, it was Salvador who hit the pause button. "Mom, I'm hungry."

"Let's go in. I'll make you some lunch. On the way back to the house Veronica watched her mother and the detectives drive away. Inside the house, Lydia was curled up on the couch. Veronica gently touched Lydia on the shoulder.

The older woman jerked awake. "Huh? What?"

"I'm sorry. I didn't mean to startle you. Would you like some lunch?"

"No. I'm just not hungry. I can't believe Al is gone."

"My heart hurts knowing Papa is dead." Salvador hugged his mother.

"Oh sweetheart, I know. It's a hurt we all feel." Lydia reached out for him. "Thank you for your curiosity, Sal. Without you we may never have known."

"Why did God make him die that way?" Salvador broke down into tears again.

Lydia took a breath. "Al believed that everything happens exactly as it is supposed to happen, Sal. Call it fate or the will of God, but it was what God wanted. Now, it's up to us to continue on with life and do the best we can with what Al left us–and know his spirit is at peace in Heaven."

Veronica found comfort in Lydia's words, but she couldn't find peace without knowing what had happened. She knew with her very soul that her grandfather didn't just fall in the stream. It was almost like she was hearing a whispered voice telling her it wasn't a simple accident.

17

The sight of her grandfather in the creek kept rerunning through Veronica's mind, over and over. Other than the horror of finding her Papa Al the way she did, her brain was trying to tell her something. An image at the back of her mind caught her attention. She suddenly knew what was wrong. Other than Brandy not being by his side, his gardening clippers weren't nestled inside their holder on his tool belt. Unless he had them in his hand, they were always in their holster. *That's what was wrong. Why weren't they there? If I can find them, I might be able to find out what happened.* Veronica didn't understand her thoughts, but something kept telling her not to say anything about them being missing.

"I'm so sorry about Brandy," said Lydia. "I'm sorry you didn't find her. I don't know what could have happened."

"I'm going to make lost dog posters and call all the veterinarians in the area and the animal shelter," said Veronica. *She's microchipped so someone may find her.* Veronica kept this thought silent and inside. She didn't know why, but again that voice inside her told her not to mention the microchip or the clippers.

"Your mother called your Uncle Jerold to let him know what happened," said Lydia.

"As if he'll care." Veronica felt the tension in her chest raise. She wanted nothing to do with Jerold Mason, her mother's brother. She never told anyone what happened when she was nine-years-old. The day he offered to care for her for an

or was a nine-year-old

afternoon while her mother was gone. The emotional turbulence of that trauma never faded. After a few years she made sure to stay away from him when he came to visit. Now, she also made sure Salvador was kept safely from him.

"I think he cares," said Lydia.

"Yeah, about how much he's going to inherit."

Lydia patted Veronica's hand, her expression resigned. "Jerold is who he is. It will be between him and God to make peace with himself."

To keep herself from making the biting comment hovering over the tip of her tongue, she took Salvador's hand. "Let's go eat lunch, *Mijo*."

After lunch, Veronica and Salvador went upstairs to her study. Salvador fell asleep on her bed while she used her computer to make a lost dog poster and start a list of phone numbers for the local vets and the animal shelter to begin calling in the morning.

***

Veronica stared up into the darkness of her room. The grey light of morning was just beginning to sneak past the edges of the window shades. She knew that meant it was a little after 5AM. She was surprised she'd slept. She sat up and grabbed her phone off her nightstand but couldn't see the screen through the tears in her eyes. Papa Al was gone. They'd never again do their morning work-out routine, then have a cup of coffee together to start the day.

By the time she dragged herself out of bed and raised the window shades, color had returned to the gardens and the cloudless sky promised another beautiful spring day. Veronica shivered a little as she took off her pajamas and slipped on a sweat suit. It would be in the high 70's later in the day, but the old inn was drafty and cold in the mornings.

After a simple workout and yoga routine she showered and dressed then went downstairs to the office to finish the lost dog posters she'd made the night before, and print them out, then make breakfast. She was reviewing the finished product when she heard the tap-tap of nails on the hardwood floor and then felt a tug on the towel covering her chair. "Up-up, up-up." The ivory-colored hook beak and the brilliant scarlet feathers of Bee Bop's head appeared over the edge of her chair.

Veronica reached down and slid her hand under the bird's feet to put her in her lap. "Hello Bee Bop." Bee Bop repeated the greeting and went about preening herself, dropping bits of feather dander in Veronica's lap, as she worked. Bee Bop watched the screen with one eye and attended to her grooming with the other. When Veronica changed the screen to show the poster she was working on, with a picture of Brandy, Bee Bop stopped what she was doing, let out a loud squawk, then whistled and added, "Here Brandy. Good girl."

Veronica stroked Bee Bop's head. "Yeah, that's the idea, Bee Bop. We want to find Brandy." She brought up a full screen photo of Brandy.

Bee Bop Squawked, stepped onto the Veronica's desk, and attempted to groom the photo on the screen with her beak and said, "Good girl."

When she stepped onto the keyboard Veronica picked her up. "You miss your friend, don't you, Bee Bop." She draped a towel over her shoulder and set Bee Bop on it. "Watch from up there. I can't have you walking on my keyboard while I'm working."

Bee Bop bobbed her head, squawked in Veronica's ear, then set about grooming Veronica's long dark hair, running strands between her tongue and upper beak. Veronica was just printing the poster when she smelled a distinctive odor. She closed her eyes and wrinkled her nose. "Yeah, I figured you'd do that." She offered her hand and said, "Up up." Once Bee Bop was on her hand, she removed the towel off her shoulder. The large bird reached for the posters still sitting on the printer and whistled.

"Yeah, we're going to find your friend," said Veronica. "But right now I need to start breakfast."

Veronica set her on the floor in the kitchen.

Bee Bop whistled for the dog and called out, "Here Brandy. Good girl."

Tears welled in Veronica's eyes. The parrot and dog loved each other. If she couldn't find Brandy, she, Salvador, and Bee Bop would mourn a double loss.

18

With a simple breakfast of oatmeal, fruit, and toast with honey or jam ready, Veronica went upstairs to wake Salvador. He was already awake, sitting up in his bed having a very serious conversation with his large, stuffed panda. He turned to face her when she came into his room. *"Buenos dias, Mama."*

"Buenos dias, Amorcito." Veronica sat on the edge of his bed. "It's Monday and you have school today, but if you would like, you can go with me to put up lost dog posters after breakfast?"

"Si. Quiero ir. I think the tires will be okay now."

"I think so to." She paused. "Sal, after we got the flat tire, you asked Bee Bop what you should look at. Then you said Bee Bop told you to look. Can you tell me about that?"

"I heard it the way Bee Bop and Brandy say things to me, but it was Papa's voice. I think he made the tire go flat right there so we could find him."

How could she argue with such a thought? Veronica swallowed the lump in her throat. "I only wish Papa Al or Bee Bop could tell us what happened."

After breakfast Veronica called Sarah, Salvador's home-school teacher, to explain why he wouldn't be in school that day.

"Why don't you let me clean up here so you can get going," said Lee.

"That would be awesome. Thank you so much." Veronica glanced over at Lydia who sat quietly and had barely touched her breakfast. "Are you going to be okay, Lydia? Is there anything I can do for you?"

"I'll be fine. Thank you, dear." Lydia took a sip of coffee. "I think I'm going to go out in the garden and try to take my mind off things. You and Sal go and do what you need to do."

Starting with the neighbors they knew, Veronica and Salvador asked if anyone had seen the dog. The neighbors, who all knew Albert Mason, expressed sorrow for her loss, offered their condolences, and asked about memorial services, but no one had seen the dog. Veronica then drove up Cold Springs Road and made a right on Placerville Drive where she tacked a poster on the wall of the feed store, Clifton and Warren's. They continued taping or stapling posters to every telephone pole they came to.

While no one they talked to had seen Brandy, all offered to keep a lookout for her. They were out of posters and Salvador's stomach was grumbling by the time they made their last stop. A driveway that split off at the top of Serenity Valley Trail.

Veronica turned onto the drive marked by an old mailbox, leaning to the side, on a rotted post. She slowed her truck to a crawl down the narrow lane. Even in her large truck she was careful to stay on the high side of the potholes and deep ruts from years of rain and wear and no care. An old riding mower, nearly invisible in the overgrown weeds and brush, was the first sign of habitation. A tangled mess of rusted field fencing was followed by various appliances and other discarded household items surrounding a house that was as dilapidated as the rusted hulk of a car parked at an odd angle next to the house. As a juxtaposition to the decay, wisteria vines, in full bloom, nearly covered the entire house giving it a sense of beauty and elegance.

Veronica backed into a wide spot away from the house, as if the deterioration might spread to her truck if she parked any closer. Salvador hugged her side as they walked toward the house, until the first cat appeared. In a flash he was on his knees, calling, "Here kitty." His entire being quieted.

Cream colored, with stripes on its dark, long slender legs, tail, and face, it was clearly part Siamese. It looked up at Salvador with vivid blue eyes and uttered a plaintive cry. Salvador called again, "Here kitty-kitty," his voice soft.

If anyone could call a cat to them, it was Salvador. While Veronica joked about her Papa calling her the rose whisperer, there was no joking about Salvador being a true animal whisperer. All their friends' dogs loved him, and even the hummingbirds that flocked around the garden's many feeders, readily sat on his fingers when he held them near the tiny perches.

True to his ability, the cat went to Salvador. After an introductory scratch around the ears and a pet along the back, Salvador picked the cat up and cradled it in his small arms. Whatever communication was going on, was truly psychic. The same communication Veronica had seen him do with Bee Bop and Brandy. The cat began to purr so loudly she could hear it from where she was standing.

Salvador looked up at his mother. "Isn't she beautiful?"

"She is." Veronica didn't have to ask how he knew the cat was a female. "Would she let me pet her?" She took a step near them but didn't reach down. If the cat decided to make a quick get-away, Salvador could get scratched.

The cat looked at Veronica, wide eyed. "Not right now, mom," said Salvador. "She's scared. She doesn't like it here, but it's the only place she can find food."

"Just be careful with her. I'm going to go talk to Addie."

Three other cats, a tuxedo cat, an orange tabby, and a steel gray cat, slunk away into the brush when Veronica approached the house. She walked carefully over the worn boards of the porch and knocked on a front door that hadn't seen any attention, be it soap and water or paint, in years. Salvador hung back in the yard petting the cat. When no one answered, she knocked a little louder.

The voice from inside called out at a near screaming pitch. "You don't have to beat the door in!" The door opened with a forceful jerk. Veronica faced a disheveled woman in a dirty dress and threadbare robe. Her bottle blond hair, burnt to a frizz from too many home color treatments, stuck out in all directions. She held a small squirming kitten in each of her hands. A cigarette hung loosely from her lips. Teeth, as yellowed as her fingers, showed when she talked. The woman's hostile sneer quickly changed to a forced expression of kindness as she stuffed the kittens in the pockets of her robe.

"Veronica dear, how nice to see you."

Veronica surprised herself at the direction of her thoughts. While the woman before her was nearly twice her age, their body types were similar, and they probably weighed about the same, but in emotion and lifestyles they were a million miles apart.

Addie Sweet looked past Veronica to Salvador. "Oh. You have my new stray. I found her wandering on the road the other day, and I'm hoping she'll feel comfortable enough to come up to the porch and eat."

Great, another stray cat. Veronica tried not to inhale the assault of ashtray breath, alcohol, and body odor. "Hi, Miss Sweet. We were just looking for our dog, Brandy. She's missing and we were wondering if you'd seen her in the last couple of days."

"Oh, is she missing? I'm sorry to hear that. And I'm so sorry to hear about your grandfather."

"You know about Papa Al?"

"The police were here asking about him … They said he was missing. If there's anything I can do for you, please let me know. I have a special touch for caring for the lost, and I can feel by your energy that you're feeling very lost right now."

19

Veronica took a step back. "Um...Yes, thank you for your concern. We'll get through it. If you see Brandy, I would appreciate it if you'd let me know."

"That dog chased my Tabytha and nearly scared her to death the other day. Something needs to be done about that dog chasing my cats."

Veronica took a deep breath. "Brandy's in a fenced yard, Miss Sweet. If your cats weren't in our yard, digging in the flower beds, she wouldn't chase them. I don't think she'd hurt them. She probably just wanted to play."

"Cats come and go as they please and she wasn't–." Addie stopped mid-sentence, then continued. "You can't control cats. You know that. I'm just grateful they feel safe coming to me in their time of need." Addie Sweet stepped out onto the porch and looked down her nose at Salvador. "Since you got that one, bring her to me." She held out her hands. When she did, Veronica noticed a long scratch down the inside of her left arm and several smaller ones on the back of her hands.

Salvador gently set the cat on the ground and gave it a final pet before it scurried away to disappear in the tall weeds.

"Why'd you do that?" Addie Sweet's voice rose to a screech. "I told you to bring the cat to me."

Not one to back down from an adult or bully of any size when it came to protecting animals, Salvador raised his chin and stood tall. "She didn't want you to touch her, so I put her down. She doesn't like–"

Veronica gave him a quick, *don't take it any farther,* shake of her head. "I'm sure the cat will let you pick her up when she's ready," she said to Addie Sweet. "By the way, did you see or hear anyone down by the creek on Saturday afternoon? Your house is closer to the creek than any of the other neighbors."

"I didn't see nothin'." Addie Sweet reached into her pockets and pulled out the squirming kittens. "Now I have kittens to care for. Goodbye." She turned and went back into the house. Before Addie shut the door, Veronica caught sight of moving boxes stacked in different areas around the front room. Cobwebs hanging from the porch rafters shook when Addie slammed the door.

Veronica walked away wondering if Addie was moving. Salvador knelt on the ground petting the cat that had come back to him. He looked up at his mother, his eyes pleading. "Would it be okay if she came to live with us, if she wants?"

"I don't know how Bee Bop would react to a cat, but we'll let the cat make her choice. Let's go home."

When she turned back onto Serenity Valley Trail from Addie's driveway, Veronica could see Arturo's battered red pickup with its wire enclosed trailer, full of gardening tools and equipment, parked near the front gate to the gardens. When she turned onto the drive to the house she saw Detective Russell's jeep and Detective Norton's car parked behind Jessica's old, repurposed police car. Both detectives were just getting out of their vehicles when Veronica pulled up. The detectives' expressions were somber.

"There's something," said Veronica.

Russell nodded. "We need to include Mrs. Mason in this conversation."

Detective Norton glanced at Salvador then looked back to Veronica. "I'm just not sure Salvador should be part of this."

"Alright. Sal, I'm going to ask Jessica to play with you in your room for a little while." Veronica felt a wave of tension and worry washed over her. "Whatever it is, it isn't good," she whispered to herself.

As soon as they walked into the house, Bee Bop started in with loud wolf whistles, Hello's, and comments that they were, "Pretty girls."

Jessica, her brown skin glistening and her long black hair up in a messy bun on top of her head, met them at the kitchen door, mop in hand. Her gaze swept between Veronica and the detectives.

"Jessica, this is Detective Russell of the Placerville police department, and this is Detective Norton with the county," said Veronica.

"How do you do officers," replied Jessica.

"The detectives are here to talk to me and Lydia." Veronica guided Jessica back into the kitchen. "Could you do me a favor and make Sal a snack?"

"*Si Hermana,*" Jessica turned to Salvador. "How does an apple with cashew butter and maybe some chocolate sound?" Getting a shoulder shrug from Salvador, Jessica addressed the detectives, "Would you each like a cup of coffee?"

"That would be nice, thank you, Jessica," replied Russell. Norton added his agreement with a nod.

"Jessica, do you know where Lydia is?" Veronica settled Salvador into a chair at the kitchen table and handed Bee Bop an almond.

"She is in her room." Jessica pulled an apple from the fruit bowl and began to cut it into wedges.

Veronica spoke softly in Spanish while Jessica worked. "When Sal is done with his snack, could you take him up to his room and hang out with him until the detectives leave? I don't know why they're here, but they're asking that Sal not be a part of it."

20

"I will take care of him for you," said Jessica.

Veronica took Salvador's hand. "Jessica is going to play in your room with you until I'm done."

"But ..." Salvador's expression was one of stubborn resistance.

"I promise to come tell you everything as soon as the detectives are finished." She turned to the detectives. "This way please." Veronica led them down the hall to Lydia's room. Lydia was on her laptop in the sitting room off the bedroom she had shared with her husband. Norton shut the door behind them. The detectives didn't sit down, there were no preliminaries. "We have the report from the coroner's initial exam," said Russell. "I can't give you all the details, but I will tell you that Albert Mason's death has now became a criminal investigation. The coroner has concluded that Mr. Mason was murdered."

"Mr. Mason was already dead when he went into the water," said Norton.

Lydia crumbled into shaking sobs. When Veronica reached over to put her arms around her, Lydia moved away. "Please don't."

Veronica collapsed into the small couch against the wall and was taken aback by Lydia's reaction. They had never been close, and Veronica accepted that everyone had their own way to mourn and express their sorrow. She was sure the older woman's response had nothing to do with the small tensions that had always been between them.

Russell and Norton sat in nearby chairs and waited for Lydia to regain her composure. "What I need to look at is who might want Mr. Mason dead and who would benefit from his death?" said Norton. "This property alone must be worth several million dollars. Did he have a will?"

"Yes," said Lydia. "Albert was very private about his finances, but I know he had a new will drawn up after we got married. In the original will Brenda and Jerold, his children, were the beneficiaries with a small amount going to each grandchild. I never saw the new will. It's with his lawyer, Marcia Waters. The only thing he told me was that when the time came, Ms. Waters would call the necessary people."

"Did he have life insurance?" asked Norton.

"He did," said Lydia. "I don't know the exact amount or who the beneficiaries are as he kept all that paperwork at the lawyer's."

"Did Mr. Mason have any reason to believe his life was in danger?" asked Russell. "Did he have any enemies, or do you know of anyone who might have wanted to harm him?"

"No!" Veronica was shocked to think that someone would hurt her grandfather. "He was–"

"It's possible," interrupted Lydia. "I'm sorry Ronnie. There are a few people who won't mourn Al's passing. But enough to hurt him ....?"

Veronica held her breath to keep her objections from spilling out. It was a moment before she noticed Detective Russell look at her then at Lydia with the kind of expression that didn't need words to tell them to talk to her. Veronica glanced back at Lydia then said, "Papa Al wasn't the easiest person to get along with. Mom always called him a cantankerous old man. When I think of my mother and Uncle Jerold, I don't think he was a very good dad."

"Al was on the spectrum," said Lydia. "When he was young he was diagnosed with Asperger's. He was beyond brilliant, in the genius range of intelligence, but he had almost no people skills. He didn't trust easily, and he spoke his mind, which often rubbed people the wrong way.

"Those who knew and understood autism accepted him for who he was and looked past his social difficulties.

"Al and I worked together for nearly two years before we began developing any kind of bond that could be considered a social relationship. We worked together for ten years. My love for Al was never romantic. I appreciated him as a brilliant co-worker. We got along. He understood my sense of humor and I was able to make him laugh."

Detective Norton asked, "Can you think of anyone who might have wanted to see Mr. Mason harmed?"

Lydia glanced at Veronica, then looked at the detectives from under hooded eyes. "I can't help but wonder who thinks they'd benefit from Al's death. One person you might want to start with is Robert Inman of Inman Genetics. Al worked for Donald, Robert's father, for over 30 years. Their relationship was never one of friendship. Donald wasn't anywhere near as good a scientist as Al, but he put up with Al's social difficulties because he knew it was Al who made the breakthroughs that made Inman Genetics' reputation and made a fortune for it.

"Several years ago Al confided in me that Donald had been taking credit for Al's breakthroughs and had patented several of Al's processes as his own. We found proof last year and brought a lawsuit against the company."

"What would that lawsuit be worth if you won?" asked Russell.

"Potentially? Millions. But the real result would be the proof of Donald's fraud, even though Donald is gone now. It's something that had bothered Al for years."

Russell gave a soft whistle. "Is there any way I could get copies of the lawsuit paperwork?"

"Of course," said Lydia.

"What about his Blue Moon?" The same wave of fear, Veronica experienced on Friday night when she and her grandfather had talked about the possible danger of having something so valuable, lapped at her nerves. *Knowing the value of the rose, did someone resort to murder to get it?*

"What is his Blue Moon?" asked Detective Norton.

"A blue rose." Veronica pursed her lips to the detective's dubious expression.

"I don't know anything about roses, so maybe you could tell me why you think someone would be willing to kill him for a rose?" said Russell.

"It's more than just a rose," said Lydia. "It's a true, blue rose. The only one in the world."

"That's important?" asked Russell.

"Important? It's more than important. It's the Holy Grail of rose breeding," said Lydia. "There are no blue roses in nature. There are very few true, blue flowers in nature of any kind. Most are blue-violet. Since genetic engineering was developed, people have been trying to create one. No one has succeeded until now."

"So that rose would be valuable?" Norton asked.

21

Veronica wanted to scream. "The patent alone would be worth millions. Having propagation rights could be worth many more millions. Once it's on the market every rose lover, from the single plant on an apartment balcony to rose gardens all over the world are going to want one–or ten."

"And Mr. Mason created this blue rose?" Detective Russell looked back and forth between Lydia and Veronica. "I'd like to see it."

"Of course," said Lydia.

"It's only in bud, but Papa told me it tested positive for blue. It hadn't started to open far enough to show color as of Saturday morning."

"I'd still like to see the actual plant," said Russell.

"It's in the greenhouse." Lydia stood up. "Let me get my keys.

"I'll come with you," said Veronica. "I know where it is."

Veronica and Lydia led the detectives across the hall. Much larger than a typical home office, it was two rooms opened up to make one big room. It contained three large desks, all with laptops and large monitors. Old fashioned wood filing cabinets lined one wall and bookshelves lined two others. "Papa Al, Lydia, and I did all our business-related work here. Papa Al had been teaching me everything about running the gardens." She glanced at Lydia. "Lydia's brilliant when it comes to figures."

"You keep the greenhouse locked?" asked Norton.

"Yeah," said Veronica. "And Papa Al always kept the greenhouse keys locked up." Veronica went to the bookshelf and took down three thick books to reveal a small combination wall safe. She put in the combination and opened the door. Inside were two sets of keys. Veronica picked up both sets. "There should have been three sets. Papa's keys are missing. He probably had them on him when he died."

"What are the keys you have in your hand?" asked Russell.

"Mine and Lydia's keys," said Veronica.

"There were no keys on him when he was found. If they fell out in the water, they may never be found," said Norton. "He had a tube of chap stick and a blue crystal like rock in his pockets, but no keys.

"The crystal was his indicolite. Blue was his favorite color."

"What's indi–whatever you said?" asked Russell.

"Indicolite. It's the blue form of the crystal tourmaline. He's carried it and his lucky tiger's eye in his pocket for years. Was his tiger's eye with him?" Veronica chewed her lip for a second then asked, "Will there be any way to get them back?"

"There was no tiger's eye. I know what that looks like, and yes, I'll make sure you get back what he had in his pockets." Russell did a quick look around the room and tapped her fingers on one of the filing cabinets. "What's in these?"

"All the business stuff. Everything from the annuals we purchase and plant, to flower pots, soil, name tags, and fertilizer costs, to utilities and employee payroll. Everything related to running the gardens. Papa Al was very organized." Veronica relocked the safe and led the detectives, with Lydia, back into the great room. She walked past the kitchen thankful Salvador wasn't there which meant Jessica had taken him to his room.

They continued into the great room, then went around the corner where the wall ended. "We can get into the greenhouse from in here."

Russell stopped at a set of heavy double doors. Solid wood and polished to a satin gleam. "What's behind these doors?"

"That's the library," said Veronica.

"Do you always keep the doors to the library shut?" Russell twisted the doorknob and push on the door just enough to look inside.

"We have to keep the doors closed because Bee Bop likes to chew on paper and wood. She'll pull books off the shelf just to shred them into small pieces if she gets in here." Veronica swung the doors open wide and went inside. This was her 'happy place.' The space was packed with books on polished wood shelves. Filing cabinets backed up against one wall. In the center of the room was a large wood table with comfortable chairs for study. There were several reading lights on bendable arms on the table.

"Wow. There are a lot of books here." Detective Russell looked down at a magazine lying on the table and read the title of the cover story. "The New Danger of GMO's. Isn't this Mr. Mason on the cover?"

"It is," said Veronica. "Friday night, Papa Al was telling me about the incident when he and his team were attacked while in El Salvador. A rival genetics company tried to steal the corn seeds Papa had created. He also told me about the lab being damaged by anti-GMO groups. I'd read the article before, but wanted to read it again. I didn't put it away because I didn't finish it."

"What's in these filing cabinets?" asked Norton.

"They're Papa Al's life study of plant genetics and roses. He saved all the magazines he was ever published in and there's research on everything from aphid control to The World Federation of Rose Society. Those files," Veronica swept her hand toward several other cabinets set against the side wall, "Are a complete catalog of roses. All the wild roses to every known rose that ever graced a garden from ancient Greece, Egypt, and China to the newest hybrids."

Lydia opened the top drawer of the filing cabinet. "Al spent weeks cataloging the new roses developed each year. Both his roses and those of all the major rose growers worldwide."

"He has just about every book ever written about the history, care, and beauty of the rose." Veronica ran her fingers along the spines of the books on a shelf. She felt the tension in her shoulders relax. She wanted to open a book and melt into it. "He was passionate about buying new rose books every year."

For a moment, she was lost in the emotional comfort she always felt in this special room. Even when she was younger she would spend hours going through the files and reading the books, absorbing the collected knowledge. Now she wondered what was going to happen to everything. Would Lydia continue Albert's work with roses and keep the gardens open, or would the house and gardens pass on to Uncle Jerold and her mom–Papa Al's children? Veronica couldn't stop the visions of the roses being dug up and carted away or bulldozed, and the books and files being taken to the dump. It would all be gone.

Veronica shook herself out of her thoughts and led the detectives back out of the library to a reinforced door in the back wall of the greatroom.

Norton ran his hand along the edge of the door jamb. "A steel door and steel door jamb with a keyed lock from the inside. This is some heavy-duty security."

"Albert was very security minded, and he wanted his roses to be safe," said Lydia. "He was very well aware of the value of what he had."

22

Veronica opened the door and stepped into a room with glass walls and ceiling. Tropical plants crowded against the glass from floor to ceiling. In the center of the room was a low glass table surrounded by several large wicker chairs, their thick cushions upholstered in tropical plant design fabric. "This is what Papa Al called the sunroom."

Russell stood in the doorway and looked around. "This is beautiful. It's like a miniature version of that big glass building in Golden Gate Park. The one with all the plants." She walked around a comfortable seating area and studied the orchids in full bloom.

"The Conservatory," said Veronica. "I love it in here. We often sat out here to finish the day. Have a glass of wine and talk about the roses and the gardens."

"I don't see any roses." Norton turned all the way around.

"No, the plants in here are tropical. The temperature and humidity are carefully controlled." Lydia shut the house door behind her.

Veronica went to the other side of the room and unlocked the reinforced security door that led into a vast greenhouse. Even through the slightly opaque glass, the sturdy steel reinforcement wire was easy to see between the dual panes of glass. In the main greenhouse, there were tables along the walls and a long table down the center with room to walk in between. Roses in pots of all sizes covered the tables. Bursts of color dotted the tops of the roses. Most just coming into bloom.

"Can you explain what we're seeing here?" asked Norton.

"Of course." Veronica led the detectives along the rubber-ized paving bricks. "This section here is seedlings from last year. Papa Al always bred a few roses every year. You never know what you're going to get with seedlings, until they start to bloom. Once the rose hips mature, we harvest them, and plant the seeds." Veronica forced herself to not stop and study each of the blooms with color just peeking out.

"So you don't know what they're going to look like until they bloom," said Russell.

"No, but that's the exciting part," said Veronica. "It's sort of like Christmas. We follow all the precautions to make sure the roses we want to breed are only pollinated with the roses we've chosen to cross them with. We keep careful records of the parent plants, so we have a vague idea of colors and pat-terns. But it's up to Nature. Papa Al patented and sold one of my roses last year. It will be pretty cool to see a "Vallejo" rose entered into the directory and in sales catalogues on the inter-net in a few years."

Veronica led the detectives to a section of roses next to the outside wall of glass. "This section is the cuttings from this year's prune," said Veronica. "Asexual reproduction is the easiest ways to make new roses bushes. Because they are from the parent plant, they are exactly the same."

"There's a lot of them," said Norton. "What do you do with them?"

"When they're big enough, we take some of them to garden clubs and farmers' markets to sell," explained Lydia. "The rest we sell here."

"So these are all roses Albert Mason created?" Russell cupped a fat bud in her hand.

"No, not all of them. Hybrid Teas like the Peace, Double Delight, and Mr. Lincoln, just to name a few, have been good sellers for years. The patents are expired on these that aren't Papa Al's, so we can reproduce them."

Veronica stepped over to the center table. "Many of the roses on this table are old roses. There's been a real interest in some of the species and subspecies roses in the last few years." She checked the name tag on a white stick. "This is Rosa Gallica Officinalis often known as the Red Rose of Lancaster and the Apothecary's Rose. Its history goes back before 1300."

"What!?" Russell's eyes were wide with surprise.

Veronica laughed softly. "Roses have been around for 30 or 40 million years. There are records of roses being grown for over 5,000 years. While it is believed it was the Greeks who started taking rose growing and breeding seriously, the ancient Egyptians and Chinese had roses in their gardens. Even Native Americans were known to have planted wild roses in and around their villages."

"So all these plants can be found in the wild?" Detective Russell touched the soft bloom of a pure white rose.

"Some of these, yes. All roses started as wild roses, then have been hybridized into what we see today. Kind of like how dogs went from wolf to Poodle after living with people for so long.

"I had no idea," said Russell.

In the very center of the green house was a steel framed structure with reinforced steel wire walls. Veronica gasped as she looked at the roses inside. She rushed inside after unlocking the door. Her gaze swept over the small roses lined in neat rows on the center table, once, and then again. "NO!" Her hands shook as she cupped each small bud in her hands, the true colors not yet showing. She knelt to look under the table when she felt her knees start to give out. It was a moment before she realized she was shaking her head and saying the word, "No," over and over. When she struggled to stand, Russell took her arm and helped pull her to her feet.

"What is it?" Russell kept hold of her arm and turned Veronica to face her.

Veronica's voice cracked. "The blue roses. They're not here."

23

"Veronica, where's the roses?" Lydia's tone was harsh. "You were the only one here yesterday afternoon."

"I didn't touch them!" Veronica felt her voice raise in volume and tension. "I only came in long enough to look for Papa Al."

Detective Norton stepped in front of Lydia and gave her a look that made her back away, then he turned to Veronica. "How can you tell the blue roses aren't here?" he asked. "They all look the same. The only difference I see is that some have deep red leaves at the top, and some don't. All the buds look the same."

"You don't understand. Papa and I have babied these plants since they were seedlings. I could tell you which one was which with my eyes closed. The new growth of the Blue Moon is deep red. And...."

Veronica counted the roses, touching each one. "Two others are missing."

"Could your grandfather have sold them without you knowing?" asked Norton.

Lydia braced herself against the table and shook her head. "No, he didn't. I would have done the paperwork. It was going to be the biggest sale in history. He'd planned for it to be an unveiling. He joked that it would be like the Vatican revealing a new Michelangelo. I was with him when he contacted some of the world's largest rose cultivars and told them what he was sure he had."

"The screenings were going to be private because Papa didn't like crowds," said Veronica. "He said how special it was going to be and that he wanted me, Sal, and Lydia there. I just wish he was here to tell us where the roses are." Her anxiety became anguish.

"Al's in Heaven now," said Lydia. "His cares are behind him. He's at peace, but someone knows where those roses are."

Veronica sniffed. "I hope so. I want to make him proud and do what he would have wanted us to do." She glanced at Lydia. There was that look again. Almost accusing.

Russell frowned. "Who else knows where the roses were? Could they have been stolen?"

"They must have been stolen when Al was murdered. That person had to have known where they were," said Lydia.

Norton ran a hand over a panel of glass in the back wall.

"All the glass is reinforced with steel wire welded into steel frames," said Veronica. "Papa said it'd take explosives and a bulldozer to get into this greenhouse. The drive, front, kitchen, and greenhouse doors are all on camera. His and my phone ping whenever something set off one of the cameras' motion sensors."

"Do you have a recording of Saturday?" There was a different tone in Russell's voice.

"The computer in the office will have all the recordings." Veronica, took her phone out of her pocket and opened the security app. "All the pictures are recorded on my phone as well. I was so busy Saturday, when I was at Davis, I didn't really pay any attention to my phone." She pulled up the app and began going through the images from Saturday. She held the phone so Russell and Norton could see as well.

There were no surprises.

"Who's that?" asked Russell at the first two people who were recorded by the cameras.

"That's Will and Nolan. They're a married couple who help in the gift shop and sell their art work there. They're probably getting the shop, ready for opening day," said Veronica.

At the recording of the next couple, she said, "That is Tim and Mary. They're neighbors and artists who also sell their work in the gift shop." They could be seen carrying things into the gift shop.

At the image of the next car, Veronica felt her gut tighten. "That's Uncle Jerold."

Lydia pulled out her phone and began going through photos. She frowned and her pressure on the keypad became more forceful. "Something ... The last photo I see is of Veronica heading for the greenhouse before she left for Davis. After that there are no more photos from the greenhouse cameras. I'd left by then and didn't look at my phone again for the rest of the day." She looked up at the ceiling of the greenhouse, then looked through the glass near the main door. She returned with her brows knit. "Both cameras aren't just off, they're not there.

"Veronica admitted to coming out here when she got home Saturday. I have to wonder how the cameras got turned off and disappeared. The sheriff came in and looked around when I made the missing person report. I was with him then, but I didn't even think about the cameras."

"Are there any other cameras that might have been active?" asked Russell.

"Several, but only at night," said Lydia. "The computer in the house should have all the recordings from the other cameras."

"Let's go look at those." The eagerness in Russell's voice was clear.

Lydia led the detectives back into the house and to the office. Veronica followed, relocking the green house and sunroom doors as she went. She wondered what Lydia was looking for. Their phones had the same apps and videos as the computers.

Just inside the office, by the door, hoping to find something she missed on her phone, she scrolled through the security app images for Saturday once again, until a noise caught her attention. She stepped into the hall. "Sal?"

The sound of running feet thumped along the hall upstairs and down the stairs. Veronica went into the great room. Salvador rushed down the steps holding out a sheet of drawing paper. "Mom, Jessica and I are making more lost dog posters."

Veronica made a show of studying the poster Salvador held out to her. "This is great. Go on back up and do as many as you want."

"Aren't you done yet?" There was a distinct whine in Salvador's voice.

"Almost. Please go back upstairs and stay with Jessica. I'll come get you as soon as I can." Once Salvador went back up-stairs, Veronica returned to the office.

Lydia had opened Al's computer to the security cameras. "This is what was recorded at night." Throughout the week the cameras had recorded deer, raccoons, skunk, foxes, cats, dogs, and a couple of coyotes, but no cars or people. The front door camera from Friday recorded the UPS and FedEx deliveries, and Jesus watering the flowers on the porch. The camera on the walkway recorded Tyler and Lee coming and going.

"I don't see your mother, the housekeeper, or your uncle," said Russell.

"They always come in through the kitchen door," said Veronica.

Lydia pulled up the video of the kitchen door starting with the previous Monday. Veronica leaned forward to watch. She nearly cried as she watched her Papa, with Brandy at his side leave the house and return, over and over. It felt as if he was still there. Veronica watched everyone in the house come and go, then she saw her mother and Uncle Jerold knock then open the door and go in. Each person eventually left. The last time they saw Albert Mason leave the house was Saturday afternoon. He never returned.

24

Nothing about her mother or uncle's movements aroused Veronica's suspicion. When Lydia activated the cameras to the greenhouse Veronica's heart leapt into her throat. There was nothing beyond Saturday morning when she went inside to say goodbye to her grandfather. It was as if the cameras on that side of the yard had been taken off line then removed.

"There's nothing there." Lydia's shoulders slumped.

"Mrs. Mason, you weren't home at this time?" Detective Russell asked.

"No, I left early to go to Folsom to do some shopping."

"Was Mr. Mason here when you came home?" Detective Norton stepped next to Detective Russell.

"Yes," Lydia nodded her head but didn't look at either detective.

"Where were you during the time Mr. Mason disappeared?" Russell glanced at Veronica then turned back to Lydia.

"I already explained this to detective Norton. I was visiting a neighbor and didn't get home until well after Veronica got home."

"Let's get back to the missing roses. Is there any place else they might be?" Detective Russell directed her question at both Veronica and Lydia.

"Ronnie, why don't you check the lab," Lydia turned from the window. "Maybe Al put the roses down there for safe keeping."

"Why would he put them down there?" Veronica asked.

"I don't know, but we have to look." Lydia ran her fingers through her still thick, gray hair. "Would you mind? I just don't have the energy."

"You have a lab here?" Russell looked over at Detective Norton, her eyebrows raised.

"Genetic engineering isn't like cooking meth. It can't be done in the kitchen sink," said Veronica. "It takes very special equipment."

Veronica stood and motioned for the detectives to follow her. "This way." She led the detectives down the hall into what had once been a lounge complete with a bar and billiards table. "This room is what Papa Al called the Way Station. A place to hang coats and put on slippers after coming in from the garage."

Tall, modern, cushion backed chairs, offered comfortable seating at the bar. Game consoles and controllers littered the stained wood top. A wide screen TV hung from the ceiling in front of the antique mirror on the wall. Veronica's heart lightened, just a little, at the memories of the evenings when she and her grandfather played billiards while Salvador, Lee and Marcus played video games.

At the far side of the room, Veronica opened a door that led into the garage. Inside the garage, she unlocked what appeared to be a storage cabinet in front of a Cadillac Escalade. That door opened to a metal security door at the back of an empty closet. She opened that door to yet another space that looked like a closet. "This goes down to the lab."

"An elevator?" Veronica heard the surprise in Russell's voice.

Both detectives followed Veronica inside. "Papa Al knew there'd be a time when stairs would be difficult for him. It also makes getting stuff up or down a lot easier."

After a few seconds the elevator door opened to a large clothes closet. Hanging on a rack were white lab coats and loose-fitting white pants. On a table were boxes of shoe covers and gloves, masks and sterile wipes. Veronica handed the detectives a package of disinfectant wipes. "The lab is a clean–secure area, so we need to gown up." She noticed Russell look down at herself. "Because we've been in the house and outside, we're contaminated. We can cover our clothes and shoes, but we need to clean our hands before we dress."

Hands sanitized, she handed the detectives pants, lab coats, shoe and hair covers, gloves, and masks. She knew well the routine. When they were covered to her satisfaction, she opened the keyed and combination locks in the correct order. The door swung open with a hiss as the seal was released. They entered a glass enclosure where a disinfectant gently misted their feet and a breeze ruffled their clothes as the air was sucked out and replaced with filtered, clean air. Inside the lab, over-head lights came on when Veronica opened the door.

Russell whistled. "Wow, this is right out of X-Men and that new James Bond movie."

"This is the heart of Papa Al's work with rose genetics." Veronica gave the detective the kind of nod a teacher might give a student who finally understood a concept being taught.

"Son of a ...." Norton looked in all directions. "My guess is that we're looking at millions of dollars-worth of lab equipment."

"Over ten million dollars-worth when it was new." Veronica described each piece of equipment and its function. "Papa Al said all this is second generation that he got used when Inman Genetics updated their equipment."

In the center of the room was a small greenhouse with full spectrum plant lights hanging from the ceiling. Through the glass sides they could see rows of small pots with tiny seedlings just popping their heads out from under the soil. Veronica pointed at the tiny plants. "These are last year's genetically altered seedlings. Hopefully some will be true blue. Lydia is hoping for tri-colors. Her dream is red, white, and blue." Veronica put her hand on something that looked like a small refrigerator. "This is the incubator, if you want to call it that, where the altered seeds are brought to full maturity before they're encouraged to sprout. Because they're genetically engineered, they take longer to mature and sprout than regular rose seeds. That's why they bloom later than regular baby-bloomers." Veronica pointed to her right. "Over there, in that enclosed glass room, are the computers Papa and Lydia use for documentation. Everything is triple backed up on two different computers and printed out on paper files. The patents are applied for from these computers, but the original patents are kept in a safe deposit box at the bank."

"If your grandfather brought the Blue Moon down here, where would it be?" asked Russell.

Veronica shook her head as she looked around. "The seedling greenhouse is the only place with grow lights. Papa wouldn't have put the three missing roses someplace without proper light. They're too valuable. They're not here."

"If they were here, could someone have come down and gotten them?" asked Norton.

"I don't think so. No one is allowed in the lab. I don't think Mom, Uncle Jerold, or Lee's brother Marcus, even know about it. Lee knows about it, but he's never been down here There's an alarm system on the doors. If anyone tries to get in without putting in the code in the proper order, the doors relock and an alarm goes off. The alarm is connected to an alarm company that knows the layout of the house and lab. I would have gotten a call if the alarm was tripped. Only Papa Al, Lydia, and I know the code."

"Alright, the roses aren't down here," said Detective Russell. "Is there any other place they could be?"

25

"No place indoors." Veronica's mind whirled into new directions. She was sure she knew every inch of the Mason House. The only place they hadn't looked was the attic. Could her Papa have set up a grow light there? The attic was big enough for an entire garden. Then she had to question if she had the courage to face the corporeal beings who frequented that part of the house. She relaxed when she realized that setting up a grow area in the attic was more than an afternoon project because there were no electrical outlets or wiring to connect them to.

After the detectives left, Veronica went upstairs to Salvador's playroom. She peeked inside to see him and Jessica coloring at his table. The table her papa had cut the legs down on to make it child sized. "Hi. Can I come in?"

"*Hola, Mama. Si.*" Salvador looked up from where he was bent over his table, marker in hand.

"Thank you, Jessica," said Veronica. "We're all done downstairs."

After Jessica left, Salvador pointed to three pictures of Brandy stuck on the wall behind him. "I'm asking God to help us find Brandy."

She didn't want to say it, but at this point she felt it really would take an act of God to find the dog. *I really do need your help, God.* Her mind went right to the child development class she had taken in junior college. Part of the curriculum was about trauma and resiliency. Her son had experienced a trauma. He was going to need all the help and support she could offer to get him through this. It wasn't about just getting over it, toughing it out, or learning to be a man. He needed to heal. To talk about his feelings and know she listened to him and understood. "How are you doing, *Mijo*? What happened yesterday was sad and scary. I'm sad and scared, so I wonder if you feel the same way."

Salvador looked up at her, tears welled in his eyes. She sat in one of the low chairs and put her arms out for him. He nearly dove into her lap and cried. She held him to her. "Cry all you need to *amorcito*. I'm here for you."

"Uncle Jerold says boys who cry are sissies."

"Uncle Jerold is wrong. Boys have feelings just like girls do. They need to be able to express those feeling and not think they're wrong. I believe Uncle Jerold would be a lot happier if he could let himself cry rather than being angry at everything."

"Do you think he's sad that Papa died?"

"I don't know, Sal, but we're not going to talk about Uncle Jerold right now. We need to focus on us."

"Mom, I feel mad and sad right now. I don't want Papa and Brandy to be gone." Salvador raised his voice and clenched his little fists. "It's not fair."

"Oh *Mijo*," Veronica rocked Salvador to comfort him. "Life isn't always fair. It's people who try to make things fair."

"I feel kind of mad that you didn't let me hear what the detectives came to say. That wasn't fair."

Veronica wanted Salvador to tell her things. Now she needed to deal with it. "I'm so sorry. Maybe you'll understand someday when you're a dad. I told you I'd tell you what they said, so I will. Right now. The detective said Papa Al did not fall into the stream and die. Someone hurt him and he died before he got into the water."

"Why, Mom? Why would someone hurt Papa?" Salvador burst into tears and buried his face in her mother's shoulder. "What did they do to hurt him, Mom?"

Veronica felt sick. *Please Jesus, help me with this.* "I don't know. The detectives couldn't tell us." At that moment the soft sound of paper fluttering caught her and Salvador's attention. One of the lost dog pictures he'd made unstuck from the tacky, putty-like substance they used to put his pictures on the wall, and fell to the floor.

"My picture." Salvador untangled himself from his mother's arms and picked up his picture. He put it back on the wall using the same tacky putty pieces. "Do you think they hurt Brandy too?"

The thought of someone harming the dog was almost too much. "Oh, *Mijo,* I hope not. We're going to keep looking for her." A sudden thought came to her. "I tell you what. I'm going to scan one of your pictures into the computer then I'll make more lost dog posters to put up and send to more vets and dog rescues."

"Can I do it too?" Salvador took his mother's hand and looked deep into her eyes. It was more than a child looking up at his mother. Veronica felt he was connecting with her mind the same way he makes a psychic connection with animals. As if he could read her thoughts more easily than he could understand her words.

"Yes, you can. I always appreciate your help."

"Will you draw with me?"

"Yeah, if you'd like me to, but I'm not as good an artist as you." Veronica had been told by many people that Salvador's artistic skill was advanced beyond a child his age. She looked at her watch. "It's almost time for dinner so what do you say we come up and draw after dinner. Then if there's time, we'll work on more posters."

26

After dinner they returned to Salvador's room to draw. Many pictures later, Veronica glanced at her watch. "It's getting late, and you have school tomorrow." She started picking up the markers and crayons scattered across the table. "We can leave your drawings on the table if you want, so we can work on them after school tomorrow. But let's put your crayons and markers away. Can I help you get ready for bed? Would you like to take a bath or a shower? I'll get your PJ's for you."

"I'm going to take a shower. I'm not a baby anymore, Mom. And I can get my own PJ's and clothes for tomorrow." Salvador put the last of the markers in the container and snapped the lid closed. Without being told, he picked up the containers and put them on the shelf against the wall.

"Can I at least tuck you in?" Veronica remained in the low chair, what little energy she had seemed to drain down her legs and leak out through her feet. Even though Salvador was only seven, she suddenly saw him growing up and becoming independent. She was losing her baby boy. "I think I'll be sad on the day you don't want me to tuck you into bed anymore."

Salvador wrapped his arms around him mother's neck. "I still like it when you tuck me in. It makes me feel safe."

It was late into the night when Veronica finished the new lost dog posters. She used Salvador's drawing of Brandy as a background with a smaller photo of Brandy in the foreground. What could be more heart wrenching than a plea from a child asking for help to find his lost dog.

***

Unable to sleep, Veronica worked at her desk in her sitting room and listed all the people she thought might want her grandfather dead, and who would benefit most from his passing. Next, she printed out everything she could find about Inman Genetics. The deeper she dug the more conflict and controversy she found within the world of genetic engineering and among the different companies and labs that competed against each other.

With the grey light of early morning peeking around the shades Veronica felt she'd found as much information as she could. She checked the time. It was 5:30. She rested her elbows on her desk, dropped her head into her hands, and swore at the developing headache. Knowing she needed to get her day started she shuffled into her bathroom, installed sometime in the 1940's. Veronica was pretty sure the claw footed bathtub, toilet, and wall mounted sink were original from that conversion.

She washed her face with the goat's milk soap, from a local goat farm, Papa Al had bought for her. Adding a soothing layer of goat's milk lotion felt good, but it couldn't beat back the feelings of loss and sadness. She went back into her sitting room with the idea of relaxing in her rocking chair, but even though she'd been up all night, she was too keyed up for such comfort. She had a new understanding of the saying of, "having the rug pulled out from under you." Her Papa was gone, so was his Blue Moon. She couldn't help but wonder if the gardens would soon be gone as well.

She sat back down at her desk and opened the computer apps to check the overnight cameras. Along with the usual deer, raccoon, fox, opossum, and the cat Salvador had made friends with, there was a person. They walked right up to the front gate by the little red barn gift shop and stood looking toward the house before continuing down to the creek. Even though they had their head covered in a hood, Veronica got the feeling the person was male. Because of their fluid movements, she thought maybe a younger man. Certainly not an old man.

She first thought of Tyson, Tyler's teenage son. Just as quickly she knew it wasn't him. Tyson's body mass was much thicker, rounder. He didn't move with the same grace as this person. Her next thought sent a surge of anxiety through her chest and stomach. Could a stranger have come onto the property on Saturday? Papa Al would have confronted anyone in the yard. Could his death have been a random act of violence? An act of impulsive rage at being told to get off the property?

Veronica got up and opened the shades over the windows. The first golden gleam of sunlight lit the tops of the Sierra Nevada Mountains, to the east. She leaned on the windowsill. Her jaw clenched as her anger stabbed outward at life. She thought of the things the detectives had said and the questions they had asked.

Was she now a suspect in her papa's murder? She was the last person seen on camera to be with him and from what Lydia said, he'd called her to tell her Veronica had come home. She wondered how she was going to prove she didn't turn off the cameras and hadn't harmed her grandfather. Her anger turned inward toward herself. "How could I be so stupid for feeling so complacent and relaxed that the gardens would be part of my life, forever?"

As the sun rose and the beautiful colors of the roses in bloom in the gardens below her intensified, Veronica's anger turned to anguish. "How could I let myself fall in love with the roses and the Gardens when it could all be taken away so easily?"

Before her anguish could reach its building crescendo, she felt a warmth spread over her like someone had wrapped her favorite blanket around her. She backed away from the window and sank into her rocker. She pulled the soft pile blanket, her grandfather had given her when Salvador was born, off the back and wrapped it around her. In that moment her heartbreak melted away and was replaced by gratitude and thoughts of her grandfather. "I'm sorry Papa. I'm not mad at you. I'm just scared."

She dabbed at the tears with the edge of her blanket and spoke to her grandfather. She felt he was there with her. "I don't know if I could ever thank you enough for what you've done for me. How much you've given me and Sal. You gave me hope for the future, Papa. A hope I'm not going to lose now, I promise you. Whatever happens, I'm going to do my best and make you proud of me."

Veronica allowed herself to cry for a moment. She closed her eyes and rocked herself until she felt she could get up and meet the day. When she stepped into the hall, she noticed the door was open to Salvador's room. She heard a voice coming from inside it. She stopped and listened. At first, she thought Sal was watching a video, then she heard his voice as if he was in a casual conversation with someone.

It was the next thing she heard that threw her into action. Crying. Like the sound of an infant desperate to communicate, but not having the words to express their needs. She rushed into Salvador's room. "Sal! What is it Sweetheart?" He was sitting in the middle of his bed, facing away from her, dressed in his pajamas, hair sticking up in all directions.

When she sat down next to him and put her arm around his shoulders, she saw he hugged a rainbow of scarlet, blue, and green feathers to his chest. It was Bee Bop who was crying, something she learned when Salvador was a baby. "Oh, Bee Bop. Baby." She stroked the bird's head. Tears streamed down Salvador's cheeks. She didn't think there was anything she could say to make things better, but she had to try. "Oh, Sal, *Amorcito*, I'm so sorry about what is happening. Losing Papa and Brandy is very sad, but I'm here for you. We'll all get through this by being here for each other."

"Bee Bop knows Papa Al is gone." Salvador took several deep, sniffing breaths.

Veronica took Bee Bop from Salvador's embrace and set her on her shoulder. "Did Bee Bop come up here all by herself?"

Salvador nodded. "Right after Papa Al woke me up."

"What do you mean?" Veronica leaned back to study her son. There was no hint of mischief or trauma in his eyes.

"Papa called my name and woke me up." Salvador sat up onto his knees, his eyes bright. "Then Bee Bop pushed the door open and crawled on my bed."

"*Amorcito*, Papa Al is dead."

"He said he was okay now. He's with your grandma, but he's not gone and Grandma is here with him.

Veronica's thoughts whirled. *Grandma, not Lydia or my mom, but my grandmother.* "You were talking to Papa Al? Did you see him?"

"Uh huh." Salvador pointed to the middle of the room. "He was standing right there. I asked him about Brandy. He said she's okay and being cared for, but she wants to come home. We need to look farther away."

27

Veronica was glad she was sitting down. She put her hands on her knees and took a deep breath. She wasn't about to tell her son he didn't really see his dead great grandfather. He'd already shared that he'd seen the ghost of Maggie Mason, so why not Papa Al? At that moment she wondered if the warmth she had felt while standing at her window and down by the stream was her Papa Al.

"Okay. I think this is something we shouldn't tell anyone about. Not even Lydia. Would that be okay with you?"

"Papa said it's okay to tell you. Now Bee Bop knows too."

"Is it possible that you were just sleepy and talking to Bee Bop?"

"No, Papa Al was standing right there," Salvador pointed to the center of his room. "And he sounded like Papa Al."

"Okay." Veronica had no idea what to say to that. Her only thought was to do what she could to find a way to return their life to some kind of familiar routine even though she knew things wouldn't be normal for a long time. "I'm going to go start some breakfast. Would you like some help getting dressed?"

"Mo-om, I'm not a baby anymore. I can dress myself." Veronica almost expected to see him roll his eyes at her.

"Would you at least let me make you some breakfast?"

"Can we have pancakes?"

"Yes we can. Lee and Tyler would probably like some pancakes too. Come down when you're ready and don't forget to wash your face and comb your hair so you'll be ready for school after breakfast. We also have Bible study this evening, if you feel up to going."

"I like Bible study. We learn lots of things about Jesus."

"I like it too." Veronica reached to her shoulder and asked Bee Bop to step up to her hand with the command, "Up up" so she could carry the parrot on her hand.

Downstairs, Veronica went to the closed door of Lydia and Papa's bedroom. She stopped and listened. She heard the shower, meaning Lydia was up and following her normal routine.

In the kitchen, she set Bee Bop on her play stand, "How do pancakes sound for breakfast, Bee Bop?" She got a squawk for a response. She started a pot of coffee, took fresh eggs from the neighbor's chickens out of the fridge, then went down to the pantry and gathered all the ingredients for pancakes. By the time she returned to the kitchen the coffee was ready.

Lydia wandered into the kitchen and took several mugs from the cupboard. At nearly the same time, there was a quick knock on the door from the basement. Tyler slid it open and nodded his thanks to Lydia for the cup of coffee she handed him as he came into the kitchen.

Veronica felt the slight tension of a smile as she thought of Papa Al's comment that the smell of fresh brewed coffee was better than an alarm clock.

Lee and Salvador came downstairs together a moment later.

***

The term, "Business as usual," kept repeating itself in Veronica's mind. Salvador was eager to go to school to be with his friend Wyatt, his teacher's son. The day's work in the gardens was both normal and joyful. What wasn't usual was that Lydia spent the day in the Garden. While she enjoyed sitting out in the garden with a glass of wine, she rarely did any actual yard work. Because of this change in behavior and routine, Veronica checked on her often. The second time she checked on Lydia, the older woman was nearly invisible where she was squeezed between camellia bushes. Veronica got down on her knees to talk to her. "Hi, Lydia. How are you doing?"

"Just fine, Ronnie."

"Is there anything I can do to help you?"

"No thank you. I'm just pulling a few weeds here and there, and Arturo said gophers are starting to become a problem again, so I thought I'd look for holes and mounds."

"Thank you. That is helpful." The day zoomed along as Veronica cared for the roses in the greenhouse, reviewed orders for supplies, and made lists of roses to take to the farmers markets that would begin the next weekend.

Lunch with the family and staff was quieter than usual. It seemed no one was willing or ready talk about the gardens or the Mason House without Papa Al.

That afternoon, when Veronica's phone alarm chimed that it was time to get Salvador from school, she closed out her computer, grabbed her purse and left by the back door.

At his home school program, Veronica greeted Sarah, Salvador's teacher and her close friend, with a hug. She got a quick review of how Salvador's day had gone, gave Salvador time to clean up the toys he and Wyatt were playing with, and say goodbye to his best friend.

When they turned onto Serenity Valley Trail, Veronica had to pull over to let a county sheriff car get past them as it came up the one lane gravel drive.

Wondering why the police were at the house, she hustled Salvador inside and sent him to his room to change out of his school clothes. She went to Lydia's room and knocked on the door. When she was invited inside she asked, "I just passed a sheriff car on the way out. What did they want?"

"They wanted to know what kind of car Al drove," said Lydia. "I took them out into the garage to show them his Escalade."

"Oh." Veronica went into the kitchen and offered to help Jessica start preparing dinner.

She had just started making a salad when her phone beeped to announce a car coming down the drive. Veronica wrinkled her nose in disgust when she saw it was her uncle Jerold. She could also see that someone was with him. Veronica walked down the hall to tell Lydia, "Uncle Jerold's here."

"I wonder what he wants." Lydia looked up from her computer. Her tone of voice was casual.

"I have a feeling we're going to find out." Veronica met her uncle at the kitchen door. Her mother was with him. Her uncle barely got in the door when he said, "Brenda and I were talking and think you and Lydia need to be a part of the conversation." He glanced around the room. "Is Lee here? He needs to be part of this."

Jerold escorted Brenda, Veronica's mother into the greatroom with a hand on the small of her back. Veronica texted Lee to come upstairs.

The response was quick. *Yeah, I saw him pull up, be right there.*

Jerold looked up as Salvador came down the stairs. "Sal, you need to go back to your room until we're done."

Salvador hesitated for only a second before he rushed the rest of the way down the stairs to his mother' side. He grabbed her hand and squeezed, hard. Veronica allowed her anger at her uncle build. She wasn't about to give him what he wanted. Never again. "Sal's a part of this family. He has a right to hear whatever you're going to say."

"No, he's too young to understand."

28

"If he doesn't understand, he'll let me know and I'll explain it to him." Veronica let her uncle know he wasn't going to tell her what to do. Needing a moment to collect her thoughts, she pulled Salvador into the corner of the kitchen near Bee Bop's closet.

Bee Bop stepped out of her closet and said, "Up up."

"Good idea," Veronica whispered. She allowed Bee Bop to step up onto her hand then set her in her cage and shut the door. "You need to stay in your cage where you're safe."

She turned to Salvador just as Lee came up from the basement through the sliding door. She kept her voice low. "I don't know what my mom and Uncle Jerold are going to say, but I have a feeling it isn't good. You can go up to your room if you want and I can tell you what they said later."

Salvador whispered back. "I want to stay with you, mom. I'm big enough to hear what they're going to say."

"Okay, but I'm going to need you to be strong. No matter what they say, don't say anything even if it makes you mad. I have a feeling we're both going to need to be stronger than we've ever been before."

"I can do it, Mom." said Salvador.

"Okay, we'll be strong for each other."

Lee put a quick arm around Veronica's shoulders, and whispered, "We can do this. We'll all be strong together."

They went into the great room together. Lydia had come out of her room and sat in her recliner. Lee sat in the other recliner, away from his father. Veronica pulled over two chairs from the dining room and set them close together. Salvador sat next to her, his feet not touching the floor, but his back straight, his chin up, and his hands in his lap. The same way he would sit in church.

Brenda said, "Jerold has made some decisions about the house and gardens, Ronnie. I know you're not going to want to hear what he has to say, but it's best to get it over with so you can start making some plans for your future."

"I'm listening." Veronica clenched her fists in her lap.

"We're going to sell the house and gardens," said Jerold. "I've already contacted several gardening clubs and rose sellers. They're willing to buy what's in the green house and whatever the new owner doesn't want that's planted in the ground."

Veronica fought her urge to throw up. She had a hundred thoughts of, "what about …?" that she had to force to stay inside. Still, she voiced only one. Keeping her voice even and matter of fact was a struggle when she wanted to scream. She asked "What about Papa Al's will? It hasn't been read yet and we don't know what he wanted."

Lydia spoke up for the first time. "I'll contact his lawyer tomorrow. We'll set up a reading at her earliest available time, but your uncle has seen the will and knows the contents."

"I was with him when he had the will written," said Jerold. Except for any money Dad has in his savings and what's left in his pension, which will go to Lydia, the property is to be split 50/50 between your mother and me, to do with as we please. Neither of us want to take on the care and maintenance of this monstrosity, so we're going to sell it. I've already contacted several historical societies who might be interested. There are even several private individuals who have expressed interest."

"When?" Veronica asked.

"As soon as all the legal paperwork is done and any outstanding debts are paid. The will was written very clearly so the property shouldn't have to go into probate. I'm thinking we can put it on the market by June. If I don't have a buyer lined up before that."

"I know we have weddings booked starting the weekend after Mother's Day. Those won't be a problem," said Lydia. "We're only booked through June. Even if the property sold right away I doubt it would be through escrow before then. We just won't book any more."

"The next issue is you and Sal," said Jerold. The look he gave Veronica was as malignant as it was unsympathetic. "You can't stay here. I believe I'm being generous in giving you a thirty-day notice. I suggest you start looking for a job and a place to live, now."

Veronica clutched the edge of the chair seat. Her head spun as if she was in a whirlpool being pulled into the depths of a hopeless abyss.

Jerold looked down at his manicured fingernails. "I'd like the structure empty when we show it."

"What do you mean, empty?" asked Veronica.

"As in no one living here," said Jerold. "If the potential buyers don't want the furnishings I've got several antique dealer ready to make offers on everything. Anything that doesn't sell will go to Goodwill or the dump."

"You'll be able to keep any personal items and your and Sal's bedroom furnishing, of course," said Brenda. "But everything else belongs with the house."

"Veronica, I suggest any rose sales you and your Papa Al had started, be finalized as soon as possible," said Lydia.

"I guess that's about it," said Jerold.

"What about services?" asked Veronica, "What were Papa's final wishes?"

"That wasn't something we ever talked about," said Jerold.

"We talked about it," said Lydia. "The family cemetery plot here on the property is still permitted, so we'll use a site there. I just don't know when it will be. The police haven't said when they'll release his body."

"I'll call the mortuary tomorrow and set up for the site to be prepared," said Brenda. "He'll be right next to Mom. I think he'd like that."

Jerold stood. "Sis, Lydia, I'll call you tomorrow. I'm going downstairs to tell that alcoholic he needs to leave. I'm not about to continue to pay for him to keep working on this dump." He glared at his son. "Lee, that goes for you too, I want you home." Jerold looked around the room at each of them. "Okay. That's it." He held out his hand to Brenda. "I'll meet you out at the car. We've got some things we need to talk about yet."

The moment Brenda and Jerold left, Veronica took Salvador by the hand and left by the front door. She led Salvador through the yard into the Victorian garden with the garden swing where they were met by Arturo and Jesus. Both men stood quietly, holding their battered cowboy hats.

29

"Jessica texted me. She told me what your uncle said," Arturo put his arm around Veronica's shoulders. "Are you okay, *Chiquita?*"

"Thank you for asking. We'll talk later." She lifted Salvador onto the seat of the garden swing then collapsed next to him. Arturo tipped his hat to her as he put it back on his head, then he and Jesus went back to what they were doing. Veronica closed her eyes and used her toe to set the swing in motion.

Salvador curled up in her lap. "I hate Uncle Jerold."

Veronica didn't want to voice out loud that she hated him too, and at that moment, she hated her mother as well. No matter how much she wanted to scream and yell, right then, she knew she needed to take care of her son. "Did you understand everything that was said, *Mijo?* Do you want to talk about it?"

"Do we have to find a new place to live?"

"Uncle Jerold and mom are sure they'll get the house, so yes. But we're not going to do anything or worry until after the will is read."

"What's a will?"

"It's a paper someone writes to tell others what they want done with their stuff after they die. Uncle Jerold said Papa wrote a will saying his children get his house and his wife gets some of his money."

"Do you get anything?

Veronica heard the anxiety raise in Salvador's voice. She wrapped him in her arms. "Oh, *Mijo*. The things I got from Papa Al are a hundred times more valuable than money or objects and they will last my entire life. Long after the money Uncle Jerold, Mom, and Lydia get, is gone."

Salvador sat up and looked into her eyes. "What did he give you?"

"First, was my love of his roses and this garden. Second, was a place to live before you were born. As a money gift, he paid for my college education, with the understanding that I would be repaying him by caring for the Gardens when he couldn't anymore. But the most important gift Papa gave me is the ability to find my strength here." She put her hand over her heart. "He also gave me the courage to believe in myself. That I can do anything I put my mind to. He believed in me and was there cheering me on to do my best raising you and all through college.

"He also believed that our mistakes are things to learn from, and when bad things happen, we have to 'pull ourselves up by our bootstraps' and keep marching. And that's exactly what we're going to do.

"I promised Papa Al that even as much as it hurts to lose him, I going to make him proud. For a couple of years now, my dream had been to take over the Gardens when he couldn't do it anymore. I dreamed of watching you grow up here, following your dreams, and becoming the kind of young man any mother would be proud of. I didn't know if you'd be interested in being part of the garden when you grew up, but whatever you choose to do in life, I plan to be there to support you and encourage you to be strong and be a good human being. I don't want to leave here, but we will if we have too."

"Where will we go if we have to leave?"

Veronica felt her heart ache to the sadness and loss they were both experiencing at the loss of Papa Al and the Gardens. "We'll find someplace nice to live. Papa Al said my knowledge of horticulture and gardening as well as knowing how to run a business are things I will be able to use all my life.

"I have two college degrees. One for taking care of plants and one in business. I'll start sending out resumes to nurseries, rose growers, and beautiful gardens everywhere."

She thought of her conversation with Gustavo in Davis on Saturday. "There may be some rough times ahead, but that's part of life, and going through tough times not only makes you stronger, but it makes you grateful for the good times. So, we're going to stay strong, keep each other and Papa Al in our hearts, and do our best.

"We're going to be okay. Now, as long as I am here, I'm going to take care of the roses which means I have work to do. We still have some time before dinner, why don't you go get your helmet, gloves, and knee pads and play on your scooter?"

Back in the house, Veronica filled her insulated travel mug with hot herbal tea, and let Jessica know where she was going. In the mud room, she grabbed her gloves and garden waist pack which held a packet of disinfectant wipes, a bottle of non-toxic waterproof glue for sealing cuts to deter stem borers, and the holster for the expensive clippers Papa had bought her. Before she left the house, she ran a sharpener over the blade a few times to hone the edge, which would make for cleaner cuts.

Without a real destination in mind, she picked up a bright orange, five-gallon Home Depot bucket and stopped at the first bed of rose bushes growing along the cement walkway that ran next the wall from the kitchen door to the gate at the end of the building.

Allowing her mind to focus solely on the plants, she checked each bud for aphids and any variety of pests that made a nuisance of themselves in the garden. Many, like leaf rollers and weevils, she picked off by hand. As she dead headed any faded blooms, she was careful to cover the cut with a dab of glue. She kept an eye open for black spot and powdery mildew, the two main problems roses gardeners had to tend with in the area. After each plant, Veronica wiped the clipper blades with a disinfecting wipe to prevent the spread of any disease that would hitch a ride on her clippers from one plant to the next.

Behind her, the kitchen door opened and closed. Veronica turned to see Salvador come out, grab his scooter and take off down the cement walkway toward the workshop and garage where the driveway was paved.

Veronica's mind was clear and focused on what she was doing and at times she felt her grandfather was next to her, dipping his head in approval of her care and knowledge. She buried her nose deep into a beautiful white Ardelle. Part of the garden since the late 1950s. It was a large rose and one of her favorites for its fragrance. She frowned as she examined the newly opened buds. She deftly grabbed a small spotted beetle between and thumb and finger and squeezed. "We've got spotted cucumber beetles again this year, Papa. This is the first one I've seen, so I hope they aren't building up a resistance to the systemic we've been using."

Finished with the Ardelle she checked under the leaves of several roses that had yet to bloom and stopped at a smaller floribunda 'Dancing in the Dark.' She ran her fingers over the deep, blood red, blossom clusters that would shade to nearly black as they aged. "Who hurt you Papa? Who was it?"

30

The questions spun deeper and deeper in her mind. The beep from her phone pulled her mind back to the surface. A dump truck had come up the driveway. She started for the gate when Salvador came running toward her. "Mom! My dirt is here! Papa got my dirt!"

"What? What dirt?"

"The dirt he said he'd get for me to play in. The man with the dump truck is here."

"Oh yeah. Now I remember." Papa Al had promised to buy some dirt for Sal to play in with his toy trucks and tractors. It was enough to keep Salvador and his friends Wyatt, Steven, and Brandon busy and happy the entire summer and fall. Knowing it would get spread all over, Papa Al had purchased a load of quality gardening soil for the area where the hillside had been cut away to make room for the shop. Now, the area would have a nice layer of garden soil and enough left over for other planting needs around the gardens.

Salvador grabbed Veronica's hand and pulled her in the direction he came from.

Out on the drive, in front of the new shop, was a dump truck, its engine running. The driver, a middle-aged man with a girth nearly as large as the cab he was sitting in, got out and smiled a greeting. "I've got an order for some soil to be delivered. Where would you like it?"

"Right over here." Veronica led him to the area next to the shop. "You're working late today. It's already five o'clock."

He shrugged. "I'm short a driver. I promised Mr. Mason I'd deliver this last week, but got behind, so I'm delivering it today. I hope I'm not inconveniencing anyone."

Veronica couldn't help but smile as she looked down at Salvador. "No, you just made a little boy very happy."

"Got your toy trucks and tractors ready?" He asked Salvador. He looked around. "There's room enough for me to get turned around here. I can't back all the way into that space, but I'll get as close as I can." The driver got back into his dump truck and began a four point turn around.

Salvador was about to wiggle out of his skin when the dirt was dumped. The driver offered a quick wave and pulled away down the drive.

Veronica scooped up a handful of the dark, rich soil and watched Salvador climb to the top of the large mound of what he called dirt. She couldn't help but smile. It was little boy heaven.

After dinner, Veronica and Salvador left for Bible study. The house of worship they attended was literally a small house converted to serve the needs of the community. It invited all worshipers no matter what race, belief, gender, sexual orientation, or environmental and political ideals they might have.

The minster who led the services had an incredible way of knowing what her followers needed. She shared her love for others and her belief that all people were worthy of God's love. While Salvador joined his friends for the children's Bible study, Veronica joined the adults for their usual prayer and study group. Two of the people who stayed by her side were Will and Nolan. A married couple, they were neighbors and while they were both trauma nurses at the hospital ER, they were also gardeners and artists. Will gardened and Nolan sold his flower motif quilts at the gift shop. As different as two people could be, Will was tall and athletic. His dark complexion was an accent to his deep voice. Nolan was Will's shadow opposite. Slender, blond and slight of build, he was soft spoken with delicate hands.

During the course of the evening, Veronica was approached by people offering their condolences and prayers. She assumed Will and Nolan had told others what had happened to her papa. Veronica began to relax. The focus of prayers that night gave her a sense that no matter what happened next, she would find the strength to get through it, which strengthened her determination to find out what happened to her Papa. Veronica met up with Will and Nolan after the prayer group. "Do you have a moment?"

"For you, always," said Nolan."

Because Will and Nolan were neighbors, she had already talked to them about her grandfather missing and they had let her know the police had told them what happened and asked them about their visit, but she needed to know more. "You were at the garden on Saturday."

Will looked over at Nolan then back to Veronica. "Yeah. Nolan dropped off his newest lap quilt to sell at the gift shop."

"Did you see Papa Al?"

"We waved to him when we saw him up by the house. Tim and Mary were there setting out up some of their art in the gift shop so we didn't need to ask him to open it," said Will.

Tim and Mary were also neighbors and artists who sold their work at the gift shop. She had called them on Monday to ask the same questions. "Did you see Lydia, Tyler, or Lee leave or anyone else come or go?"

The couple conferred with each other through a look once again. "We didn't see Lydia. And Tyler left a little before noon," said Will.

"What about Lee?" Asked Veronica.

Will looked at his partner. Veronica was sure there was some sort of unspoken communication going on between. There was something they weren't telling her.

"I don't remember seeing him leave," said Nolan.

Veronica eventually thanked them and went to pick up Salvador.

He greeted her with the story coloring sheets he had done, but he was quieter than usual. On their way through the parking lot, to get to the truck, Salvador asked, "Mom, what's a state?"

An easy question to answer for a change. She explained what a state was, that states made up The United States, and that they lived in the state of California.

"Is California west?"

"Except for Hawaii, which is way out in the ocean, and Alaska which is up by the north pole, California is as far west as you can go before you step into the ocean. Oregon and Washington are states in the west also. They are north of California.

"Did your Bible class study states today?" she asked as she opened the truck door for Salvador to climb into his booster seat.

"No, we studied about ...." Salvador paused as he settled into his seat.

Veronica leaned toward her son. She saw that look of deep concentration she had been seeing more often. "What is it *Mijo?*"

"During bible study we went outside to look at the beautiful world God made, and Papa Al was there."

31

Veronica took a deep breath, realizing this was something that might happen more often. "Did he talk to you?"

"Yes, he said we'll find Brandy at the end of the western states."

Veronica did what she could to try and figure out what Papa Al meant. Thankfully, Salvador's next question stopped her mind from spinning.

"A hundred is a lot, huh?"

"One hundred?" Relative to what? She thought. Miles, dollars, questions on a test? "It can be. What makes you think about 100?"

"Papa Al said Brandy is at the end of the western states 100. What did he mean?"

"I don't know Sal. Maybe it means to look one hundred miles away."

"Could Brandy have run away that far?"

"Not in this short of time, but if someone who lived one hundred miles away found her and took her home, then yes, she could be one hundred miles away. I'll start looking that far away tomorrow when veterinarians are open."

***

The next morning, Veronica began her day making her list of which growers to call and looking up cameras to replace the ones that were missing. The next task was almost overwhelming. The list of veterinarians within a hundred miles to the west. She began calling animal shelters and vets in the Sacramento area and as far away as Davis, Vacaville, Elk Grove, and Woodland, sending each of them the poster she had created with Salvador's art.

It was after lunch before she got to garden business following her Papa Al's plan of offering his new roses for sale to breeders and responding to requests for photos of his new roses when they came into bloom. She ordered a rose book from the American Rose Society for herself which caused her to worry about what her mother and uncle would do with Papa's books and rose files. From that growing tension, a new kind of determination bloomed. She was going to do all she could to save Papa's files, books, and roses. She would give them away to gardening clubs if she had to, to save them.

The next thing she did was to begin working on creating a job resume. She was going to need a job to support herself and Salvador. Her phone alarm beeped. It was time to go get Salvador from school.

When they got home, Salvador headed right for his dirt pile with his toy trucks and tractors. Thankful for the diversion from the day's thoughts, Veronica followed him out to spend time with him. She sat at the edge of the pile with her back against the shop. She focused on Salvador's running dialogue about the road he was going to build and the imaginary crew he was going to hire.

That sent her brain into thoughts of her own job search when Bee Bop's loud scream interrupted her thoughts. Bee Bop must have come out through the dog door, as she often did to follow Papa Al or her around the yard.

"Bee Bop," called Salvador. "Where are you going?"

Bee Bop landed in the weeds at the top of the bank cut into the side of the hill.

Veronica got up and walked toward her. "Bee Bop. Here pretty girl."

The macaw turned her head and looked at Veronica. She made kissing sounds and greeted herself, "Hello, Bee Bop.

Pretty bird." She then began rooting through the grass and dirt with her beak, picking up small stones and twigs and tossing them aside.

Veronica held out her hand, hoping to lure Bee Bop to her. "Up up, pretty bird." Bee Bop turned toward her with a stone in her mouth. She rolled it between her tongue and upper beak. Veronica stretched out her hand, palm up. "Please don't eat a rock. Up, up."

Bee Bop waddled toward Veronica's hand and dropped the stone into her palm.

The gold and brown stripes of the stone oscillated in the afternoon sun. She knew the stone in an instant. "This is Papa's tiger's eye. How did it get out here? How did it get out of his pocket?" She closed her fingers around the smooth, polished stone and put it into her pocket.

She reached out to Bee Bop again, "Up up." Instead of stepping up onto her hand, Bee Bop took her thumb in her beak and pushed her hand away.

Salvador reached out his hand, "Come on, Bee Bop." Bee Bop pushed his hand away too, then turned and hopped along the edge of the bank with a flap of her wings.

Veronica followed from below until Bee Bop headed into the brush away from her. By then the bank Veronica was walking next to was only knee high. She stepped up into the grass to follow Bee Bop.

Keeping the bright red, blue, and green feathers in sight wasn't difficult, but trying to keep up with the rainbow moving through the underbrush was challenging. Veronica couldn't figure out what Bee Bop was doing or where she was going. She called to Bee Bop, "Cracker? Here pretty bird. Cracker."

The bird ignored her. As she worked their way through an area of thick brush that Bee Bop went under, Veronica could hear they were getting closer to the stream.

At a thicket of blackberries, Veronica had to go around where Bee Bop easily went under. At the other side she stopped and looked around. No Bee Bop. Worried about losing the macaw, Veronica called, "Bee Bop. Here Bee Bop. Cracker?"

A squawk came from inside the thicket near where she stood. It was then that Veronica noticed an area of new growth had been bent and broken. From inside the thicket, Bee Bop squawked and appeared to be pulling at something hung up on the canes. Veronica's heart jumped into the throat. The bright orange coating on the handles was unmistakable. Bee Bop had found her Papa's garden clippers.

Veronica got down on her stomach and tried to reach into the thicket to get the clippers but the sharp thorns poked and scratched her hands and arms. When she scooted around to try to reach into the thicket from a different angle, she saw something red, caught in thorns of a broken branch. It was a small scrap of cloth. Near the piece of red material was a small piece of blue fuzz. The fuzz looked familiar, but she was too focused on the red flannel to give it more than a glancing thought. She started to reach for the red scrap, then stopped herself. It was a piece of flannel from the shirt Albert Mason had been wearing when he was killed.

Veronica pulled her phone out of her belt pouch and called Detective Russell. Nearly breathless, she explained where she was and what Bee Bop found in the blackberry canes, including how Bee Bop found her Papa's tiger's eye. At Russell's request, Veronica changed the phone to 'facetime' and showed the red flannel, the blue fuzz, the tiger's eye and Bee Bop still trying to retrieve the clippers.

32

Detective Russell instructed Veronica not to touch anything and do what she could to prevent Bee Bop from moving the clippers any more than she already had.

"Mom, where are you?" Salvador called from up the hill.

Bee Bop was the first to respond with several loud screams. Veronica tried to talk over Bee Bop's screams, "Sal's looking for me," she said to Russell. Veronica looked up from her phone and shouted. "I'm here, Sal."

"What are you doing down here?" he asked coming through the thick brush.

"Following Bee Bop. I need you to do something for me."

"*Si, Mama.*"

"Can you crawl under there and get Bee Bop? She found Papa's clippers. I'm on the phone with Detective Russell and she asked to try to keep Bee Bop from moving them."

"How did Papa's clippers get in there?"

"I don't know, that's why I called Detective Russell. But we need to get Bee Bop."

"I can get her." Salvador studied the thicket from different angles. He got down on his stomach and wiggled through the only opening he could see.

"Please be careful. Those thorns are sharp." Veronica knelt near where Salvador went into the thicket and spoke softly. "Come on Bee Bop. Pretty bird."

From inside the tangled mass of blackberry canes, she heard Salvador let out a few, "Ouch. Ow." Then he said, "Hi pretty bird. Up up. Let's go get a cracker. You want a banana cracker?" A moment later Veronica heard Salvador say, "Good girl, Bee Bop. Up up."

Veronica waited with nervous anticipation as Salvador slowly wiggled out, feet first, using his toes and elbows to move backwards.

When he was out from under the thicket with Bee Bop perched on his arm, Veronica hugged him and kissed the bird on the top of her head. "Can you do something else for me?"

"*Si Mama.*"

"Take Bee Bop to the house and put her in her cage, then bring Detective Russell here when she gets to the house. She's on her way."

Veronica walked with Salvador back the way she'd come. She stopped where she could still see the thicket and waited. It wasn't long before Salvador came back leading the detective through the brush toward her.

The first thing Russell did was to ask to see the tiger's eye Bee Bop found and asked if Veronica was sure it was the stone her Papa always carried with him. Next she photographed the pieces of material and the clippers, then the surrounding area. "Is this part of your grandfather's property?"

"No, it's Addie Sweet's, who lives just up that slope."

"I met her when I was talking to neighbors. I'd like to know the story behind that woman."

Veronica grimaced, "Yeah, she's not very friendly and that's probably not her real name. She considers herself a cat rescuer, but seeing how she handled the two kittens she had in her hands when I went to ask about Brandy, I felt sorry for them."

Russell nodded, tapped a contact on her phone, and held it to her ear. "Phil, this is Jillian Russell. I've got something …" She walked away down toward the stream.

Veronica couldn't hear the conversation, but she had to believe it was important. She plopped down in the drying grass to keep herself from walking too close as she couldn't stand still. Her nerves jittered and poked her as if blackberry canes had suddenly grown inside her. She rubbed her arms and legs and ran her fingers through her hair as her mind created new worries about what the police would find and what they would think. It was only when Salvador sat next to her and laid his head in her lap that she was able to still her nerves.

Detective Russell walked back up to Veronica as she put her phone in her pocket. "Detective Norton is on his way to Miss Sweet's for permission to go onto her property and retrieve the evidence. If she doesn't us give permission, we'll have to get a search warrant. I've also sent for the CSI team."

Salvador looked around, "We're already here. Can't we just reach in and get the clippers?"

Russell gave Salvador a knowing smile. "Sounds easy enough doesn't it, but we have to follow police procedures. So what we're going to do now is go to your dirt pile and wait for the CSI team. If you grandfather's lucky stone was there, there might be more things to find."

Norton called Russell as they waited for the CSI team. Sweet refused to give permission for anyone to go onto her property, so they had to start the procedure to get a search warrant. A short time later the CSI team arrived and went to work on the bank where Bee Bop found the tiger's eye. Veronica pointed out where Bee Bop landed and found the stone then where she stepped up the bank to follow her. — bank?

Salvador stood close by watching the proceedings. "Are you going to take my dirt away?"

"No Salvador. We're not going to take your dirt away." Russell assured him. "We just need to look around before you can play in it. Do you have your trucks and tractors ready?"

Salvador's eyes lit up. "They're over there." He pointed to the far side of the pile. "Would you like to see them?"

"Yes, I'd like to see them, but you're going to have to keep working over there so you don't get in the way of the CSI team."

Salvador scrambled over the top of the pile just as one of the CSI team members held up a small plastic bag and said, "Bingo."

Russell was at her side in a second. "What do you have?"

"A button. It's a perfect match for the missing button ~~the~~ ~~on~~ the deceased's shirt," said the investigator. She had what appeared to be a small flashlight in her other hand. "My guess is that he was murdered here and dragged up the slope into the brush." The investigator then shined the light on the ground. Spots on the bank glowed. When she aimed the light at the grass where Bee Bop found the tiger's eye, more spots glowed. The technician photographed, then began scraping at the glowing spots and putting the bits of dirt into a plastic bag.

Russell's phone rang. She walked away to answer it.

Veronica leaned toward the CSI team member closest to her. "What kind of light is that and what's glowing?"

A technician shined the light on the ground where areas glowed. "It's similar to a black light. Body fluids glow in the light. In this case it's blood."

33

Russell walked back to them, putting her phone back in its holder on her belt. "That was Norton. He's on his way."

Detective Norton drove up to the shop and parked behind Veronica's truck. He offered a polite greeting to the CSI team, then said, "All right let's go."

"You got the search warrant?" asked Russell.

"Don't need it. Sweet, and that isn't her real name by the way, doesn't own the property or the house she's living in. It all belongs to a man named Aaron Rogers who lives in Pollock Pines. He gave us verbal permission to go anywhere on the property and take anything we need for our investigation. Since we aren't going into the house, we don't need a warrant."

"What's Sweet's real name?" asked Russell.

"Doris Norris," said Detective Norton.

"Why would she change her name," asked Salvador.

"People change their names for different reasons," said Russell.

If that was my name, I'd definitely change it, thought Veronica.

With permission to go onto the property, the CSI team once again put up yellow tape to block off the area, then began photographing, scraping, and gathering bits of dirt and grass to put into evidence bags. Veronica pointed out the route Bee Bop had gone to the blackberry thicket. The CSI team used their black lights. From their reactions there appeared to be a trail of blood marking a clear path away from the shop and into the thicket following the way Bee Bop had gone.

Veronica wasn't allowed to go with them so she followed their progress by watching from the back yard. She realized that whoever killed her papa made sure to stay far enough away to be out of sight from the house.

The CSI team eventually deduced that Albert Mason had probably been killed at the bank and carried, but sometimes dragged, as far as the tangle of blackberries where Bee Bop found his clippers. The discovery of the fuzzy blue material and the piece of red flannel suggested his body got tangled in or dropped in the briar on the way down a particularly rocky area to get to the stream. When the detectives and the CSI team were finally done, the entire area was closed off with crime scene tape.

Veronica waited for Russell before she went back to the house. "Will they be able to do a test to see if that's Papa's blood, even though it's been in the dirt for a few days?"

"Yes. They'll do a blood type and DNA test," said Russell. "Because your grandfather was in the water for so long it was difficult to get an exact time of death, but what you found might tip the scales as far as evidence. That was nice detective work from you and Bee Bop. The city might have to hire you two as a detective team."

Veronica heard friendship in the detective's voice. She felt a warmth toward this woman. *You'd have to include Sal. He's the one who talks to Bee Bop and Papa's ghost.*

She wasn't about to say that out loud, but there was something she did want to tell Russell. Veronica and Russell walked together toward the house. "Can I tell you about a couple of things?" asked Veronica.

"Does it have something to do with your grandfather?"

"Kind of, yes. I think so."

"I'm all ears, Veronica."

"Mom and Uncle Jerold came by yesterday and announced that they were going to put the place up for sale as soon as the will was read, and Uncle Jerold gave me a 30 day notice to leave. And– " Veronica clamped down on her lip as her anxiety built.

"Well that's not going to happen," said Russell. "Now that there's an official murder investigation going on here, no one can leave and the place can't be sold until the investigation is over, no matter if it takes a month or a year.

"If I may ask, I would like you to write down everything you remember about the conversation and email it to me. It could be helpful in the investigation."

"Okay, I can do that."

"Thank you. Now what else do you need to tell me?"

"Yesterday, when I got back from picking Sal up from school, a sheriff's car was just leaving from here. Do you know what they wanted?"

"I do, but that's part of the investigation and I can't share that with you."

"Oh, okay. Do you have any idea when Papa Al's body might be released for funeral services?"

"I can't answer that either, Veronica. Because I just don't know. I do know it will be after the full autopsy and toxicology report is finished. I'll let you know as soon as I know something."

"Thank you."

"We need to have a conversation with Mrs. Mason," said Detective Norton, walking up to Russell and Veronica. "Is she available?"

"She's in the house, in her room. I saw her move the curtains and peek out the window earlier. I'll let her know you need to talk to her."

Back in the house, Veronica knocked softly on Lydia's door. "Lydia, the police need to talk to you."

The older woman opened the door. She made eye contact with the detectives. "Is there something you need officers?"

"We need to speak to you for a few minutes, if you wouldn't mind," said Norton.

"Of course. Come in." Lydia stepped back allowing the detectives into her room, but she moved in front of Veronica. "Shut the door on you way out, won't you dear?"

"Uh, sure. Let me know if you need anything." Veronica understood she was being excused and not wanted as part of whatever conversation was going to happen.

It wasn't long before the detectives left and Lydia made it known that she wanted to be left alone and would eat dinner in her room.

Her mind nearing the stage of burn-out, Veronica curled up with Salvador on the couch in the great room and watched a movie on TV. Even with Salvador asking questions about why the characters did what they did, she couldn't focus on anything except becoming homeless and how she would care for Salvador.

***

The next morning, Veronica woke well before the sky signaled the dawning of a new day. She was surprised that she fell asleep so quickly and slept all night long. Her pillows propped up behind her back, she grabbed her phone off her nightstand and went through the photos from the motion sensor cameras during the night. There were deer, two silver foxes, Salvador's visiting cat, and a raccoon. She also checked all the garden's social media apps and email. There were the emails from rose gardens replying to her invitation to view her Papa's new roses, requests for information about weddings in the gardens, and the usual junk she deleted right away.

When she finished, Veronica got up, dressed, and went downstairs to make herself a cup of coffee before starting breakfast. She missed her morning workout with her grandfather, and made plans to get back into the routine when her energy allowed.

As Russell requested, she went into the office and began writing a detailed account of the conversation she'd had with Lydia, her mother, and her uncle Jerold. Veronica didn't know if it had anything to do with her grandfather's death, but Russell wanted her to write it down so she did.

She had just finished when Salvador came in, still in his pajamas. Without saying anything, he crawled onto her lap and tucked his head into her shoulder.

"What is it Mijo? Did you have a bad dream?"

Salvador shook his head. "No. I was hoping Papa would come visit me again, but he didn't. Do you think he's gone now?"

"Papa's spirit will always be with us. Maybe he wanted to let you sleep or maybe he didn't have anything important to tell you today."

"I miss him."

"So do I *Mijo*, but I still think God and Papa Al wants us to do the best we can and continue with our lives. Now, that means you need to get ready for school and I have work to do as well."

"Are you going to go to school again?"

Veronica laughed. "Not right now, even though there are still wonderful and exciting things I want to learn about."

34

"Are you going to be going to school when you get old, like Papa?"

"I don't know. Some people love to learn and want to make their lives better no matter how old they are. When I was in college there were a lot of old people going to school. Papa was almost eighty years old and he still studied and worked at making new and better roses. Scientists say that to keep your brain working you need to keep learning. It's like exercising. Even when you get old, if you want to stay strong and have fun, you need to keep your body healthy by exercising."

"Is that why you exercise?"

"Yes it is. I'm not old, but it makes my body, as well as my heart and brain healthy. And now I need to start breakfast. Do you want help getting dressed and ready for school?"

"No, Mom. We got my clothes out last night. I can do it."

"I forget how grown up you're getting." Veronica stood. "Come down as soon as you're ready."

Downstairs, in the hall, Veronica knocked on Lydia's door.

A quiet, "Yes?" was Lydia's answer to her knock.

She opened the door and peeked inside. Lydia was still in bed. "I'm going to make breakfast. Would you like something?"

Lydia let her head drop back into her pillows. "I don't think I have the energy to get up this morning."

"Would you like me to bring you breakfast?"

"You are such a dear, Veronica. That would be wonderful. I just can't summon the energy or interest to get up today. All I really want to do is lie here and cry."

"If you need to talk or a shoulder to cry on, I'm here."

"Thank you, but I'll get through this," sniffed Lydia.

After breakfast Veronica took Salvador to Sarah's for school.

Unable to focus on her own work when she returned home, Veronica went out into the garden with her tools and bucket. Arturo and Jesus were just pulling the mowers out of their trailer. They paused their preparations when she came up to them. Arturo greeted her with a hug and a kiss on the cheek, *"Hola, Chiquita. Como estas?"*

The conversation continued in Spanish. "I'll be okay. Thanks."

Jesus put his arm around her shoulder and pulled her to his side. "If you need anything, we're here for you … At least for as long as we can be part of the garden even though your uncle is planning to sell the place."

Veronica turned into Jesus' side and put her arms around him. "Oh, Jesus. Let's not go there right now. Detective Russell said nothing can happen until their investigation is over so let's just get everything ready for opening day."

After leaving Arturo and Jesus to their mowing, Veronica lost herself in the glory and beauty of the roses coming into bloom. In the sales garden she made sure each plant was labeled with its name and class. Miniature, floribunda, tea, grandiflora, shrub, climbers, ramblers, English, or old world. Each variety was in its own distinct area, clearly labeled. At the beginning of each section, she uncovered the information signs describing the cultivation and care requirements of each variety. To make sure the information signs made it through the winter in good shape, they had been covered when the gardens closed in October. Next Friday she'd bring out the fat-tired wagons to make it easier to cart multiple roses, selected for purchase, to the giftshop where the cash register was.

Veronica's phone buzzed in her back pocket. She recognized the number. It was Detective Russell. "Hello Detective Russell."

"Hello Veronica. I have a small request. I need you to come to the station for an interview. There are some questions I need to ask you."

Veronica's hands shook and her voice cracked. "Am I being arrested?"

"You were the last person to see your grandfather alive. You admitted to going into the greenhouse. At the same time the cameras went down. We need to talk. You can come down now, on your own, or I can send a car to come get you. Your choice."

"I'll come now. Where do I go?"

"My office is at the police station on Main Street. Just come in the front door. The receptionist will let me know you're here."

"Okay. I'll leave shortly. I want to put Bee Bop in her cage and change out of my grubby clothes."

Veronica went into the house and put Bee Bop in her cage with enough food and water to last a couple of days. Her anxiety simmered in a soup of fear that she couldn't cool. She knew she hadn't murdered her grandfather, but she didn't know if she could prove her innocence. The knowledge that the American justice system was based on a person's innocence until proven guilty wasn't a comfort at the moment.

At the police station, she handed over her purse, did as she was asked when she was searched and fingerprinted. She was read her rights, then escorted to an interview room complete with camera and a bare table with three chairs.

"Do I need a lawyer?" she asked Russell.

"Do you feel you need one? You have a right to a lawyer. If you don't have one, we can get you a court appointed lawyer."

Veronica's anxiety rose a notch when Phil Norton came in. Her first thought was, *oh my God, they're going to do the good cop-bad cop routine on me.* "I think it would be the smart thing for me to do, so yes, I would like a lawyer."

Detective Norton got up and left the room. It was a while before she was escorted to another interview room where she met a dour faced older man. "Veronica, this is Joseph Thurman. He will be representing you if need be."

"Nice to meet you, Veronica," Mr. Thurman offered his hand. "I'm very sorry about the loss of your grandfather. Please have a seat and we'll get started." He sat down opposite her at the small table and opened the file he carried with him. He took out a pen and pad of yellow, legal-size paper. "Now, please tell me everything that happened on Saturday, the day your grandfather went missing."

"I was taking my son to the Davis Picnic Day. I went out to the greenhouse to talk to Papa Al before I left," she began. She told about the day then looking for her grandfather when she got home.

Mr. Thurman eventually said, "Alright, I think I have all I need for right now. We're going into the interview with the detectives now. I want you to pay attention to me and only answer the questions I agree you should answer, and to stop talking immediately if I tell you to stop." They returned to the interview room with mirrors and cameras.

"Veronica, I'd like you to tell us about going into the greenhouse to talk to your grandfather, Saturday morning," began Russell.

35

Veronica heart sank a little deeper into the abyss of hopelessness when she explained about going out to the greenhouse alone with her grandfather.

The questions continued. She surprised herself when part of her attention was not only on answering their questions as best she could, but on what questions they asked, in what order, and how they were asked.

From the detectives' questions about where she was and what she did that Saturday evening, Veronica got the feeling they were going on information or a report that someone had heard or saw something that pointed a finger at her. She also had the feeling that they thought she had turned off the cameras, then removed them so her movements wouldn't be recorded.

Detective Russell asked, "Do you own a blue coat?"

"I have three coats. I have a long wool coat with a hood. It's tan in color. It's more of a dress coat, that I wear to church and school when it's cold out. I have a heavy winter coat for wearing around town and sometimes to school. It's bright purple and waterproof. I also have a rain coat I wear around the garden. It's black. I got it at the thrift store so I don't have to worry about tearing it on a rose thorn."

"Do you have any other coats?" asked Detective Norton.

Veronica thought. Was she missing one? "No, I have sweaters, and hoodies, but no other coats."

She was proud of herself for keeping her act together through the questioning, until they got to the conversation with her mom, her Uncle Jerold, and Lydia.

"Veronica, I have here a conversation you told me about, of what your mother and uncle said about selling the Mason House." Detective Russell pulled several sheets of paper out of her file and handed them to Veronica. She recognized them as a copy of what she typed up and emailed to the detective that morning. "Could you tell us about this?" Russell handed everyone a copy.

Veronica read aloud what she had written. Her sense of loss over her grandfather and the gardens she loved was overwhelming. She was thankful Russell offered her a box of tissues and a bottle of water.

"I understand that this is very difficult for you," said Thurman. "I want to assure you nothing in the house or gardens can be touched, except in the everyday business of running the gardens, until this investigation is over and the case is solved."

Veronica was equally comforted when Russell said, "I'm going to ask you to call me if Lydia or your Uncle Jerold start taking or selling items or showing the place to potential buyers or real estate agents before this investigation is over."

Detective Norton's next question knocked her off balance so thoroughly she could only stare at the detectives. Detective Norton asked the question again. "What can you tell us about your brother?"

Veronica almost asked what brother, as there were times she forgot she had a brother. She shook her head as if to reorganize her scrambled marbles. "Nothing. My father took him away when I was two. I don't even remember him or my father except from pictures Papa Al has. My brother was five years old when my father left. I know his name is Carlos, like his dad, and everyone called him CJ for Carlos Junior, but that's all I know. I don't know where they went after they left me and Mom. I never saw either of them again. Why are you asking about him?"

"We're trying to get an idea of everyone who had any kind of connection to your grandfather. Friend, family, or business. We're pretty sure two people were involved in the murder," said Russell. "Your grandfather was not a tiny man, even for his age. It would have taken two people to carry him from the yard to the stream where his body was found."

"Am I going to be arrested?" Veronica's thoughts went to Salvador. What would happen to him? Where would he go? Who would care for him?

"No, you're not being arrested," said Norton. "But don't leave the area."

Veronica saw a certain kindness in his eyes, but she knew he had a job to do, and felt he was determined to do it well. Veronica fought to hold herself together. It wasn't until she reached for another tissue that she realized she was crying again. "I'm sorry, I don't mean to fall apart, I'm just worried about my son. I didn't do anything to harm my grandfather, but I don't know if there's anything I can do to prove that."

"You don't have to prove anything," said Norton. "That's our job. The best thing you can do let us do our job so we can find out who did harm your grandfather."

When the interview was over Veronica spent a few more minutes with Mr. Thurman where he instructed her not to talk to anyone about what was said during this interview. She thanked him, took his card, and agreed to call him if she needed to, or had any questions.

Veronica pulled over twice on the short drive from Placerville to the Gardens to gather her wits and dry her tears. Her thoughts were filled with worry for Salvador. What would happen if she couldn't be there for him? That's when the idea came to her. Would Sarah and Dale be willing to take Salvador? Sarah Harvey was more than Salvador's home school teacher and sometimes babysitter. Salvador loved her like a second mother, but more important, Veronica trusted her.

What got Veronica's attention as soon as she walked through the door at home, was the quiet. Usually quick to call out if she was in her cage, Bee Bop was silent. Worried that her uncle had taken her to sell her, Veronica rushed to Bee Bop's cage. The large macaw sat quietly on her perch and looked at Veronica with ruffled feathers.

"Hello pretty bird." Veronica opened the cage door and offered her a slice of dried banana. "Pretty girl." Bee Bop didn't move to accept the offered treat. Even more concerned now, Veronica reached her hand to the bird and said, "Up up?"

This offer Bee Bop accepted. Once outside her cage, Bee Bop made kissing sounds, offered her dry tongue version of a kiss on Veronica's nose and said, "Hello," quietly several times.

After some head scritches, Veronica put Bee Bop on her play stand, refilled the bowl with fresh water, and headed down the hall. She knocked on Lydia's door. When she didn't get an answer she peeked inside. She wasn't there.

"Lydia?" Veronica called her name softly as she walked around the bottom floor of the house. A quick check in the garage told her Lydia was home, both vehicles were there. Not finding her inside, she went out the front door. Two white, straw cowboy hats moved among the old-world roses. Veronica pursed her lips into a thin line. If Arturo and Jesus hadn't had their hats on, she probably wouldn't have seen them. She went into the Old-World Garden. *"Hola, Arturo, Jesus?"*

36

Jesus backed away from the large shrub rose he was dead heading, removing the spent blooms. "Si *Hermana?*"

"Have you seen Lydia? She's not in the house, but her car is here."

Arturo joined them. "*Si.*" He pointed up the hill toward the back yard. "I saw her earlier out behind the greenhouse. She appeared to be looking for something behind the azalea bushes back there."

"She said she was helping look for gopher mounds in case we needed to set out traps," said Jesus.

"That's nice of her."

"Yes, but she hasn't mentioned seeing any," said Arturo.

Veronica returned to the house and went into the office.

She opened the notebook she had started using to keep track of her calls to veterinarians around the area. As she started flipping through the pages to get to the list she got distracted by the ideas for sales promotions she had written down in the notebook as part of one of her business classes at Davis. She'd continued working on the ideas after she graduated, but when she thought about the Gardens being sold, she lost all interest in what she was doing. Needing a distraction, she got up and headed for the lab.

Once she was inside, she opened the small greenhouse, and took out a tray of long test tubes, filled with water. Tiny cuttings with their stems immersed in the water rested in the open tops. She put the tray on a table and sat down just to stare at them.

They were part of her senior project to test starting success and growth rates of the cuttings. She'd used tap water from the kitchen, distilled water, three different types of commercial spring water, commercial "health" water with a ph of 9.0, and two natural sources of water. She'd gone to Coloma to get pure river water from the American River each week, and water from Hangtown Creek, which at one time was heavily polluted.

All the cuttings were from one rose, a *Rosa Mundi,* which can be notoriously difficult to start in a non-commercial setting. Because her instructor, who came to the gardens to see her Papa's growing setup, was so impressed with the lab and the greenhouse, he approved her idea for the project even though it had probably been done before.

She utilized long test tubes to make measuring root growth easier so she wouldn't have to disturb the cutting to get a precise measurement. With exacting care she had taken weekly measurements of root growth, stem growth, and the size of each new leaf.

Now that she had graduated, she had to decide what to do with the cuttings. When she started the project she'd planned to plant them in the Gardens. Her Papa had been delighted with the idea of an entire hedge row of Rosa Mundi gracing the front yard. Now she wasn't sure what to do with them. The dense weight of depression began to settle over her.

Veronica put the cuttings back in the greenhouse and checked the moisture, temperature, and light over the seed pots. She felt a surge of excitement when she noticed a few more of the seedlings just starting to poke their heads out of the soil. "Look Papa! The blues and tri-colors are sprouting." She spoke out loud, as if her Papa was with her. "These seedlings look healthier than the ones last year. I think you were right to change to the new soil mix."

Keeping with her papa's routine, she noted the numbers of the pots, which corresponded with the records of how that seed had been genetically engineered and charted the date they sprouted. There were moments, as she worked, she almost shivered to the feel of her Papa standing next to her, smiling his approval at her attention to detail in checking the moisture level in each pot and recording her findings. She also backed up the information on the computer and made a paper copy for the records.

Finished in the lab, she went up to her bedroom to continue her search for rescues and vets within a hundred miles west of Placerville. Her focus fully on her project she barely heard the familiar tap tap of nails on the wood floor in her bedroom, but the greeting of, "Hello, hello," got her full attention. She hit save and went into her room. Bee Bop was nowhere to be seen, until she noticed the bright blue and red tail feathers disappearing into her closet through the partially open door. "That's what I figured." She crossed the room and opened the door all the way.

Bee Bop picked up the shoe she'd been chewing on for the past few weeks, tossed it toward her and said, "Hello." Veronica knelt to the floor, handed the shoe back to her and gave the bird head scritches, while she double checked that there was nothing on the floor except the blanket Bee Bop and Brandy nestled in, the chewed-up shoes, and a partially shredded shoe box. She also checked that all the plastic storage containers were shut tight. She gave Bee Bop one final pet. "Chew on your shoe and box. I need to work on finding Brandy."

Veronica's stomach growled. She realized she'd missed lunch being at the police station. She asked Bee Bop to step up onto her hand. "Let's go down and get a snack then I have to go pick up Sal." Out in the wide hallway, Bee Bop launched herself off of Veronica's hand for flight and disappeared down the stairs in and graceful open wing glide.

In the kitchen Jessica was chopping cilantro for what she was making for dinner. She turned when Veronica walked behind her to get into the refrigerator. "Hungry. Just getting a snack before I get Sal," said Veronica.

"Would you like me to make something for you?" asked Jessica setting the knife down on the cutting board.

"*No, gracias.* You're busy with dinner." She pulled out a carton of almond milk and something wrapped in foil. "Is this that banana bread you made?"

"*Si.*" Jessica held out her hand. "Let me cut a couple of pieces for you while you pour yourself a drink."

As soon as Jessica unwrapped the banana bread Bee Bop flew onto the floor and nibbled at Veronica's ankles. "Cracker, cracker."

Both Jessica and Veronica laughed at her timing and antics. Jessica put two pieces of bread on a small plate then cut a third small piece that she picked up with her fingers. She set the plate on the table for Veronica and offered Bee Bop the small piece she held. "Here you go Bee Bop. Pretty bird." She then sat down at the table across from Veronica. "*Estas bien?*"

Veronica took a sip of almond milk she'd poured for herself and looked up at the housekeeper whom she considered a friend as close as a sister. "I don't know, Jessica. Things are hard right now."

"Jesus and I are here for you, if you need us." Jessica put her hand on Veronica's. "No matter what happens." She pushed the plate closer to Veronica. "Eat. You have a little one to care for as well as a big business to run. You need your strength."

"*Gracias, Hermana.*" Veronica gave a soft laugh, then asked, "Have you talked to Lydia today?"

Jessica shook her head. "No. She ate lunch in her room, but did not speak to me. Then she went outside."

"Losing Papa Al has been hard on her," said Veronica. Her thoughts suddenly surged in a different direction. Lydia had admitted that she was never romantically close to Albert, so her loss of him probably focused more on her losing her free ride and now having to find a place to live and paying her own way.

37

After she finished her snack, Veronica grabbed her purse then went out the kitchen door and around to the far end of the greenhouse. There she found Lydia sitting in a flower bed under a large native Toyon bush. "I'm going to go pick up Sal from school. Are you okay?"

"I'm fine. I just don't have a lot of energy, but I want to help out in the garden."

"Thank you, Lydia. We're all here for you if you need us." Veronica turned and left. She was careful to drive the speed limit. When she made a left onto Mallard Drive she noticed a tan Jeep not too far behind her. *No, I'm not a flight risk Detective Russell. I really am just picking up Sal from Sarah's. Then we'll go right home.*

Veronica texted Sarah to let her know she was there and went inside without knocking on the door. Salvador and Wyatt, Sarah's son, greeted Veronica at the door to the school room with hugs. "Mom, can Wyatt and I finish our game?" asked Salvador.

"You'll have to ask Miss Sarah if she has a few minutes to spare," replied Veronica.

Sarah looked at Veronica with the sight of a mother and schoolteacher that can read between the lines. "That would be fine. You boys go into the playroom. Veronica, can I offer you a cup of tea?"

"I would love one. Are you sure you have time?"

Sara put her arm around Veronica's waist as she guided her into the kitchen. "I always have time for one of my best friends."

Veronica sat down and fought off her tears while Sarah started water to heat and set out teacups with a selection of herbal tea packets in a bowl. Veronica chose a Stash, pomegranate-raspberry green tea, tore open the packet, and set the bag in her empty cup which Sara then filled with hot water from a glass tea pot.

Sarah sat down across from Veronica at the small kitchen table. When Veronica sniffed, Sarah reached back to the kitchen counter and picked up a box of tissues. "What is it, Love?"

Veronica took a tissue from the box, dabbed at her eyes and blew her nose, then took a deep breath. "I have a huge favor to ask of you."

"Okay. You know I'm always here for you."

"There's a possibility I may be arrested for Papa Al's murder." She kept her voice at a near whisper so the boys wouldn't hear.

Sarah gasped. "Veronica, what happened?" She moved around the table to sit next to Veronica so the conversation could continue in whispers.

"The police wouldn't tell us the details, but Papa Al was murdered. I don't know what kind of evidence they have but they asked me to go into the police station for what they called an interview that was more like an interrogation. They searched me and read me my rights. I'm worried they're going to arrest me."

Veronica accepted Sarah taking her hand. "I didn't do anything to hurt Papa Al, Sarah. Not even by accident."

"Have you thought about getting a lawyer?"

"I had a lawyer from the courts with me for the questioning. He was okay. Now my only thought is for Sal. That's what I need to ask you about. If something happens, could he stay here, with you?"

Sarah moved closer and took Veronica in her arms. "Yes, we'd be glad to care for Sal. Dale and I both love him, and I know Wyatt does too. And I'm going to give you the name of a good criminal lawyer."

"You know a criminal lawyer?"

"Do you remember when my little brother got into trouble a few years back? He was guilty, but he was a stupid kid, not a criminal. A lawyer named Robert Gartner took his case. I think you might want to talk to him. I have his information in the office. I'll email it to you."

"Thank you. What do we do for Sal? Do we need a lawyer for that too?" Veronica took a sip of her tea.

"I'm sure we will." Sarah took a small notebook out of her apron pocket and began making notes. "It's probably something that needs to be set up through the courts and social services, but I want you to let me get that started. We'll have to do it together, but you have enough to worry about right now."

"Thank you, Sarah." Veronica felt her eyes begin to water. "You are such a great friend. If something horrible happens, I can't think of anyone I'd rather have to take care of Sal."

"Now tell me what else is happening. What's happening with Lydia, your mom, your uncle Jerold and the Gardens? Sal said something about you having to move and the place being sold."

Veronica and Sarah sat and talked for another twenty minutes about Veronica's plans if she had to leave the gardens. Their conversation was interrupted by Sarah's husband, Dale, walking into the house. Home from work as the head mechanic at the county road department. Dale was a big man, but Veronica had never seen him without a smile on his face.

Dale set his large metal lunch pail on the counter and scooped up his wife for a man-sized hug and kiss. "How you feeling today, Sweetpea?" He put his hand on Sarah's stomach and grinned over at Veronica. "Did Sarah tell you? We're expecting another crumb cruncher. In October."

Veronica flew to her feet with one of those girl screams of pure joy. "You didn't tell me. Congratulations!"

All three adults were in a hug when Wyatt and Salvador came into the kitchen to find out what all the commotion was about. "Hi Dad!" Wyatt flew to his father, arms up for a hug.

Dale scooped him up. "How's my big man today? What are you and Salvador up to?"

"We're playing colony, but a blob monster is eating our town."

Dale put on a very serious face. "Hmm. That can happen to colonies in unknown lands. Where was your colony?"

"We decided on the planet of Earth 2."

Dale laughed and set Wyatt back on his feet, "My little superhero is an explorer now. How was school with your mom today? What hidden corners of the mind did you explore?"

"We learned about where babies come from and watched a baby chick be born on YouTube. Mom said maybe we can get one of those ink-you-bator things and hatch our own baby chicks. Can we Dad?"

"We'll talk about it."

Salvador's face lit up. "Mom! Can we have a baby too? Just like Wyatt's going to have?"

Dale laughed a full hearty laugh. Veronica hugged Salvador. "That's something we'll talk about later. After we know where we're going to be."

There was a quick whispered conversation between Dale and Sarah. After more hugs, Veronica and Salvador headed for the door. She took Sarah's hand and spoke softly. "You two talk. Okay. Two's company but three might be a crowd."

Dale's gaze bounced between his wife and Veronica. "What?"

38

Sarah took Dale's hand, kissed it, and said, "I'll explain everything, later." She gave Veronica one last hug and whispered, "It's going to be okay."

When Veronica left Sarah and Dale's she felt emotionally better than she had in days.

After turning onto Mallard Drive, from where Sarah and Dale lived, Veronica noticed a car sitting up on the hill alongside a side street, that pulled out onto Mallard right behind her. She got the weird feeling she was being followed and hoped like everything it was the police making sure she went home and didn't go on the run. In a strange way having the police so near was comforting.

That's when another concern hit her. Even though she was going to be jobless and homeless, with a seven-year-old child, soon, she was worried about the Blue Moon. Her thoughts were burdened about what happened to the blue rose and what someone might have done, or yet do to get it. If it had been stolen, it was easy to think about what someone would do to prevent her from finding out who did it. If it was hidden, what would someone do to find it?

She turned onto Serenity Valley Road and stopped. She turned to Salvador. "I'm going to get the mail."

Salvador's focus was out the back window. Veronica followed his gaze. The car that had been following them crept past at a snail's pace then went out of view behind the thick brush that blocked her view of the road. Veronica grabbed her mailbox keys. "I'll be right back."

When she stepped beyond the narrow drive, onto the wide turnout next the road, she saw the car parked just beyond the mailbox. Her nerves scattered like a herd of frightened deer. She couldn't think what to do. She paused at the mailbox, but kept an eye on the car. The driver appeared to be a woman. She was on the phone. Veronica relaxed, slightly. It wasn't unusual to see someone parked alongside the road to talk on the phone. She fumbled with her keys to open the locked security mailbox when she thought she saw the woman look into her rearview mirror.

Thinking only of getting back to Salvador, she grabbed the armful of mail, slammed the box door shut and hurried back to the truck. Again, she hoped it was the police just checking that she went home.

Veronica headed for the office while Salvador remained in the kitchen to say hello to Bee Bop.

She had just gotten started going through the mail when Salvador came into the office, school pack hanging over his shoulder. "Can I do my homework at Papa's desk?"

"Yes, of course. Let me know if you need help and when you're ready for me to see what you've done."

Veronica had asked Sarah to give him homework every day. Not only did his homework give him the advantage of working at a level above the other students his age, but it set him up to have good study habits for when he was older and to help him be self-motivated as well as be responsible.

His willingness to take on the responsibility of doing his homework was fed by her attention to what he was doing and praise for doing his work with care. She looked up from her work to see him bent over his paper, pencil gripped tightly in his hand. He appeared to be drawing, rather than writing. "What are you working on, *Mijo*?"

Salvador got up with his drawing in hand and set it on her desk in front of her. The image was of a person, probably himself, holding a baby. "Can we have a baby like Wyatt's going to get?"

While her actions, at the age of sixteen, may have been impulsive and borne of childhood trauma, the result was the most precious gift from God she could ever have. While she lived through the roses, her purpose in life was Salvador.

Veronica looked to Heaven to ask for guidance. "Sal, that's something we'll have to talk about later. After we know where we're going to be and what kind of job I get." The next thought jumped into her mind like a frog into a pond. If she was going to be arrested for the murder of her grandfather, she had Salvador to worry about, even if they let her out on bail. That was another part of her fear. Bail for murder had to be a lot. She had a small savings, but she didn't own property she could use for collateral. She was pretty sure her mother and uncle wouldn't help her and she wasn't sure about Lydia.

After dinner, Veronica went up to Salvador's room where they read stories, colored pictures, and did puzzles. "Mama, are you sad?" Salvador seemed to notice she was lost in thought while putting together their puzzle.

"I just realized that trying to figure out who killed Papa Al is like putting together a puzzle. First you have to find the pieces, then you have to try to figure out where they fit. That is probably how detectives do it."

"Do you think the police will find out who killed Papa?"

"Yes, I do."

***

Veronica didn't fall asleep until after midnight, but her day started at 3:30am when Salvador's crying woke her. Hyper alert to his voice, she was out of bed and across the hall when he was just crawling out of his own bed. *Amorcito!* What is it?" She picked him up, sat down on his bed and rocked him. "It's okay, *Mijo.* I've got you. You're safe."

"I had a dream there was a bad person." Salvador buried his face into her shoulder. "They wanted to hurt you."

Veronica felt helpless. She couldn't tell him that no bad person was going to get her. "Can you tell me about your dream? Did you see the person?"

Salvador shook his head, rubbing it into her shoulder. "I couldn't see them. I could only see you."

"It was just a bad dream. A lot of scary things have been happening. It's been enough to give anyone bad dreams. Let's go to my room where we can be together in case you have another bad dream." Veronica stood with her son in her arms. Walking across the hall, she realized he had gotten too big to carry.

She sat against her pillows and rocked him in her arms until he fell asleep, then laid him down next to her. Unable to relax, she had her own visions of someone coming after her, and worries that Salvador's dream was more than the bad dream of a child who had just experienced a trauma. Her brain kept circling around to the idea that the dream was a message from her grandfather and that she was in danger.

As the grey light of another day peeked around the edges of the window shades, Salvador wiggled his way up to sit next to her as she ran through the security camera app on her phone. When she went through the camera feed of the front parking lot and gift shop, the person caught Salvador's attention. "Who's that?" He pointed to the person with the hood over their head, standing near the front gate of the gardens.

"I don't know. Maybe a homeless person looking for something to eat." *Or something to steal. Or could it be the person who killed Papa?*

Before her thoughts could go too far in that direction, Salvador pointed at the next piece of camera feed, "Mom look! There's the cat. She came. Can we put some food out for her? I think she's hungry."

Veronica put her phone down and put her arm around her son. She didn't want to think that the stranger had come to do them harm. She turned her attention toward her son and the cat. "Yes, we can. We'll stop at the feed store and see what kind of quality cat foods they carry, but I have a feeling we'll be feeding half the wild animals in the area as well. I'm glad you got back to sleep. How are you feeling this morning?"

"Okay, but can we stay here for a while?"

"No, it's time to get up." Veronica kissed him on the cheek as she swung her legs off the bed to get up. "You have to go to school, and I have work to do."

"But what about the bad person in my dream?"

"I think it was just a bad dream, *Mijo,* but I'll do everything I can to keep myself safe and be very careful around people I don't know."

"But what if it's someone you know?" Salvador's voice rose an octave.

That's an even scarier thought. She recalled Phil Norton's comment that most murders are committed by someone known to the victim frightened her. "Then I'll keep myself safe even around people I know–except you."

39

Friday brought another beautiful day in the paradise that was the Sierra Nevada foothills. Lee returned from his dad's and went right to the basement to start work on whatever Tyler needed him to do.

After taking Salvador to school, Veronica began her workday in the greenhouse. There wasn't much that needed to be done, but being locked inside a secure area among the roses she loved soothed the raw edges of her nerves. The buds of one of the roses she had bred the year before were just developing, the sepals not yet unfurling to show the bud's colors. She had crossed a Gold Bunny with a Purple Tiger in hopes of getting a flower with purple and yellow stripes. Resisting the urge to spread the sepals a little to get a look at the colors was almost painful. She felt a little like her grandfather, had said he felt a kid at Christmas wanting to peek into her presents. She laughed at herself. "Oh Papa, how did you resist peeking–most of the time?"

The vision of her grandfather bending to look closely, with a slight nod of his head, then moving on to the next plant, brought a smile to her lips.

Finished in the greenhouse and careful to lock the doors when she left, she went out into the gardens to wander among the roses. With her bucket, disinfecting wipes, and her clippers in their holster on her belt, she lost herself in the beauty of the Serenity Valley Gardens. She felt as if her soul was being soothed.

She greeted Arturo and Jesus when they entered the Victorian garden with rakes, hedge pruners, and wheelbarrows to begin their work in that garden. She clipped a perfect red blossom of a Ruby Wedding and sat down on a bench overlooking the gazebo where the weddings were to be held. Beautiful blooms of the climbing Swan Lake covered the gazebo in bridal white.

Veronica looked into the blossom of the rose she held and wondered if she would ever walk across the lawn to the gazebo for a wedding of her own. The thought had come to her from time to time since Salvador was born, but she always shook it off. Other than Salvador and the gardens, there was nothing else in life she wanted. She didn't need another tragic love story as part of her life.

There would probably never be that special someone who would sweep her off her feet. But somehow, the idea of a lifelong partner was comforting. What surprised her most was that not only was she was totally open to a platonic relationship, lately she had begun to visualize that special partner being a Ms. Right.

The camera app on her phone beeped to a car coming down the drive. A familiar, full-sized SUV pulled up next to the gift shop, behind Arturo's truck and wire enclosed trailer. It was Tim and Mary Archer, neighbors and artists who offered their artwork for sale, and worked in the gift shop on the weekends the Gardens were open. Veronica watched as Mary unlocked the gift shop with her key while Tim pulled boxes out of the back of their vehicle. Mary's paintings of birds and flowers went into the gift shop and Tim's garden creatures, welded together from pieces of old tools and scrap metal, went into the small fenced section next to the gift shop.

The Archers waved and made their way toward Veronica.

Tall and skinny with a beaklike nose, Tim didn't walk so much as he seemed to flow across the ground. Nearly as tall as her husband, Mary was built solid with big hips and thighs. There was nothing delicate about that woman. In their thirties, they had two boys who were nearly the same age as Salvador and were two of his good friends.

The Archers' expressions, when they got closer, spoke of genuine care, but Veronica couldn't help but wonder if they were the kind of people who would harm someone for an imagined slight or political difference. The detectives said it took two people to take her Papa to the stream. The Archers clearly fit the police description of the strength needed.

Mary was the first of offer Veronica a hug with benefactions of support and caring. "Oh Veronica, how are you doing? I can only imagine how hard this week has been for you after Al's passing."

"If there's anything we can do for you, please let us know." Tim's hug was firm, then they sat on either side of her on the bench.

Mary took Veronica's hand. "How are Salvador and Lydia doing?"

"Salvador's hanging in there. I'm trying to help him get through this the best I can. Lydia's withdrawal into what seems like depression has me a little worried. While we've never been close, I still wish there was something I could do for her."

"She's a strong woman. She'll get through this," said Tim. "And how about you? You going to be able to manage these gardens by yourself?"

"I don't think that's going to be a challenge, Tim." Veronica felt tears pressing against the back of her eyes. "Mom and Uncle Jerold are going to inherit the Mason House and Gardens, and plan to sell it. Uncle Jerold has already given me a thirty-day notice to leave."

Mary in her usual openness and willingness to make lemonade out of lemons put her arm around Veronica's shoulders, "Oh, Sweetheart, you have nothing to worry about. With your education and skills, you'll be able to go anywhere in the world and get a job."

"Thanks Mary. I've created my resume and have started sending it out to different botanical gardens."

"So what kind of environment would like to see Salvador grow up in?" asked Tim, "There are gardens all over the world, and not all of them are in big cities. You could even homeschool Salvador if you wanted."

"Speaking of homeschool, we're thinking of changing school systems for our boys," said Mary. "Does Sarah have room for a couple more kids?"

"I'm sure she does." Veronica looked between Tim and Mary. "What's happening?"

"We're just getting disillusioned with the public school system and want something better to meet the education needs of the boys. Salvador seems to be doing so well at Sarah's, and he really likes her and her school program."

Veronica took a breath. She had to start somewhere. If she was going to save herself, she had to know more than the police knew or were willing to tell her. "You were here Saturday afternoon when papa Al disappeared. Did you see anyone do anything that seemed off to you?"

"That's the same thing the police asked," said Tim.

"I know, but they won't tell me anything. They're even pointing a finger toward me. Maybe you thought of something after you talked to them."

Mary raised her voice. "They're crazy to think you would have hurt your grandfather. You weren't even here."

"We only came to drop off some paintings and sculptures," said Tim, his chin resting on his chest in thought. "Will and Nolan came right after we opened the little red barn, but I do remember something." Tim pointed to area above and behind the shop, thick with brush and live oaks. "I thought for sure I saw a flash of blue of someone walking through the trees, up on the hillside. I didn't actually see anyone, just the flash of blue. Bright sky blue. Almost bluer than the sky is today."

40

Their conversation was interrupted by the arrival of a large delivery truck pulling up to the front gate. "That should be the tables and chairs for the weddings," said Veronica. "Thanks. I'll talk to you guys later."

"We'll head that direction, too," said Mary. "We want to get started on the outdoor displays for Tim's new artwork we brought."

Veronica met the truck driver at the gate and directed him back to the paved drive that went along the sales garden to the house, and where to park for the easiest access to the basement.

Once the delivery driver took in the tables and cartons of chairs, Veronica signed the delivery invoice and tucked the copy he gave her in her back pocket.

Tyler and Lee stopped work on tiling the bathroom and started opening the boxes. "Let's see what we've got," said Tyler.

He and Lee set up the two folding tables for outside where the weddings would be held. He checked their sturdiness and that the legs folded and unfolded smoothly. "These are nice. They'll work well. Now, let me show you how to store them." With Lee's help, Tyler refolded the tables and showed Veronica how they would be stored on a rolling platform that slid in and out of a custom-made closet. Veronica was impressed with the ingenuity of the design. It worked so well she could pull out and set up the tables by herself.

The thirty outdoor plastic chairs hung on a rack that slid out of a closet. Tyler settled his bulk on one of the chairs before he hung it on the rack. He wiggled some then nodded his approval. "These are more comfortable than I thought they'd be, and they feel sturdy. Good choice."

The tables and chairs put away, Veronica went upstairs to the office and sat at her papa's desk. He was truly a modern man, he read books on his kindle, had the latest iPhone, and the newest computer, but he used a land line phone for the gardens, and kept a copy of all his records on paper. She turned on his computer to see if there were any new emails from people they had contacted. Because she was so involved in helping with running the gardens, he had given her all his passwords.

Papa Al's phone logs, which she'd already gone through, offered a brief explanation of who he'd talked to, but the emails were often more detailed. Within a short time, Veronica had a list of growers and breeders she needed to call. She wasn't surprised that the list was worldwide. Her grandfather had done work in countries all over the world.

She glanced down at the time on the tool bar at the bottom of the computer screen. It was too late to call any of the overseas companies, but she could call the nurseries in the US. She started on the East Coast and worked her way west. She was able to reach about half the people on her list. She explained who she was and that her grandfather had passed away and she was trying to continue his work, so if any potential deals had been made for rose sales she needed to know so she could honor that sale.

She got six hits for roses that were identified only by a number, and two for the Blue Moon. Those two were sending someone to see the rose.

One of the growers was surprised that their rep, Daniel Benson, hadn't called yet. "He should have been there by now," said the woman on the phone.

The rosarian, Mr. Benson, came every year, and Veronica knew him well. He was an older man, almost frail looking, but he was pleasant and knew his roses.

The feeling of loss and sadness at selling these roses, other than the blues, was almost overwhelming. Veronica had fallen in love with two of them. There was the hybrid tea that was deep yellow with orange in the very center of the flowers, known only by a number. Her favorite, a silver and red striped, she'd named Fire and Ice.

Following her grandfather's protocol, Veronica offered assurance to each of the breeders who were interested in the numbered roses. "Yes, the roses are still available for sale, they are in bud, and should be in bloom by the end of the next week. If you can't send a representative, I can call and do a live video feed of the roses once they bloom."

Because her grandfather had done business with all the breeders over the years, there was trust that the color wouldn't be photo shopped. She remembered her papa's words, "What you see is what you get."

Veronica also assured the breeders, "Yes, each one of my grandfather's new roses have been engineered with the gene to be resistant to black spot and powdery mildew."

She hung up the phone from her last call with a sense of completion. The two rose companies that were the breeders her Papa Al most admired were local. One in California and the other in Oregon. Both expressed their sense of excitement in anticipation of the Blue Moon blooming by the end of the week as her Papa had told them it would. When they mentioned sending a representative the moment color started to show on the bud, Veronica had to tell them that her grandfather was dead, and the Moon was missing.

What she hadn't said was that Serenity Valley Gardens would be closing and all the roses would be put up for sale, because that loss was just too hard to talk about.

Lydia followed Veronica outside after lunch. Lydia stayed in the backyard while Veronica went into the garden with the Old World and Species Roses. She wandered among the large rambling bushes where she clipped off the faded blooms and checked the leaves and growing tips for rust, black spot, and powdery mildew, the three problems the old roses were most prone to develop. Her phone interrupted her thoughts when it beeped to a vehicle coming down the drive. She saw a Jeep pull into the drive and park next to her truck. With a sigh of anxiety, she recognized Detective Russell. She grabbed her bucket and headed for the house.

Veronica called out, "I'm down here Detective Russell." She waved her arms to make sure she was seen.

Russell waved in acknowledgement and came toward her. She started out in her usual business-like way. "Is there somewhere we can talk in private?"

"Yes, of course." Veronica looked up at the inn. Privacy wasn't a problem if she wanted to be alone-unless you included the inn's apparitions. The problem was sound proofing. "Let's go to the sunroom where we can sit and talk." Veronica was sure that even if Lydia was nearby, she wouldn't be able to hear a conversation through the double pane glass walls unless she had her ear pressed to the glass, but they would see her if she did.

Russell set her briefcase at the corner of the low coffee table and directed Veronica to pull up a chair, so they faced each other across the corner. The detective started pulling files out of her case. "Do you know an older man by the name of Daniel Benson?"

"Yes. He's a rosarian who buys some of Papa's roses every year for Lighthouse Roses."

Russell pulled an 8x10 photograph out of an envelope and put it on the table in front of her. "Is this him?"

"Yeah, that's him." Veronica looked at the picture of the kind old man who always bought some of her grandfather's roses. A wave of worry washed over her. "Why are you asking me about him?"

"I'm asking because your name was found in his motel room."

"It's understandable that he'd have my name. He's here to buy some roses. He comes every year. I didn't talk to him, but Lighthouse Roses told me he should have been here already. Did you ask him why he hasn't called or set up a time to come see the roses Papa Al was going to sell to him?"

"I couldn't ask him. He was murdered earlier this week."

"Oh my God!" Anxiety and fear washed over her. "He was such a nice old man. Do you know who did it?"

"It appears he was killed the same way your grandfather was. Where were you Tuesday night?"

"Sal and I were at Bible study."

"Where was your Bible study?"

When Veronica told Russell the location of the church, she could see the tension increase in Russell's body.

"That's right across the street from the motel where Mr. Benson was staying. Were you alone at any time while you were there?"

"Not usually. Let me think. Oh, there was a short time when I needed to use the bathroom just to take space with so many people offering their sympathy over Papa Al's death."

Russell pulled out another sheet of paper. "Is this your signature?"

41

Veronica studied the paper. "That is my name, but that isn't my signature. I mean it's close, but it's too wiggly."

"Do you have a sample of your signature somewhere?"

"Yeah, lots of them in the office. Oh! And here." She leaned forward and pulled her copy of the signed delivery slip from her back pocket. She unfolded it and laid it on the table in front of the detective. "The wedding tables and chair were delivered this morning. I signed for them, and the driver gave me this copy."

Russell set the signatures side by side and studied them closely, then photographed them next to each other. "I'm not a handwriting expert, but these are definitely different. I figured you would know which company sent Mr. Benson and might use your name and not your grandfather's."

The tension in Veronica's back eased. This was something she could handle. "I just talked to Lighthouse Roses and told them of about Papa Al dying. They told me Mr. Benson had been sent to buy some roses but didn't know why he hadn't contacted us yet."

"He hadn't called you to let you know he was here?"

"No, I checked all of Papa's messages and emails, and didn't see anything from him."

"Do you have a record of your grandfather's phone messages and emails since his death? And do you have something else you signed within the past few weeks? I'm going to need another sample of your signature."

"Yes, and yes and okay. We'll have to go into the office. Everything is there."

Veronica led the detective to the office. She got into the cabinets against the back wall and pulled out different files. Both she and Russell started going through them with the detective photographing some of them. Once Russell felt she had enough example of Veronica's signature, she asked for information about sales representatives.

Veronica offered to print out a list of every company they dealt with, and the week's emails related to roses.

"That will be very helpful," said Russell. "While you're doing that, may I get on your computer?"

The tension returned to Veronica's back and shoulders. She thought for a moment. What would she be looking for on my computer? All the things on her computer ran through her mind. She knew there was nothing that could link her to her grandfather's murder. "Be my guest. Most everything on it will probably be boring. There's nothing personal on it, no love letters to anyone, no angry rants to neighbors, not even any juicy emails to past classmates. You can even get on my social media if you want. There is nothing the entire world hasn't already read."

Veronica wrote down her password to get onto her desktop and her email password. "I have a laptop upstairs as well, but it's linked to this password, so what you see down here is the same as on my computer upstairs in my room. If you want to get into anything else that needs a password just let me know."

From her papa's desk, she picked up a notebook and handed to the detective. "This is the list of all the rose breeders Papa sold roses to. The highlighted the ones are calls from the breeders interested in his roses this year."

Russell looked at the list and her papa's phone log, side by side. "Many of these contacts are dated today." There was a hint of surprise in her voice.

"There's stuff I have to do." The sadness that engulfed her diffused the tension in her stomach. "If Mom and Uncle Jerold get possession of the Gardens, I want to make sure any deals Papa had started are able to be finished. But mostly I wanted to know if he sold the Blue Moon."

"Is that what the buyers are coming to see?"

"No, they're coming to see some other roses. Buyers for the Moon want to see it in bloom. They want to see proof it's real. People have been photo-shopping blue roses for ages. There are pictures of blue roses all over the internet, but none of them are real.

Veronica's voice wavered. "I had to tell all the buyers that Papa had contacted that the Blue Moon is missing."

"Why has it been so hard to create a blue rose? I understand that there aren't any blue roses in nature, but with genetic engineering what's taken so long?"

"Most of it has to do with the fact that genetic engineering is an exact science, but it's not always successful. They've gotten shades of purple and mauve, but not blue."

"Well, maybe when God created the blue sky, blue fish, and so many blue birds, he or she said, that's enough blue for a week's work."

Veronica laughed, "Maybe that's why there are no blue dogs or blue and white zebras."

"Yeah, it would be fun to see zebras dressed in something other than your basic black and white. But blue dogs? I don't know. That would take some getting used to." Russell's tone became serious. "Now that I'm learning more about roses, I'm understanding how it would be that someone would commit the ultimate crime over a flower. Who– " Russell's phone rang interrupting her comment. She answered it with a simple, "Russell ... Phil, what have you got? ... Hang on. I'm at the gardens now. I'll call you right back." Russell looked up at Veronica. "I need to take this call in private. I'll be in the library." Without saying anything else she got up and left the office.

Veronica followed Russell out of the office as far as the stairs. "I'm going to use the bathroom upstairs."

She went up the stairs. Directly over the great room she opened a door and went into the bathroom that put her over the library. Closing the door quietly behind her, Veronica knelt next to the heater vent on the floor. She carefully opened the grating and settled to the floor with her ear next to it.

"Phil, this is Jillian. You got the report from CSI and the coroner?" Detective Russell's voice traveled through the heating system as well as her mother and grandfather's voices had when she and Lee were ten and had accidentally discovered how voices carried from the library to the bathroom.

"The same knife or the same kind of knife? ... The same knife. That could explain why we didn't find it with Mason's body. ... The same multiple stab wounds? ... In the same places. That's interesting. The fingerprints on the paper are a match for Veronica's?... Hmm, no the signature doesn't match. I had her sign on a piece of paper and I have enough signatures on documents from over the past 12 months to prove she signs the same way each time and it's not a match for the letter. ... No, not yet. I don't believe she's a flight risk and the evidence we have right now is just too circumstantial. I want to wait until the DNA on the coat comes back. ... Yeah, thanks ... Her cooperation seems to be 100% so far ... Yes, all right, I'll touch base with you when I'm finished here."

42

For a moment Veronica thought she was going to pass out. Black spots popped in front of her eyes, then she heard a soft knocking on the door. Unsure her legs would hold her up, she crawled to the locked door and said, "Yes?"

A throaty voice replied. "Hello? Cracker?"

The barest of smiles twitched at Veronica's lips. *Bee Bop to the rescue.* She opened the door then held her hand out to the feathered rainbow on the floor. Bee Bop took Veronica's thumb in her beak and went through the motions of regurgitating to feed her as an act of bonding. Veronica smiled and said, "I love you too, pretty bird." She scooted out into the hall to sit cross legged next to Bee Bop.

Bee Bop crawled into her lap then rolled over on to her back, let out a loud, wild laugh then said, "Give me kiss?"

Veronica smiled at the big bird's antics. She picked Bee Bop up and held her in her arms like a baby then kissed her on the beak. Bee Bop made loud kissing sounds until there was the sound of footsteps coming up the stairs. Veronica re-positioned Bee Bop to sit on her hand so she could hold her at eye level and see who was coming up the stairs. It was Detective Russell.

Russell made eye contact with Veronica, came the rest of the way up the stairs, then squatted in front of Veronica. "I was wondering what all the noise was up here."

Bee Bop bobbed up and down, let out a wolf whistle and said, "Hello baby."

Russell laughed. "Hello to you pretty bird."

Veronica kept a close eye on Bee Bop's eyes for any sign of pinning. Her pupils shrinking to the size of a pin prick.

"Do you think she'll let me pet her?" asked Russell.

"We can try," said Veronica. "Try stroking the top of her head, but keep an eye on her pupils. When a parrot pins their eyes at you, it's time to back away. If she bows her head, it's safe."

Russell slowly reached out. Bee Bop bowed her head to allow the touch. The detective gently stroked her feathers. "This is so cool. I didn't realize she'd be so soft."

"Parrots like being groomed at skin level, it's called scritches in parrot language, but you don't want to go beyond their head and neck." Veronica gave Bee Bop scritches on the top of her head to show Russel how.

"Scritches not scratches. Why don't you want to pet them anywhere but on their head and neck?"

"For a parrot, petting them anywhere else is stimulating."

"So you end up with a lascivious parrot."

Veronica could see Russell was trying to contain a laugh. Veronica said, "Yeah, not the role model you want with children in the house. Parrots are ruled by hormones as it is. You don't need to add fuel to the fire."

"Sounds like having a mare." Russell relaxed to sit with her knees bent, her feet under her.

"A mare?"

"A female horse. They're pretty much ruled by their hormones as well. People either love them or hate them. There are even jokes about having a bad mare day, but I wouldn't trade my mare for anything."

"You have a horse?"

"A mustang I adopted from one of the prison mustang gentling programs."

"They put horses in prison?"

Russell laughed. "No. They round up wild horses then take a few to different prisons around the country. Inmates get a chance to give back to society by getting the horses gentled and ready to be adopted. In return the inmates learn patience, humility, and what it means to develop trust. These programs are great, and more than a few inmates have gone on to work with horses when they're released."

"How long have you had your horse?"

"Almost six years now. She's my bud and partner. I mostly do trail riding, but we're just starting to get into competitive trail riding."

"What's that?"

"It's where riders take their horses out on the trail and go through obstacles such as jumping logs, going through water, and opening and closing gates. Each horse and rider is judged at the obstacles and the ride is timed. They're fun and challenging. Thankfully they're not long. I don't think I could do endurance races."

"What are those?"

"Long distance races. They can be anywhere from 25 to 100 miles. They're held all over the world but one of the toughest is the Tevis, or Western States 100."

Veronica almost dropped Bee Bop. *Could that have been what Papa meant when he told Salvador to look at the end of the Western States?*

"What is the Western States 100?"

"It's a 100 mile race. It used to be just for horse and rider, but now they've opened it up to people-runners. It goes from up near Lake Tahoe, cross country over mountains on some of the toughest trails there are, and ends in Auburn. It takes a human about 24 hours, but a horse can do in about 6 or 7 hours." Russell shook her head. "I'm just not up for sitting in the saddle for 7 hours."

Auburn. The end of the Western States 100. That's what Papa meant. Auburn's not that far away, but how would Brandy have gotten to Auburn? Veronica's mind jumped into that blender on high speed. She felt like her thoughts were going a hundred miles an hour. It made her dizzy.

Russell rose to one foot and one knee on the floor. Her voice and the concerned look on her face brought Veronica out of her thoughts and gave her eyes and mind something to focus on. "Veronica. What just happened? Are you all right? Do you need me to call an ambulance?"

"What?" was the only thing Veronica could think to say.

"The color just drained from your face. You looked like you were going to pass out."

Veronica held Bee Bop to her chest and whispered to the top of Bee Bop's head. "What do I do? Help me, Papa."

Bee Bop squirmed away from Veronica's grasp to climb down to the floor. She tilted her head to look up at Veronica and said in her grandfather's voice, "Tell her." Bee Bop then turned to Russell, bobbed her head and said, "Tell pretty girl."

"Veronica, what just happened? That wasn't the parrot's voice."

Veronica leaned forward, hands to the floor, to keep herself upright. She felt the tears drip down her cheeks. *Oh God, if I don't end up in jail for something I didn't do, I'm going to end up in a mental hospital.* "That was Papa Al's voice. He's been talking to Salvador and through Bee Bop since Sunday, helping us find Brandy."

"What are you supposed to tell me?"

43

"It was something Papa Al said to Sal on Tuesday. To look for Brandy at the end of the Western States 100. He must have known we'd have this conversation, or he–" Veronica looked up at Russell. She wondered if she'd end up in a straightjacket before she was put in handcuffs. Bee Bop crawled back into her lap and made kissing sounds.

"Veronica, what do you mean, your grandfather told Salvador?"

In for a penny, in for a pound? It was something her grandfather always said about getting involved in something. She took a breath. *I'm not crazy detective Russell, really I'm not.* "It was Papa who told Bee Bop to tell Salvador to look in the stream after the flat tire. Salvador is sure it was Papa who made the tire go flat at exactly that spot.

"Salvador has a connection to animals. He's an honest to God animal whisperer. Animals, like the stray cat at Addie's, come up to him. Twice now, Salvador has talked to Papa Al. Once in his room to tell him he was okay and he was with grandma, and again on Tuesday in the garden at church to tell him to look at the end of the Western States 100 to find Brandy."

Veronica sank into a relaxed state of radical acceptance of whatever was going to happen next. "I had no idea what that meant until you just explained what the Western States 100 was, and I probably just convinced you I'm totally nuts."

"Veronica, I'm not one who can pass judgment on what you've experienced." Russell pursed her lips. "I'm going to be honest with you. I've only been on the Placerville police force for two years, but even in that short of time I've heard stories from officers, from over the past 60 years that many of them, good, honest, officers have seen ghosts or spirits in this area.

"Different officers have reported seeing the same person in certain locations only to have them vanish into thin air. Most of the officers don't talk openly about their experiences but the stories are shared now and then to those they trust."

"Ghosts are common in Placerville." Veronica said. "You've probably seen the books written about them. Have you ever been on the 'ghost walk' through town?"

"Yes. It was led by a docent, highlighting the places ghosts are seen most often," Russell gave a little shiver. "The docent talked about The Cary House Hotel in town, the Vineyard House in Coloma, The Bee Bennett Mansion, The Hangmans's Tree, and the Gold Bug Mine. One of the retired detectives I know told me about the ghosts he and other officers have seen at Lyon's Park. I bet even this place has its own visitors from the past."

"From the past and present," said Veronica.

Detective Russell laid a hand on Veronica's arm. "The only thing I'm going to ask is that if something like this happens again with Bee Bop or Salvador, please tell me. And if you find you dog in Auburn, I especially want to know about that."

"Okay." Veronica looked at her phone. "It's getting late. I need to go pick up Sal from school. If you need me to stay I can call Sarah and ask her to keep him for a little while. It will probably be all right, Sal and Wyatt are good friends so they'd enjoy some play time together."

"No, you go pick up your son." Russell stood and offered a hand to help Veronica to her feet. "I've downloaded most of what I need to my work computer, so I can continue from the office or home. I'd appreciate it if you make any calls to your contacts and find anything out about other representative that are coming, that you let me know who and when."

"Sure. I'll text you or call if I find out something worth knowing."

"Sounds good. I'm going to get going and let you go get your son." The detective and Veronica walked down the stairs together. Bee Bop, on Veronica's hand, whistled, and asked for kisses, and crackers until they reached the kitchen. The scent of onions and chicken sautéing in chili sauce filled the air. Russell reached for the door, but looked over at Jessica stirring what was on the stove. She nodded toward the stove and then spoke softly, "That smells really good."

Veronica glanced toward Jessica then smiled at the detective. "When all this is over, can I invite you to dinner? Jessica is an excellent cook."

Russell gazed into Veronica's eyes and said, "I accept that invitation. I hope we can do it soon."

"I do too."

Once Detective Russell had gone, Veronica knelt to set Bee Bop on the floor where she made a beeline for her closet, whistling until the door closed behind her. Veronica stood and stared out the kitchen door window, wondering about what had just happened between her and Russell. Were the vibes she was feeling real? Or a police ruse to gain her trust and let slip a confession about murdering her grandfather?

Her phone rang. It was Sarah. "Hi, can you stay a little while when you come to get Sal? Dale's bringing home an old garden tractor for the boys to take apart and eventually learn how to fix. That would give us a chance to talk about the information I got from the lawyer."

"Sounds good. I'm on my way." Veronica felt like the weight of a thousand pounds had been taken off her shoulders in knowing she was doing her best for Salvador. That no matter what happened to her, he would be cared for.

***

She parked in front ~~to~~ of Sarah's house with the same sense of comfort she always felt when she picked up Salvador. It was the solace that he loved his school environment and was succeeding to such a high degree as a student, even as young as he was. The tension drained from her body when Salvador and Wyatt ran from the open garage with shouts of joy and greeting. Salvador stripped off his disposable gloves and grabbed his mother's hand. "Mom! Come see the tractor Mr. Dale brought home. We're going to fix it." He pulled her toward the garage. Inside, the machine in the middle of the garage was old, faded red and rusted, but it was a real tractor.

Dale met her with his usual smile, but his tone serious. He addressed Salvador first, "Sal, go get the gloves you dropped. If you need a new pair, put those in the garbage and get some new ones." He turned to Veronica, lowered his voice and nodded his head toward the door into the house. "Sarah's waiting for you in the house." His smile broadened. "I'll save your hug for when I'm cleaned up. Right now, I have two young mechanics to take care of."

Veronica put her hand on Dale's arm. "I can't believe how happy you've made a certain little boy." She clenched her lips between her teeth for a second and added, "And you won't believe the sense of relief you've given that little boy's mother."

She went into the house where Sarah led her into the living room.

As soon they were settled next to each other on the couch, Sarah said, "Dale said yes, absolutely. He loves Sal. He said Sal can stay with us as long as you need him to. He's always welcome." She gave Veronica a quick hug then held her hand and added, "I contacted a lawyer with family services and got the paperwork started. We have an appointment to go over the forms Monday."

44

"I can't believe you got so much done so quickly." Veronica gripped Sarah's hand in an effort to prevent her tears from building. "Thank you. I love you both. I hope I won't need to take you up on your kindness, but it eases my heart to know he'll be safe with you."

Veronica paused for a moment to take a deep breath. She looked back at Sarah. "I don't know what's going to happen, but somehow I will pay you back for what you're doing."

"You don't have to pay us anything. We're your friends and we're doing this because we love both of you." Sarah leaned back into the soft cushions of the couch. "Can I get you some tea while the guys play tractor mechanic? It'll be a little while before hunger pulls them away from what they're doing. In the meantime, we can have a cup of tea and a blueberry muffin I made this morning. How does that sound?"

"That sounds awesome."

Veronica stayed longer than she expected, but Dale and the boys were still elbow deep in greasy tractor parts when she and Sarah went out into the garage. "Are you guys about done for the day?" asked Sarah.

"Just finishing up," grinned Dale.

"It's going to take you a while to clean up, so I'm going to take a quick run to Raley's." Veronica pulled out her keys and walked toward the open door of the garage. With the store only a quarter mile away, the trip would be quick. "I'll be right back."

Veronica set the bag of cat food on the back seat. Back at Sarah's, Salvador leaped into his booster seat and held the bag all the way home. "Do you think the kitty will like this food?"

"As expensive as it was, I hope so. And if she's hungry enough, she'll eat it." As she drove down the driveway, she slowed and hugged the edge of the road as Arturo and Jesus were using the weed eaters along the drive. When she stepped into the house with Salvador at her side, Bee Bop let out a loud scream from the top of her cage then in a quieter voice, said, "Hello, hello. Cracker? Cracker?"

Salvador dashed to the counter to grab some almonds and banana chips, then climbed onto the step stool next to her cage so he could reach the top. "Hello, Bee Bop." Veronica stroked the top of Bee Bop's head.

Salvador gave her an almond. "I love you Bee Bop."

"Bee Bop loves you." Veronica kissed Salvador on the cheek. "Why don't you take an early shower. There are smears of grease on your arms and face. I'm so glad Miss Sarah let you wear some of Wyatt's clothes when you were working on the tractor. That black grease would never wash out of your good school clothes."

"I'll wear my old clothes to work tomorrow," Salvador's voice rose with a tone of excitement. Sarah and Dale had invited Salvador over to work on the tractor.

"That's a perfect idea. And take some clean clothes to change into when you're done. Maybe we'll go out for pizza, afterwards."

When Salvador headed upstairs, Veronica walked down the hall to Papa Al and Lydia's sitting room. She knocked and waited until she heard Lydia say, "Yes?"

Veronica looked around as soon as she went in. "You've moved everything around." The furniture had been rear-ranged. This surprised her as the desk, small couch and chairs were heavy. "Did you do all this yourself?"

"Heavens no," Lydia laughed. "Lee helped me."

"That was kind of him." The one thing that stood out to Veronica was that the desk had been moved so that the computer monitor faced the back wall and Lydia could look up and see anyone coming into the room without turning, and no one could see her computer screen when they came through the door.

"I needed something to take my mind off things," said Lydia. "I don't have the interest to do much of anything else. Is there something you need?"

Veronica noticed a touch of irritation in Lydia's voice. "I just wanted to ask if there was anything I can do for you?"

Lydia reached for a tissue and dabbed her eyes. "I'm fine, Ronnie. It's just been a rough week."

"Yeah, it's been hard for all of us. I'll let you know when dinner's ready."

Back in the kitchen, Veronica set a gentle hand on Jessica's arm. "I'm going down to talk to Tyler." She reached for the sliding door that led down into the basement.

"I'll leave this door open." She didn't want to say out loud that she didn't feel safe with Tyler. That she couldn't help but wonder if he was responsible for her grandfather's death.

Jessica nodded. "I will be close by." She glanced toward the mudroom where her husband, Jesus, was washing up for dinner. "We will both be close by."

"Thanks, Jessica." Veronica started down the stairs, her mind considering the plausibility of Tyler drinking again, going into a drunken rage at Papa Al saying Tyler's son Tyson couldn't come onto the property anymore, and something horrible happening when no one else was around. Tyler was large enough to overpower any of them, even Lee, Arturo or Jesus.

As she turned the corner at the pantry, she was hit so hard she was nearly thrown off her feet. Suddenly she was grabbed by the shoulders which kept her from tumbling backward. The profanity that went with the grasp was right in her face. "Sorry Ronnie! Sorry. Darn. I was charging up the stairs like a bull elephant."

Veronica looked up into her cousin's face. "Thanks for catching me. I wasn't paying attention to what was in front of me."

"I guess I wasn't either. Are you okay?"

"Yeah, I'm just going to talk to Tyler for a minute. Is he downstairs?"

"He's in the apartment." Lee passed her and trotted the rest of the way upstairs.

Veronica went around the corner in the basement just as Tyler was coming out of the newly rebuilt apartment he'd been calling his home. "Tyler, can we talk for a minute?"

He stopped and faced her, his voice gruff. "What's there to talk about? Your uncle told me to get out."

"Tyler, I know what Uncle Jerold wants, but I also know Papa Al told you that you could stay here as long as you wanted, or needed, as long as you continued to work on the house. He saw the quality of your work and was very happy with what you'd done so far."

"That doesn't matter anymore, does it?"

45

"Yeah, it does. Detective Russell said my uncle cannot do anything concerning the Mason House while the murder investigation is going on. Detective Russell said to keep doing things as normal until the case is closed.

"I know Uncle Jerold and Mom plan to sell, but they both said that even if the property sells right away it will be a month or so before escrow closes so we can have the weddings already booked. The gardens are going to open next weekend, and we have our first wedding in three weeks. I need you to be here to finish the basement."

"What about you and Lydia?"

"I don't think Lydia knows what's in the will, and from the comments she's made, I think she's looking for someplace to move to. Uncle Jerold felt he was being kind to give me a 30 day notice. He probably gave her the same notice." Veronica felt her anger building. She sniffed and clenched her fists. "I love this old place and the gardens. I can't imagine my life without these roses. However, I have no choice but to leave once the investigation is over, the will is read and the place sells."

Tyler set a hand gently on Veronica's shoulder. "You're going to do okay, Veronica. With those degrees of yours and your brains, any garden in the world would flourish under your care and guidance. If you were my daughter I'd encourage you to think about where in the world you'd like to live and where the most beautiful rose gardens are."

Veronica nodded and moved away from his hand. "Thanks. I have a little bit of money saved up. Maybe Sal and I will start by visiting our top choices."

"There you go." Tyler's expression darkened. "Now, I want you to allow Tyson to come back. He's my son. I need to be in his life as much as I could use his help for the short time I'll be here. He's a good worker. Between him and Lee, we'll get a lot done."

"Tyler ...."

"Yeah, I know he's made some mistakes, but haven't we all? Your grandfather saying he couldn't come here anymore was just wrong. I don't want to sound cold, but now that he's gone, I want you to let Tyson come back."

"I don't know if I can make that decision. I'll have to talk to Lydia."

Tyler's response was a huff that sounded almost like a growl as he went up the stairs into the house. Veronica followed him a moment later. She paused at the landing with the pantry door. The image of someone coming onto the property during the night flashed into her mind. Could that have been Tyson coming to see his dad? Had he been back? Could he have figured out how to get to the house by staying outside the view of the cameras? Or could Tyler have told him how? Tyler knew the boundaries of the cameras and how to close them down at the circuit breaker box. Was her papa's trust in Tyler a fatal mistake?

As she took a step toward the stairs that led to the kitchen, she hit a spot of air that was so freezing cold it stopped her. She was almost sure she noticed a wavering shadow around her. She backed up a step back and responded with an attitude she'd never had before when encountering an apparition on the stairs. "Really?" She put her hands on her hips and let out a loud sigh. "Do you have to stand in the middle of the stairs so I walk through you? If you want my attention, just say something or tell Salvador. I know you know what's going on, but you have to understand I'm doing the best I can."

171

Without hesitating she headed up the stairs. The cold spot was gone.

Upstairs, Veronica found Lee and Salvador sitting on the floor of the kitchen feeding Bee Bop little pieces of walnuts as Jessica worked around them to finish dinner. Bee Bop repeated Lee's exaggerated kissing sounds and laughed when Salvador did. Veronica caught Jessica on her way back from the table. She glanced in the direction of Lee, Salvador, and Bee Bop. "Are those three in your way?"

"No," said Jessica with a soft laugh. "They are fine. It is nice to see they can find joy during a time of such loss."

"Jess, when the time comes, you're going to make a great mom."

Jessica put a hand on her stomach. Her smile was shy. "Maybe that time won't be too far away."

"Are you …?" Veronica felt her breath catch in her chest with a sense of excitement.

"No, not yet, but we are making plans."

"That is so awesome. With you and Jesus, I feel like I'll have a niece or nephew.

After dinner, Veronica got up from the table when Lydia did. She followed the older woman into the great room. "Do you have a minute?"

"Let's go out front." Lydia went out the front door and sat down on the porch swing.

Veronica sat next to her. "I talked to Tyler earlier. He wants us to let Tyson come back to work with him. At least until the place sells. Would you be okay with that?"

With a wave of her hand, as if she was brushing away a fly, Lydia said, "Do what you want. It doesn't matter to me anymore."

Veronica fought off the tension she felt building. "Lydia, do you know what Papa Al's will says? Being his wife, will you get the Mason House?"

For the first time in days, Lydia looked up at her and made eye contact. An honest connection, not just a glance. "I have no idea what your grandfather's will says, Ronnie. Al was very private about his finances and wishes. I know he made several trips to the lawyer, but he never told me anything. You know as much as I do. If Jerold and your mother think they know what it says, maybe he told them. I don't know."

"Okay. Thanks Lydia." Veronica went inside to help Jessica clean up from dinner. After saying goodbye to Jessica and Jesus for the weekend, she went into the office, leaving the door open. She got on her computer and began putting the finishing touches of a half page newspaper ad to come out the next Wednesday for the garden's opening on Mother's Day. In full color, the advertisement was a version of the full page ad she had put in the local El Dorado County magazines. One that came out every month and the one that came out several times a year.

Satisfied with what she'd created, she got up from her computer and left the office to stand in the hallway and listen. The Mason House was quiet. She walked into the lounge at the end of the hall; it was empty. She went to the bottom of the stairs in the great room and called out. "Sal? Are you here?" There was no answer.

Only slightly concerned as he usually lets her know where he's going, Veronica got into the camera app on her phone to see if she could see him outside. She smiled when she found him and Lee at the dirt pile next to the shop.

She walked around the shop to where she could see Lee and Salvador kneeling in the dirt. Lee offered suggestions to keep the cut along the side from collapsing on Salvador's road while Salvador explained what he wanted to do with his toy tractors. Veronica hugged herself to the pure joy of watching her son. She cherished this child so much. He was her life and purpose. The thought of not being there for him if she was arrested for killing her grandfather nearly made her sick. The determination to do whatever she had to do to make a good life for him if they had to leave the Gardens set itself into cement in her soul. She loved this child more than life itself.

173

Veronica walked up behind her son and cousin. "How's it going gentlemen?"

"Mom!" Salvador left his tractors and threw his arms around her.

Veronica hugged him back and asked, "How's work going?"

"We're making a road to our new house. Lee said he'd help me build it with wood left over from stuff they're building."

Veronica made eye contact with her cousin. How could she ever thank him for being such a great role model and friend? "That's very cool. By the way, we got so busy talking about other things, I forgot to ask how school was today."

"Fine," Salvador looked up at her, his eyes squinting to thin lines, as if wondering why she asked such a question because one day at school was just as good as the last. His expression morphed into delight. "I made something for you. It's in my school pack."

"Well thank you, *Mijo.* Would you like to go inside, or would you like to stay out and play some more?"

"I need to park all my equipment in the shop, then I'll come in." Salvador stepped away from his mom, squared his shoulders and clasped his hands behind his back. "Dale says a man should always put his tools and equipment away when he's finished for the day."

Veronica inhaled a breath and smiled. Salvador looked and sounded more grown up every day. *Where's my little boy gone?* This was an influence she hadn't seen from Dale before. *Oh, I know exactly where he went. I'm losing him inside an old dirty, greasy, tractor.* "Dale is absolutely correct, and six hands can make the work of two hands go faster and easier. Would you like some help?"

"Sure Mom." Salvador's eyes lit up. "If you can take the shovel and bucket Tyler gave me, I drive the trucks." He turned to Lee. "Lee could you help me with my tractors?"

"Will do, Boss." Lee touched his forehead in a mock salute.

With the tools and equipment lined up neatly in the corner, Tyler had cleaned out for Salvador's toys, the three of them went inside talking about driving real trucks and tractors someday.

46

In the kitchen, Salvador opened his school pack and pulled out a plastic bag with what appeared to be an orange tinted glob inside. "Here, Mom. This is what I made for you today."

"Oh, how interesting. What is it?" Veronica took the bag, almost afraid to open it.

"Soap. We made soap in science. It has all kinds of healthy, natural stuff in it." Salvador dug into his pack and brought out a slip of paper. "This is all the stuff that's in it."

Veronica smiled as she read the ingredients. A natural glycerin soap bar melted to add shea butter, raw cocoa butter, and mint oil, then shaped into a ball by eager little hands before it re-hardened. Sarah was into the natural, raw, and organic.

"This is great." Veronica opened the bag and raised it to her nose to smell the mint and cocoa butter. "Oh, this smells really good, Let's put it in a bowl here by the sink where we can use it to wash our hands before making something to eat." After placing the soap in a glass bowl, she took Salvador's hand, relishing the touch. "I have some work to finish. Do you have homework?"

"Yeah. Can we work together in the office?"

"Yes, we can."

Back in the office, Veronica sat at her Papa's desk. Salvador glanced at her desk across the room. "Can I sit at your desk?"

"That would be a good idea. I'll be right here if you need help with anything, and I'd like to see what you're working on."

This attention was something she'd craved from her mother, but never got. When she became a mother, she was determined to give to her son what she never got as a child. The idea of being a different kind of mother was never far from her mind.

The last thing Veronica did that evening was help Salvador put a bowl of food and water out on the front porch for the kitty. Once Salvador crawled into bed, she read a chapter of the story book she had been reading to him. Veronica knew that reading to a child every day was the best way to instill their love of reading when they got older. She made a point of taking him to the library to check out books or going to the thrift store to buy books, so they always had something to read. Salvador took pride in the little library he had created in his playroom. He kept his books dusted and she often found him curled up on his beanbag chair with one of his books, sounding out the words he knew by heart from her reading the books to him so many times.

Later, she settled into her rocker with her book of psalms. Her feeling of completion almost seemed unreal. A month ago she had graduated from college. The dream she'd worked so hard for. Then reality hit her. In four weeks she'd likely be homeless … or in jail. As she had done when she was Salvador's age, she got down on her knees at her bedside and prayed. She didn't pray for her troubles to go away, she asked for the strength to get through whatever trials faced her in the coming weeks, months, or even years.

When she crawled into bed, she was more at peace than she had been for days. She fell asleep quickly, but her dreams were unsettling. It wasn't so much the actual images that bothered her, it was the feelings she was left with that were disturbing. There was the sense she was being targeted with hostility. She felt useless and helpless, unprepared for what was happening to her and feeling alone without help or support. Right before she woke up she dreamed she was a kite, let loose and adrift. She rose higher and higher into the darkening sky until she jerked awake. The feeling of her dream still permeating her entire being well into the morning.

After taking Salvador to Sarah and Dales for the day she returned to find a car next to the gift shop. She pulled up next to the small barn like structure and went inside. Will and Nolan greeted her with joyous enthusiasm. They showed her their creative displays of Mary's flower paintings. Outside in a newly fenced area, there were Victorian gazing balls that had become popular in gardens again and cement garden creatures from frogs to garden fairies. Tim's garden creatures made of rusted shoves, rakes, pick axes, and old spoons and forks, welcomed guests at every turn, and seemed to beg for a forever home. Tile and stone decorated flowerpots of all sizes, made by one of their older neighbors, conjured up inspirations to beautify every corner of a porch or deck. Whirly gig art objects that moved and changed shape with the slightest breeze were engaging and mesmerizing.

Veronica was so taken by the beauty of a piece that looked like a dandelion puffball she wanted to buy it on the spot, until reality hit her so hard she took a step back. In a month, all this and the gardens including herself, could be gone.

Back in the little barn, Veronica reached out for the hands of each of her friends. "Oh, this looks so good. Thank you, guys."

Will took Nolan's hand so they made a small circle. "Let's say a prayer to the goddess of gardens and all things beautiful."

Veronica smiled at Will's often repeated notion of multiple deities as he asked for blessings for all things beautiful and creative, the wisdom to always see the beauty in nature, and to have courage to make it through life's struggles.

At lunch it was her and Lydia. Tyler and Lee were gone for the day. "Did Mom or Uncle Jerold call you about the reading of the will?"

"No, I haven't heard anything," said Lydia. "Either they're going to do it without us, or they haven't called the lawyer yet.

It makes no difference to me. No matter what happens, I'll still be a widow and alone again."

Veronica thought it probably wouldn't make any difference to her either. "I'm glad to see you up and about." Veronica forced her expression into a soft smile. "I hope you don't mind me saying that you look better today. I've been worried about you. Are you starting to sleep at night?"

"A little better. Thank you for caring." Lydia caressed the papers laying on the table. "I've been researching places to live."

"Have you found someplace you might like?" Veronica began to relax. Lydia was more like her old self again. Veronica hoped she was coming out of her depression.

"I used to live in upstate New York. I really liked it there, but now that I'm getting older, maybe I'll retire in Florida. I have a little bit in my savings, and with what Al left me, I should have enough to make a new life for myself."

Veronica got up to clear the table of the lunch dishes. "I hope you find your happy place, Lydia."

47

Veronica started washing the dishes when she felt a weight on her foot, then heard the familiar, "Up, up. Cracker?"

"Mooch." Veronica smiled as she reached down for Bee Bop to step up onto her hand. When she raised Bee Bop up to eye level, she kissed her on the beak.

Bee Bop responded with loud smacking sounds and, "Cracker?"

"Sure, you can have a cracker." Veronica took a few almonds from the bowl on the counter, then set the macaw on top of her cage and put the almonds in the bowl on top. "Here you go pretty bird. I've got some things to do, so behave yourself and stay out of trouble."

Upstairs, Veronica stood by the window and looked out at the beauty of the roses. She got her phone out of her purse and called her mom. She wanted to get this over with. "Hi Mom, how are you today?" She tried to sound positive and happy.

"Hi Ronnie. Is everything okay? You don't usually call me on Saturdays."

Veronica frowned at the condescending tone of her mother's voice. *That's because you usually don't want to talk to me, and how often do you call me? Never.* "Everything's fine. I was just wondering if you'd heard anything about Papa Al's will being read. Lydia said she hadn't heard anything."

"Your Uncle Jerold is handling that, so you'll have to ask him."

Yeah right. I'll be reading my own will before I call him for any-thing. In her attempt at small talk with her mother, Veronica got the usual non-replies in response, so she told her mother she loved her and said goodbye.

She sat down at her desk, elbows in front of her keyboard and her hands raised to rest her forehead against them. She felt a headache coming on so she went into the bathroom for a couple of aspirin.

Unable to focus on anything work related, she went down-stairs to the library. She found herself looking through the sec-tion which held Papa's collection of fiction. She stopped at the section of murder mysteries and picked out a classic, with a cat as the sleuth.

Doing something she had never done before, she went down into the pantry, poured herself a 4oz. glass of wine, then went back upstairs and into the greenhouse sunroom where she curled up in one of the large comfortable chairs and opened the book.

She was deep into the plot of the book when her phone rang. It was Sarah. "Hi, Sarah. How's things?"

"Couldn't be better. From what Dale says, I think you have a budding mechanic on your hands."

"He could be interested in worse things," laughed Veronica. "Is he ready to come home?"

"Yes and no," Sarah's voice was bright. "Dale is getting ready to barbecue some hamburgers and I'd like to invite you to join us for dinner."

"I'd love to. What can I bring?"

"Your smile and your appetite," laughed Sarah. "I have everything else. Even ice cream for dessert. So just bring yourself."

"I'll be there in a flash." Leaving her book on the glass table and putting her wine glass in the dishwasher, Veronica went into the great room where Lydia was watching a movie on TV. "Sarah and Dale have invited me to a barbecue dinner at their house, so I'll be gone most of the evening. There's beef stew and baked potatoes in the fridge from last night for your dinner when you're ready."

"That sounds good. You go and have a good time with your friends. I'll talk to you at breakfast."

For the first time in a week, Veronica was able to relax and even laugh. The evening was one of friendship and joy. There was no mention of losing the gardens or her possibly needing to give up her son. The focus was on the boys–their interest in tractors and growing up.

Saying goodnight was almost difficult and the hugs extra-long. "Thank you so much for such a wonderful evening," Veronica was nearly in tears.

"Both of you are always welcome here," said Dale. "Let's plan to do this a few hundred more times over the next sixty years."

"It's a deal." Veronica hugged both Dale and Sarah once more, then headed for home.

***

After tossing and turning most of the night, and staring up into the dark, Veronica finally sat up in bed and turned on her bedside light at 3:30am. She rubbed her forehead with her fingertips. "This just sucks. Please tell me this isn't going to be my new sleep habit." She reached for her phone and opened the camera app to the driveway and doors. She smiled at the sight of the cat coming all the way onto the front porch at midnight, eating, then jumping up on to the porch swing for a cat nap.

The solitary, hooded figure came an hour later. He sat down on the bench outside the little red barn and answered or made a call. Veronica noted that he didn't seem to be up to mischief, he didn't check the lock on the front garden gate or get close enough to the gift shop to trip the motion sensor light over the door. Except to look up at the house a few times, his conversation was without animation. Eventually he put his phone in his back pocket and walked away toward the creek.

Veronica wondered if he was just a homeless person wandering onto the property from the creek. Or if there was some kind of connection to him and the murder of her grandfather? She'd show the video to Detective Russell.

When the light of the sun broke over the peaks of the mountains to the east, Veronica opened her eyes and realized she'd fallen asleep. She took her time getting up, doing her morning workout, and dressing before wandering downstairs to start breakfast. Pulling out farm fresh eggs purchased from the neighbors and organic bread from the co-op, she started the fixings for French bread.

Salvador, who couldn't stop talking about working on the tractor, had Lee, Tyler, and even Lydia smiling. After breakfast Veronica sat on the front porch and soaked in the warmth of the morning sun. She sipped her coffee and let her mind wander. "I needed yesterday and with what's coming in my life I need to take that break more often." She looked up at the peeks of the snow-covered mountains, visible from the front porch. She stood and took a deep breath. "That's it. That's what we're going to do today."

Veronica walked down the hall where she heard Lee and Salvador playing video games. On the wide screen TV, spaceships regrouped for another assault against the aliens.

"Hey you two. How would you like to go play in the snow today?"

48

Lee and Salvador's faces lit up at the suggestion to go play in the snow, the game controllers forgotten in their hands. Salvador wiggled in his seat. "Really!?"

"Really." Veronica smiled. She had their interest. "We'll go up Mormon Immigrant Trail as far as we can or until we find a good place to pull over. I'll put together some lunch, and lots of hot cocoa. We'll have snowball fights, maybe make a snowman, and take the snow saucers."

"What about going to church?" asked Salvador.

"We'll go to the Sunday evening gratitude service if we have time when we get back. I'm sure God won't mind if we go to enjoy the beauty of the world he created."

"All right. I'm in!" Lee high fived Salvador.

"Get your day packs. I want to see three extra pairs of socks, two extra sweatshirts and sweatpants, two pairs of pants, your winter coats, gloves, and snow boots. Add your slippers for on the way home." Veronica pointed toward the doorway. "Okay troops. You have your marching orders. Park your spaceships and let's get ready to go."

On the way back to the kitchen, she let Lydia know where they were going, then packed sandwich makings and a variety of goodies and treats. She paused when she heard the sound of bulky snow boots tromping down the stairs. Salvador came into the kitchen, his arms full of extra clothes. "Mom, can I ask if Wyatt can come, too?"

"What a great idea," said Veronica. "I'll call and ask." Within ten minutes the plan for the day was set. Dale and Sarah and Wyatt were coming. They had a truck with four-wheel drive, so Veronica would follow in her truck. She felt safe that Dale wouldn't lead her into trouble, and if she did get stuck, he'd be able to pull her out.

The day was filled with snowball wars, a snowbear, and daring plunges down snow covered hillsides. It was as much fun as Veronica hoped. Lunch was around a large propane heater Dale brought. While the guys were out sledding, Sarah leaned closer to Veronica. "Anything happening with the investigation into Papa Al's death you haven't told me about?"

A wave of fear washed over Veronica. If she told Sarah everything the police knew, would Sarah begin to believe she really had killed her grandfather? "Nothing I haven't already told you, except ...." Veronica looked over at the guys. A little boy scream of laughter caught her attention. Wyatt's saucer careened down the hillside. She refocused on Sarah. "One of the sales reps for a rose garden was found murdered in his motel room."

"Oh my God!" Sarah gasped. "Do they think it had anything to do with Papa Al's murder?"

"They think it probably did. He and Papa Al were pretty good friends. He came every year to buy roses." Veronica mourned Daniel Benson's death. She liked him. "I'm pretty sure he knew about the Blue Moon." She didn't say it but she wondered if he knew where it was and that was why he was murdered. Did he give up her Papa's secret or take it to his grave.

It was late before the guys were ready to settle around the heater for cups of cocoa with marshmallows and change out of their wet clothes for something warm and dry.

Later that evening as Veronica and Lee watched the moon rise over the Sierras from the front porch swing, she laid her head on Lee's shoulder. "I really needed today. Thanks for coming with us."

"Thanks for inviting me." After a moment's silence he added, "I'm really going to miss this place when Dad sells it. I mean it's more like a home to me than being at Dad's."

"What are you going to do when he sells the place?"

"I'm going into construction with Tyler. He said he'd hire me when he gets his business going again. What he promised me in salary will be enough to get a small place of my own eventually."

"Is that what you want?" Veronica leaned forward and looked into her cousin's eyes. "You always said you wanted to be a doctor."

"I only said that because I wanted Dad's approval. He was totally against Marcus wanting to go into the theater. Dad called him worthless and said he'd never amount to anything. I guess I was like most kids who just wanted to be loved by their parents. I felt really bad for Marcus. I mean I've always tried to be there for him, but by the time he was fifteen he just sort of drifted away. I guess I can't really blame him."

"Do you like doing construction?"

"You know, I really do." Lee sat back and took a deep breath. "It is so cool to look at your day's work and say, "I made that." Doing roofing and plumbing isn't so much fun, but I really like building things. I'm the one who designed the closet for the tables and chairs in the basement."

"You designed those?"

"Yeah, I came up with the idea when Tyler was talking about building a storage closet."

"Lee, you're a genius."

"Thanks cuz." Lee put his arm around Veronica's shoulders and hugged her. "From what I've seen of your incredible promotions for the Gardens, I'd say we were definitely related. And you know what else? For the first time ever, I feel comfortable with who I am."

"What do you mean?"

"Uh, okay. If Bee Bop can come out of her closet, I guess I can, too. Ronnie, I'm gay."

Veronica suddenly knew what Will and Nolan were hiding from her. "Is that where you were last Saturday? With someone special?"

"Yeah. He's a friend of Will and Nolan's, but just a friend. We spent the night together, just hanging out and talking." Lee took a breath and looked down at his hands in his lap. "I'm sorry I wasn't more honest with you about where I was. I was worried you would reject me."

"Lee, I'd never reject you for knowing who you are. You're my cousin and I love you." Veronica held her breath for a moment and wondered if she was having the same kind of closet to come out of.

49

Veronica spent Monday morning working on Garden book keeping and beginning of the month's payroll. Even though it was done automatically through the bank, there were still records to be kept. Finished with that, she called one of the rose growers who was sending a buyer. She got through to Harold Garland, an older man who had been to the gardens to buy roses several times over the years. "Harry, this is Veronica Vallejo, Albert Mason's granddaughter."

"Yes, Veronica. We talked last week. What can I do for you?"

"I know you were sending someone to look at some roses for purchase. Who is it you're sending?"

"Her name is Katherine Seaton. She's a rosarian. She should be there Wednesday. I sent you an email Friday that she's on her way."

"Lydia must have gotten the email because I didn't get it, but that works fine." Veronica felt her anger build. Why didn't she get the email? Did Lydia get it and delete it? Has someone hacked into her papa's computer? Veronica clenched her teeth and took a breath. Might as well get this over with. "Did Papa mention a rose he named Blue Moon?"

There was a pause at the other end of the line, then Harold Garland said, "The rumors about a blue rose have been buzzing through the rose world like a hummingbird. Is it true?"

"Papa Al was sure he got true blue this year. All his preliminary DNA checks tested positive for blue. I helped raise those roses, there are three of them with blue DNA. They should be in bloom by now–however, they were stolen when he was murdered. My concern now is someone trying to sell them as their own."

"So you don't have them?"

"No. I have the ones Papa described when he first contacted you for sales. They're in bloom now. They're unique and beautiful. My favorite is a high centered, red and silver striped. I just don't know what happened to the blue roses."

"Well, I can tell you that if they show up on the market, the entire rose world will light up. They'll be found."

"Can I make a request? Could you send any future emails directly to me? I didn't get your email, so that could mean Papa's computer has been hacked. I'm going to close out his account and up the security on mine."

"That's a good idea. Give me your email and I'll make a note to send everything directly to you from now on."

After Veronica said goodbye to Harry, she had an unsettled feeling. It wasn't the rose buyers coming, or the missing blue rose. It was the need to sell all the roses. Before her grandfather died, they had spent hours discussing which roses to sell and which to keep and patent for sale later. Because of the high cost of a patent, that was always a big decision and an important one.

They had talked about keeping the Blue Moon and entering it in the Annual International Rose Trials. It had a chance of winning the American Rose Center Gold Medal. The most prestigious award at the trials. Up against roses from all around the world, a gold medal from the International Rose Trials gave a rose instant world-wide fame.

Her next call was one she'd been thinking about since her Papa died. The phone was answered on the second ring. "Inman Genetics."

Veronica spoke in her most professional voice. "This is Veronica Vallejo, Albert Mason's granddaughter. Is Robert Inman available?" She was surprised to find out he was, and he would take her call.

"Miss Vallejo, this is Robert Inman, how may I help you?" The voice sounded almost feminine.

"Thank you for taking my call, Mr. Inman, I wanted to let you know of the passing of my grandfather, Albert Mason."

"Oh? I'm so sorry. I hadn't heard." Inman paused. Veronica could hear him taking a breath. His voice softened. "The world has lost one of its greatest scientists. Had he been ill?"

"No," Veronica clenched a fist. This was something she had to do. "He was a crime victim. The police determined it was homicide."

There was a longer hush at the other end of the line. Finally, Inman said, "How horrible. Do the police know who did it?"

"No, not yet." She wasn't about to announce that she was their prime suspect. "But I'm calling about the lawsuit Lydia and Papa Al had against your company."

"That's not something I want to talk about over the phone."

"Could I come meet with you?"

"I can do that. I have time in about an hour. Could you come then?"

"I'll see you in an hour."

Veronica stood in front of her closet and stared at her clothes. She wanted to look professional. She ended up choosing the dress and matching low heels she wore when she graduated. It was a simple blue dress, but the design was elegant, and the fit was perfect for her body. She put on some makeup, matching blue earings, and added a necklace of a simple gold rose. She switched to a simple, but dressy, tan leather purse and headed out the door.

Inman Genetics was in El Dorado Hills, just south of Hwy 50. The address and the sign, painted on the side of the building that said, InGen were neutral in tone and discreet. Because she got there a bit early, she sat in her truck, brushed her hair, and put on a dab of lipstick, then checked her phone for emails about Brandy. She kept a close eye on the time and headed for the office with five minutes to spare.

The reception area was clean and classy, but not opulent. The receptionist at the front desk, introduced herself as Mrs. Steel. An older woman, she was slender with an up-swept hair do and no makeup. Her greeting was friendly, but professional. She picked up the phone and announced that Veronica had arrived. "Mr. Inman is ready for you. I'll take you back."

She led Veronica down a long hall hung with photographs of smiling farmers surrounded by lush, healthy crops. From the appearance of the surroundings and the clothing worn by the people, the photographs looked to have been taken in different countries around the world.

After a quick tap on a solid wood door, Mrs. Steel ushered Veronica inside. The office was large, done in neutral colors. The photographs on the wall of individuals and flowers were more artistic than the photographs in the hall. A man stepped out from behind a large desk that reminded her of her papa's desk. The man was just a bit taller than she was and of medium build. His graying hair was just starting to thin and recede. He held out his hand. "Robert Inman. Nice to meet you, Miss Vallejo. Your grandfather meant a lot to this company. I'm very sorry to hear of his passing."

50

He gestured to a pair of chairs near the window. "Please, have a seat and make yourself comfortable. Would you like a cup of coffee, soda, or water?"

"Water would be nice. Thank you," said Veronica.

"Would you like a cup of coffee, Mr. Inman?" Asked Mrs. Steel.

"Please. Thank you, Mrs. Steel," replied Mr. Inman.

Veronica watched her go through a side door into what appeared to be a small kitchen. She returned a moment later with a cup of coffee and a bottle of spring water and a glass on a silver tray. She set the tray on a low table between the chairs and said, "Buzz me if you need anything," and promptly left the office.

Robert Inman sat down once Veronica sat. She clasped her hands in her lap. "Thank you for taking the time to see me, Mr. Inman."

"Please, call me Robert. We don't need to be so formal. Is it all right if I call you Veronica?"

"Yes, that's fine."

Robert Inman leaned toward Veronica, rested an elbow on the arm of the chair and his chin on the back of his hand. His gaze was direct, but relaxed. "When I talked to your grandfather he said you were quite competent in the lab."

"You've been in contact with my grandfather?"

"Off and on, yes." He leaned back and crossed his legs. His demeanor calm. "Your grandfather was brilliant, and his retirement left a big hole in the lab. My father eventually talked him into doing contract work, mostly evaluating some of the work we were doing. We're going to miss him now that he's gone. It's so sad to hear of his death."

"I hope you don't mind me asking about the lawsuit. I didn't even know about it until Lydia mentioned it to the police. She hasn't been willing to give me any details."

Robert Inman rubbed his chin in thought. "To be honest, that lawsuit has me in the dark as well. Without permission from our lawyer to talk about it, I can't tell you much, but I have to wonder why the suit was started. I had a feeling from talking to your grandfather that he wasn't that interested in following it to the end, because it probably would have gone to court."

Veronica almost felt as if she'd stuck her finger in a light socket. She struggled to keep her cool. "Are you saying the entire idea may have been Lydia's?"

"I'm sorry, I can't answer that."

"I know she's seeking financial damages. So I guess the suit is for financial gain?"

"You have an excellent understanding of Lydia's mind," said Inman. "Much of the work Mrs. Black did for us centered on how our work could be of financial benefit to us. She was creative and had a real mind for figures and promotion."

"Mrs. Black?" Veronica's mind spun. She was glad she wasn't standing, she probably would have fallen over.

"I'm sorry, I mean Mrs. Mason. When she first started working for us she was Mrs. Norris. If I remember right, there was a tragic accident, and she became a widow at a fairly young age."

"When was she Mrs. Black?"

"She married Lester Black, was one of our technicians, shortly after she began working for us."

"So Lydia had been married twice before?" Veronica picked up her water glass and took a sip.

"She was a widow, twice." Inman shook his head and his gaze turned to look out the window as if he was seeing into the past. "Lester disappeared while we had a team in Costa Rica. Lydia was there when it happened and took it pretty hard. We were all happy for her when she and your grandfather got together."

"And now it's happened again." Veronica said. "Poor Lydia. No wonder she's withdrawn into such a state of depression."

"I'm sure it has been hard on her." Inman's mind appeared to switch gears. "How are you doing? I know you lived with your grandfather. This has to be a horrible loss for you too. Your grandfather told me you just graduated from UC Davis with a double degree. Are you looking to start a career now?"

Veronica sensed her feelings do that whirlpool swirl inside her. She had to fight the urge to grab hold of the chair's arms to steady herself. "With my papa's recent passing I haven't decided what I'm going to do. His will hasn't been read yet so I don't know if Lydia or my mother and uncle will get the Gardens. Either way, I'm sure I'll be looking for a job and a new home."

"Could I interest you in taking a position here?"

"My degrees are in horticulture and business administration, not genetics."

Inman gave a short laugh. "To me, degrees mean a person has the willpower and intelligence to complete a demanding course of study. It would be an entry level position, but from what your grandfather has told me about how you helped him in his own lab, we could use someone like you." He wrote something down on a sticky note and gave it to Veronica. "This is the salary we could offer someone with your knowledge and experience."

The figure he wrote made her head spin. This could be the answer to all her problems. She would have a well-paying job when she left the gardens. She could still live in Placerville and Salvador could stay in school with Sarah. Veronica noticed

Robert Inman watching her closely. If he was looking for her reaction, he got one even though she tried to merely nod. "This sounds enticing," she said.

Inman smiled. "I'd like very much to show you our setup here, if you have the time."

"I'd love to see it." The next thought that sprang to the front of Veronica's mind was the question of whether she was willing to abandon her education and dreams of a life in Gardens for a life confined inside a lab, but then she thought of the stories her grandfather told her of traveling around the world.

Inman led Veronica out the door and down the hall to an elevator to the second floor of the two-story building. In a small room leading to the lab, Veronica quickly went through the process of donning sterile wraps, shoe and hair covers, mask, and gloves.

Inman smiled. "You know the process."

Veronica allowed herself a slight smile. "It's the same routine Papa always followed in his lab."

"Dad saw your grandfather's set up. He was impressed with what he'd done with secondhand equipment." Inman paused. "I know of your grandfather's work. Did he ever get that blue rose he was trying for?"

Veronica's mind raced. *The Inmans know about the rose, or at least the potential of it. Could their desire to cancel the lawsuit be enough to commit murder? Could they have stolen the rose? And why is Inman offering me a job? Control? Insider information? Or am I being used? Is Inman's offer a ruse to draw me into a good job to get me to drop the lawsuit?* She imagined taking the job, dropping the lawsuit, then being laid off or fired for some reason so she was left with nothing.

51

By the time she got home, Veronica had just enough time to change clothes and leave to go get Salvador. She grabbed her purse and keys, then headed for the kitchen. Jessica was slicing a thick hunk of beef into thin strips.

The knife she was using was an old butcher knife. Probably one of the knives from when the place was an inn. The wood handle was dark with age and use, but the blade was well made and kept very sharp. Watching Jessica's skill with her precise cuts was a little frightening. Veronica's mind went to the conversation she overheard with Detective Russell. The same type of knife had been used to kill her grandfather and Daniel Benson at the motel.

Veronica glanced at the antique knife holder. A large block of wood, tilted at an angle, with slits for holding knives. There were spots for twelve knives of all sizes, from small paring knives to a large cleaver. Two slots were empty. She looked back at Jessica. She had one of the knives, but where was the other one? She checked the sink. It wasn't there or on the counter.

What got Veronica's attention was that the missing knife was the knife she most often used. She looked in the ceramic crock crammed full of wooden spoons and other wooden kitchen implements. The knife wasn't there. She looked through the three drawers that held the silverware and other kitchen tools. The knife wasn't there either.

Veronica ran her fingers over the handles of the knives in the block. She spoke in Spanish, "Jessica, have you seen the other knife that should be here?"

Jessica stopped slicing the beef. "No. It has not been there. Is it lost?"

"I don't know. It must be." She moved toward the door. "I'm going to get Sal. We'll be back soon."

Veronica's phone rang as she was driving down Cold Springs Road. She answered it with her hands-free device, but pulled over as soon as she heard Detective Russell's voice. "Okay, I'm stopped. What can I do for you?"

"I just have a couple of questions. Do you have a cat?"

"A cat? No. Nothing with fur except Brandy, and she's still missing."

"Did you pet or hold a cat recently? Maybe a friend's cat?"

"No. I've seen a cat on the nighttime camera, but only on camera. Salvador held a cat at Addie's house when we went to look for Brandy last Sunday, but I didn't hold it or pet it."

"What kind of cat did Salvador hold?"

"I think it was part Siamese."

"Long or short hair?"

"I don't know much about cats, but I think it would be considered a short hair. That woman has lots of cats, so if you found cat hair on something related to Papa Al, it could have come from one of her cats. They're always in the yard digging in the flower beds. Umm …" Veronica thought for a moment. Should she say something about the missing knife? She wasn't supposed to know about how her papa was killed, but it might be important.

"Umm what?" asked Russell.

"I don't know if it's relevant or not, but there's a knife missing at the house."

"What kind of knife?" The tone in Russell's voice changed.

She explained how she watched Jessica cutting meat and noticed another knife missing.

"How long was it? Do you know?" Asked Russell.

"I know it was longer than six inches, but not ten inches. I looked through the kitchen drawers. It wasn't there."

"Why do you think I'd be interested in a knife?"

"I overheard your conversation with Detective Norton when you were in the library. I heard you ask about the knife."

"Veronica! That was a private conversation and official police business. How did you overhear that?"

Veronica closed her eyes, rested her forehead against the steering wheel, and swore. She took a deep breath. "Help me Papa," she whispered to herself. "I'm in manure so deep you might as well soak me with a hose and call me compost."

"Veronica. Are you still there?"

"I'm sorry. I'm here. I'm just stressing." She explained how she had learned about voices traveling through the vents when she was young. "I know I could get in a lot of trouble for listening to your conversation, but you already think I'm the one who killed my papa. How much more trouble can a person be in than being a murder suspect? I didn't kill my grandfather! The only way I'm going to prove that is to find out who really did it."

"Veronica, that's Phil's and my job. Let us do it."

"Yeah, but if someone is trying to frame me and the evidence is pointing at me, you may not look further. I didn't see Papa Al when I got home on Saturday. I looked all over the property for him, just like I told you."

"Then you need to help me. Is there anything else you haven't told me?"

Veronica hesitated a moment. "There might be one thing. I was talking to Tim and Mary Archer. Tim said he thinks he saw someone wearing something bright blue up on the hill behind the shop on that Saturday before I got home."

"He never said–"

"I know he didn't tell you that. When I asked him why he didn't tell you, he said it slipped his mind and he didn't think anything of it when he saw them."

"Do you think he could identify the color of blue if he saw it?"

"He's an artist. He works in 3-D, but he still has the sight of an artist, so he probably could."

"Okay. Where are you now?"

"I'm sitting along Cold Springs Road. I was on my way to pick up Sal. Do you need me to come in so you can arrest me?"

"Veronica, you're not being arrested, but I would like you to come in to sign a statement regarding what you just told me."

"Would tomorrow be okay?"

"That would be just fine. How about one o'clock."

"Yes, that's fine. I'll be there tomorrow at one o'clock."

"All right. I'll see you tomorrow. Stay out of trouble between now and then and leave the investigating to the police. I know you've been calling rose growers and have asked about Mr. Benson."

"Those were calls I had to make, as part of the garden business. I needed to know who is coming to look at roses and when. I think someone has hacked Papa's computer because I didn't get the emails they said they sent with that information."

"Bring you papa's computer with you when you come. We have someone who can get into it and find out what happened to those emails."

"Okay, I'll see you tomorrow."

52

Sarah pulled Veronica to the small office upstairs, out of earshot from where the boys were playing in the playroom downstairs. She handed Veronica a thick manila envelope. "I just picked this up. All the paperwork is done. I made an appointment for you to drop everything off tomorrow."

Veronica sat down to ward off her sudden sense of light headedness. "This is all of it? It's done?"

"I asked Mr. Winters to rush this." Sarah sat next to Veronica on the small couch. "If something happens, we need to have all this done now. To protect Sal."

"I don't know how to thank you." Veronica wrapped her arms around her friend in a fierce hug. "I don't know how I'll be able to repay you for what you've spent on all this, but I will pay you back. When's the appointment? I have to go into the police department tomorrow afternoon. If something happens it will be a huge load off my mind knowing Sal is safe."

"Eleven thirty tomorrow morning. Same office on Cedar Ravine. They'll be waiting for us."

Veronica exhaled. "Thank you. This works out perfectly because I have to be at the police at one. One more thing. How's Sal doing in school? Are you seeing signs of stress?"

"Ronnie, that kid amazes me. He's as focused and positive as ever with his schoolwork. I try not to press him about his stress level other than to ask him how he's doing in the morning, which I do with all the kids. I don't want to cause more stress if he's not ready to talk about it."

"You are so intuitive when it comes to dealing with kids. He's pretty open with me about his feelings and we sort of decompress from the day right before bedtime."

"Then get your son and go home and decompress."

As soon as they got into the truck Veronica asked Salvador, "What were you and Wyatt playing? Sarah and I could hear you all the way upstairs."

"Wyatt and I were pretending we were dragon macaw superheroes. We had to get the bad guys. Wyatt names them dra'caws. They're kind of loud, like Bee Bop is sometimes. We told the police where the bad guys were and had to fly away to get them." Salvador became animated in his booster seat, flapping his arms as if he was flying. "We had to fight the bad guys and take them to jail."

Veronica hoped like everything Salvador wouldn't have to experience his mother being taken to jail.

When she turned left on Mallard Lane instead of right to go home, Salvador asked. "Where are we going?"

"We're going to Clifton and Warrens. We need to get food and water bowls for the kitty."

"I hope the kitty wants to live with us," said Salvador.

Veronica was astounded at her son's comments. It wasn't that he hoped he could keep the cat. His comment was from the cat's point of view. Would she want to stay? At that moment, she thought about what would happen when they had to leave. People moved with pets all the time, so she had to start planning to move a macaw, a cat, and in her dreams, a dog.

Clifton and Warren's, the small country feed store, which catered mostly to the needs of ranchers, felt like another world. Near the door there were bags of treats for everything from horses to goats. The older woman behind the counter directed them to the back of the store where the entire wall was devoted to everything cat and dog.

As Veronica and Salvador started in that direction, the sound of peeping caught Salvador's attention. He raced toward the sound and plastered his face against the wire mesh of the brooder to look inside. Each section had a different type of chicks. Taped to the front was a picture of what they would look like when they grew up and what color of egg they laid. "Mom, look! Chicks. Just like in the video we watched at Sarah's. Can we get one?"

Veronica peered inside at the little fluff balls of down–not yet real feathers. "Oh *Mijo*, maybe someday, but not right now. Remember, we don't know where we'll be living. We came here to get cat bowls. You can stay here and look at the chicks if you like, but I'd like you to help me pick out the bowls."

"Okay, Mama."

Before she could explain the importance of stainless-steel bowls, Salvador grabbed a plastic dog bowl covered with paw prints, hugged it to his chest, then collapsed to the floor and began to cry. Veronica knelt to his side, "Sal, what is it?"

"I miss Brandy. We're never going to find her. Somebody took her. She's gone!"

Veronica gently took the bowl from him and held him up in her arms. "We're not going to stop looking, *Amorcito*. We have to trust that Papa knows where she is and he'll guide us to her."

"But he hasn't come to visit me again."

Veronica kept her voice low. "Maybe he's busy helping God with his garden. We just need to trust." She picked up two no-tip stainless steel bowls with plastic paw prints glued to the sides. "Come on, let's go home, and set up the kitty's food and water. I'm sure Bee Bop would like some of your attention."

Veronica stopped at the top of the road to get the mail, then turned back to Salvador. "I need you to do something for me after dinner."

"What Mama?"

"I want to talk to Lydia. Maybe you could take Bee Bop to your room and play tug of war with paper."

"Can't I come with you?"

Veronica quickly rethought her need to talk to Lydia in private. Salvador and Lydia had always had a good relationship. "Maybe that would be a good idea. For a short time, anyway. Maybe she could use some little boy hugs. Then you can go play with Bee Bop so Lydia and I can have some private time."

"Why do you want to have private time?"

"You know how you and I go someplace private to talk about our feelings? I need to talk to Lydia about her feelings, and just like you and me, that talk should be private."

"Okay, Mama."

After dinner, Lydia retreated to her room. Veronica knocked on Lydia's door, with Salvador at her side. She waited to be invited in. She found the older woman sitting at her desk. While Veronica pulled up a chair and sat down near her, Salvador went right up to her, arms outstretched for a hug.

Lydia responded by wrapping her arms around him and pulling him to her. "How's my little munchkin?"

"I miss you," said Salvador.

"I'm sorry, Honey. I just need some time to myself. Losing Papa Al the way we did was very hard on me."

"Are you still feeling sad?"

"Yes, but only a little bit now. Now I'm worried about where I'm going to live when Jerold and Brenda sell the Mason House. Just like you, I'm going to have to move."

"Lydia, do you have a few minutes so we can talk?" Veronica was comforted by how good Lydia looked. She had dressed, her hair was combed, and she had just a touch of makeup on. Maybe she was coming out of her shell of depression.

53

"I'm going to go play with Bee Bop." Salvador wiggled away from Lydia and left the room. Veronica closed the door behind him and returned to Lydia's side. "How are you doing? We've been worried about you. Sal's missed you."

"I'm feeling better." Lydia's hand went to her mouse and clicked several times. The reflection of light from the monitor on Lydia's face disappeared. "This has been so hard. There were days when I felt totally lost." Lydia patted Veronica's hand. "I'm fine, really. With becoming a widow, again, and the thought of having to leave here, I've been busy getting my finances in order and looking for someplace to go."

"Have you found someplace you like?"

"I'm still making a list of choices. I've been reaching out to old friends and people I know in different states. Asking them about how they like where they're living."

"I'm glad to hear you're connecting with friends."

Veronica watched Lydia's gaze shift. She scooted her chair back from her desk. "Now, I want to shower and relax for the evening. This has been a difficult time for me, so I'm going to ask you leave."

"It's been hard for all of us. I'm sorry if I upset you." Veronica had a strong feeling that Lydia was holding something back. She didn't want to lose the connection they were making so she quickly changed the subject. "Just one question. Did you have a chance to call Uncle Jerold about when Papa's will is going to be read?"

"No I didn't. I'm sure your uncle will call us. Maybe he's just been busy." Veronica had the feeling Lydia was eager to change the subject as well.

"I've been checking Al's emails about rose sales," said Lydia. "You're doing a good job taking over that part of the business. Nolan and Will have the little red barn looking good. I think the Gardens will be ready for this weekend."

"I just wish we could find the blues. None of the rose breeders I've talked to have been contacted about their sale, so if someone has them they might be going to keep t.hem. The babies in the lab are looking good. I've got my fingers crossed for your tri-color. I just hope they're big enough to make it outside of the greenhouse by the time we have to ...." Veronica couldn't finish. The reality of having to leave was too much.

"Have you thought about where you're going to go?"

"No. I've been so busy, but I have been sending out resumes do different botanical gardens."

"You should get away now. Just pick up and leave with Sal. Go travel around and be together. It would give you a chance to go visit rose gardens where you could apply for jobs."

Yeah, that's just what Detective Russell needs me to do, thought Veronica. Another thought pushed into her mind. "How well do you know Addie Sweet?"

"Who?"

"Addie Sweet, our neighbor up behind us with the cats."

"Oh, not very well. I've only talked to her a couple of times. Why do you ask?"

"Her name is really Doris Norris, the same name you had at one time." Veronica tried keeping her voice tone light.

Lydia's expression darkened for a second, then she laughed. "Oh, isn't that funny. I didn't know that. Norris is such a common name. My last name was Black before I married Al. I was widowed at a young age. There are probably as many Norris' as there are Blacks, Masons, and Vallejos. How did you hear about my name being Norris?"

So who's lying? "When I went to talk to Robert Inman about the lawsuit, he mentioned it. We started talking about the work Papa did there and he mentioned you by name."

"What did he say?"

"He was very positive and impressed with the work both of you did."

Lydia exhaled a short laugh. "Of course. I'm sure he was being nice so you'd drop the lawsuit. He's just like his father. The acorn doesn't fall far from the tree."

***

Back upstairs Veronica found Salvador in her bathroom. The shower was on and he was leaning over the tub. "I'm giving Bee Bop a shower. She likes showers."

Veronica knew meant that both of them would end up thoroughly soaked. "Thank you for taking such good care of her. Baths are important for birds." She was also thankful it would keep them busy for a while. "I have some work to do at my desk, so I'll be right out here. Let me know when you're done, it will be dinner time soon." Veronica sat down to carefully read through the papers from the lawyer. She signed all the sheets that needed her signature. She was nearly in tears by the time she finished.

She was convinced she was doing the right thing, but that didn't make it any easier. The painful thought of losing Salvador was like being stabbed in the heart. Only it wouldn't kill her like it killed Papa Al, it would just go on hurting forever.

Finished with the papers from the lawyer, she started going through the day's mail. She separated everything into three piles. Mail to Lydia, her mail, and anything to her papa and the gardens. As her papa had taught her, she went through the house mail first. Most of it was junk mail. Next, she started going through the garden mail, opening each envelope with an old fashioned letter opener her Papa had used. It was very old, and beautiful, real silver with a carved ivory handle. The mail that drew her attention was from rose breeders asking for photos of his new roses, membership renewal for the various rose associations her Papa had belonged to, and invitations to this year's rose shows in the US, England, and France.

Her heart beat a little faster at the announcement for the prestigious American Rose Center Rose Trials as part of the International Rose Trials. There would be rose trial judging in 16 countries around the world. The one her papa entered was in California. She fantasized about winning the American Rose Center Gold Medal for the Blue Moon.

At the bottom of the pile was an envelope that got her attention. Her name and address were hand printed. The stamp was the recent Wildflower Forever stamp. The post mark was Sacramento. There was no return address.

"Mom, Bee Bop's done with her bath."

Veronica set the letter aside. She went into the bathroom and shook her head at the mess of wet towels and water on the floor. Salvador was fully dressed but just as soaked as Bee Bop. Lord, give me the patience to get through this, she thought to herself. She gazed into Salvador's bright, smiling face and could have sworn that Bee Bop was smiling as well. How could any parent be angry at such joy? She rolled her eyes in wonder at how one little boy could get so wet giving one macaw a bath. She assumed he was in the tub as well. "Your turn." She pointed to the tub. "Take a quick one, it's almost dinner time. I'll get your PJ's."

Right before bedtime, Salvador checked that the kitty had food and water for the night. He had taken extra care placing the food and water bowl in a protected corner of the front porch the night before, now he asked, "Can we make a bed for the kitty? She doesn't have anywhere to sleep."

"Yes, we can. I think there's an old blanket in the hall closet. I'll get that." Veronica pushed the coats to one side so she could get to the storage tubs on the floor until something stopped her. She stood staring at the closet for a moment trying to figure out what was wrong. Then it hit her. Her blue cover up was missing. Definitely not a coat, it was more like a thick, floppy-fuzzy sweater she wore around the house during the winter to ward off the usual chill in the huge old place. What got her attention was the fact that the bright blue color, which stood out, wasn't there.

She almost forgot to breathe. Could that have been what Detective Russell was asking about? It wasn't a coat, so she hadn't thought of it, and she hadn't opened this closet since the beginning of March. She moved each of the coats hanging on the bar. Not finding it, she checked the floor of the closet and behind boxes of stuff that closets collected over time. There were other closets in the house, maybe it had gotten put in one of them. She wondered if maybe Jessica moved it to make room for more storage boxes. She'd ask her when she came tomorrow. She thought of calling the detectives right away, but if Jessica had put it in a different closet, she would feel ridiculous for calling first without checking. She decided to wait.

54

Veronica had to force herself to return her thoughts to Salvador and the cat. She picked up the plastic storage tub with the blanket and headed outside. "Here you go." She set the tub on the porch.

Salvador's eyes lit up. "We can use the tub as a kitty house." Kneeling on the floor, he tipped the tub on its side, pushed it against the wall next to the food bowls and arranged the blanket into a soft pile inside it. "I think the kitty is going to like this. I hope she comes again tonight."

"Why don't you think real hard about inviting her, and picture the bed and food in your mind. You talked to her once with your mind, maybe she'll hear you again."

It was late by the time she got Bee Bop settled in her closet for the night and had Salvador tucked into bed with the light out. The house seemed quieter than usual as she sat back down at her desk and picked up the envelope addressed to her. Again, she studied it. There was no company name or return address.

It felt like there was no more than a single sheet of paper inside but there was an unevenness that was intriguing. She slid an old-fashioned letter opener under the sealed flap, careful not to tear the paper inside. She could see areas of color thought the piece of printer paper. Unfolded, Veronica studied the images cut out and glued around a short message in the center. There were roses and other flowers as well as a graduation cap with the words, "congratulations" and the year.

At the bottom was a photo, of two very young children, a boy and a girl, holding hands. That photo sent a shiver up her back and down her arms.

The short message in the center was simply addressed to her.

Ronnie,

Congratulations on your graduation from U C Davis. Kudos on your hard work and dedication. The majors you chose and the degrees you earned are going to take you anywhere in life you want to go.

CJ

Veronica burst into tears. It was from CJ, her brother. She was sure then that that was who had been coming onto the property and sitting on the bench. She carefully folded the letter and slipped it back into the envelope, then put it in her desk drawer, and began making her plans to contact her brother.

With her alarm set to wake her a half hour before the hooded figure usually arrived, she watched the camera on her phone. She saw the cat, the raccoon, and the deer, but no human. She fell back asleep, disappointed.

Waking at 6AM, she began her day as usual. After taking Salvador to school, she had plenty of time to spare before her meetings with the lawyer and Detective Russell, so she took her time getting dressed. To her outfit of a pair of jeans and a soft cotton, button down shirt in light green, she added a pair of cut crystal earrings the same color of green as her shirt.

She walked through the lawyer's door at precisely 11:25. Both Sarah and Dale were already there. "How are you doing?" asked Sarah.

"Okay, I guess. This is just hard," said Veronica.

"We're going to get you through this," said Dale. He hugged Veronica from the side nearly squeezing the breath out of her.

The receptionist looked up from her computer. "Mr. Winters is ready for you."

They walked down the short hall together. Mr. Winters stood and greeted them with handshakes. "Nice to meet you

Miss. Vallejo." He motioned to the comfortable chairs in front of his desk. "Have a seat. We'll get started."

Veronica was glad to sit down. Mr. Winters got right to work explaining the forms Dale and Sarah need to sign to get legal custody of Salvador if for any reason Veronica couldn't be there to parent him. There was also a clause that stated she could rescind that right for any reason at any time to regain custody of her son.

Veronica felt at peace when she left the lawyer's office knowing Salvador would be well cared for, but at the edge of that comfort was the worry that she would need that agreement by the time she was done with Detective Russell that afternoon.

Dale had to get back to work, so he left right away. They waved as he drove out of the parking lot. Sarah turned to Veronica. "You've got 40 minutes before you have to be at the police station and it's only three minutes away so why don't we go across Main Street for a cup of coffee and a piece of pie.

"That sounds good, but I don't think my stomach can handle coffee."

Sarah put her arm around Veronica and guided her to her truck. "Then I think a cup of cocoa is in order. I'll meet you there."

They sat outside near the sidewalk. Veronica wanted to stay away from any conversation related to the two meetings, so she asked about Sarah's school program. "So, tell me more about how you want to expand your program."

"My Dream is to include music and more art. Things that are as basic to education as math and reading but missing from public schools." She reached across the table and took Veronica's hand. "The other thing I'm really hoping for is the possibility of a small garden program. I'm not a gardener, so I would love to have your help. Dale and I have the space in our yard and I've been reading up on gardening in our area. I discovered the entire world is divided into zones and I think the one

Placerville is in means we can grow flowers and some vegetable all year long."

"If Sal and I are able to stay in the area, I'd love to help." Veronica felt her own excitement building. "I got a job offer with Inman Genetics in El Dorado Hills. I might take it so Sal can stay in school with you, and we can still see each other."

"Dale and I know enough people in the area that we might be able to help you find a cute little place to rent, somewhere nearby."

"Veronica looked at her watch when she felt the alarm buzz against her wrist. "It's 12:45, I've got to get going." They stood together.

"I'll get this." Sarah picked up the bill.

"Thank you for being such an incredible friend."

At the police station, Veronica grabbed her grandfather's laptop out of the back seat and went through the front door. She stopped at the thick glass window separating the small reception area and the officer at the front desk. "My name is Veronica Vallejo. I have an appointment to see Detective Russell at one o'clock." She didn't even have a chance to sit down before Russell came through the door to get her.

"Hi Veronica, come on back," said Russell, holding the door open.

Veronica handed Russell Papa Al's lap top. "I hope your person can find out what happened."

The detective led Veronica down a short hall. "We'll see what our magician can do with it." She paused at an open door, stuck her head in, and held out the computer. "I got it. Do your magic."

55

Russell directed Veronica back up the hall. Instead of the interrogation room, Russell led her to her office. It was a small space, just enough room for a desk and two chairs, but it had a window. "Have a seat." Russell motioned to the chair closest to the corner of the desk. Veronica looked around as she sat down. The walls were covered with police awards of distinctions and a large map of the City of Placerville. On the corner of her desk were two pictures of Russell on her horse. The horse was brown with a long black mane and tail. It had black up its legs past its knees. The only white was a wide white stripe down its face to its nose. In one picture Russell was riding through a beautiful mountain stream, and in the other picture her horse had a pretty blue ribbon hanging off her bridle.

"This is your horse?"

"Yeah, she's my bud." Russell opened a file and handed Veronica a sheet of paper. "Could you read through this and make sure the details are correct?"

It was a narrative of their phone call about the knife. When she finished, she looked up at Russell. "I think it's just what we said. You must have recorded the conversation and typed it up."

"I did exactly that, but what I would like to have is a better description of the knife." Russell set her phone on the desk. "I'm going to record this as well. Now, if you can, describe the knife in detail to the best of your memory."

Veronica described the knife as she would a rose blossom. The shape, color of both the handle and the blade. She answered Russell's questions about the thickness and stiffness of the blade and that the edges of the blade's handle could be seen where the two pieces of wood were connected to it with some sort of brass rivets.

Russell typed while Veronica spoke. When she was done, Russell printed the description for Veronica to sign.

"I know you and detective Norton are the ones doing the investigation, but can I ask a question?" said Veronica.

"What would that be?"

"The last time I was here, you asked me about my brother. Can I ask why you asked about him? I was totally honest when I told you I haven't seen or heard from him since he was five. Did something happen to him?"

"I'm going to trust you with this information. Apparently he showed up at your uncle's and at your mom's. Phil talked to your mom. It seems he went to her house, but she refused to open the door and threatened to call the police if he didn't leave. She insisted she didn't know who he was. We were wondering if he'd made contact with you."

"In a way, he has. He sent me a short letter of congratulations for graduating. I'm hoping he's the person who's been coming to sit on the bench at night. He's my brother. I want to see him, providing he's not involved in something that would be a bad influence on Sal. And there's something else."

"What would that be?" asked Russell.

"You asked me about a blue coat. I was honest with you when I said I didn't have a blue coat, but ... I do have a bright blue cover up. And it's missing from where I've always keep it."

"Can you describe it for me?"

"It's bright blue, fuzzy, and soft. I only wear it in the house in the winter. I haven't worn it or even gotten into the closet where I keep it since March. I noticed it missing last night when I got into the closet."

"And you couldn't find it anywhere?"

Veronica felt her anxiety build. "I didn't look for it other than in the closet. I was busy with Sal, and then it slipped my mind. I was going to ask Jessica if maybe she put it somewhere. I just got busy and forgot this morning." Veronica's phone began ringing in her purse.

"Go ahead and answer it," said Russell.

Veronica didn't recognize the number, but her phone service was pretty good at identifying possible scam numbers so she answered. "Hello? ... This is Veronica Vallejo ... Oh, Ms. Waters, thank you for calling. Is there going to be a time to read Papa's will? ... What? ... Could I call you back in a moment? ... All right. Thank you." Veronica hung up.

"Are you okay?" asked Russell. "You look a little pale."

"That was Marcia Waters, the lawyer who did Papa's will. She said there isn't a will, but she needs to talk to me."

"Would you like to call her back and put it on speaker? I can record it for you to listen to again later if you need it."

"That might be helpful. I don't know if my brain is working right now."

"Scoot up to my desk and put you phone on the corner here. I'll put my phone next to yours to record the conversation."

Veronica put her phone on speaker and dialed the number. The answer was right away. "Marcia Waters."

"Ms. Waters, this is Veronica Vallejo. You said you needed to talk to me, that Papa Al didn't have a will?"

"Veronica, your grandfather came to me two years ago and dissolved the will he'd made some years before. Instead of a will, he created trusts for TOD's, Transfers on Death accounts and asked me to be the plan administrator. He was very specific about his beneficiaries and the amount of assets each beneficiary was to receive from which account. One account is to be divided between his two grandsons, Lee and Marcus Mason. His wife, Lydia, is the beneficiary of his remaining retirement account, and his son, Jerold, and his daughter, Brenda, are the beneficiaries of a life insurance policy that was paid up years ago."

214

"Thank you for letting me know," Veronica was happy for her cousins. What they were getting meant they could start a new life away from their father. But she felt as if her heart dropped to the floor. She was getting nothing. She was exactly where she started, broke and homeless. She was surprised that the first thought was, I can do this. I'll get a job, and Sal and I will be fine.

56

"We're not done yet," said Ms. Waters. "There is the matter of his estate and his rose breeding and selling business. The assets known as The Historic Mason House Inn and the properties surrounding it known as the Serenity Valley Gardens, which covers some five acres and the undeveloped property which covers another ten acres, goes entirely to you, his granddaughter, Veronica Vallejo. Because he understood the cost of running the business of the gardens and restoring the historic property, he added the amount of two million dollars, from an annuity account to help you cover the costs and continue breeding the roses he loved so much."

Veronica couldn't even breathe. She felt her mouth working, trying to find some air. She understood the term of being a fish being out of water.

Her head was suddenly pushed from behind, down toward her lap. She heard Russell's voice, "Breathe, Veronica."

She gulped air into her starved lungs.

Marcia Waters continued, "Now, what I'm, going to need is for you to come down to my office to sign for the distribution of funds. Your grandfather arranged for some accounts to be closed and his business account to be moved to your name upon his death, which I have done. I will also need to re-title you as sole owner of both the property and Gardens, and the annuity accounts. Could you come by today? I have an open time in about an hour, if you're available."

Veronica looked up at Russell. The detective nodded. "I'll be by in an hour." Veronica was surprised she could even talk and that the words that came out of her mouth were intelligible. Veronica thanked her and hung up.

"Congratulations." Russell had pulled up the other chair to sit next to her.

"I ... I ...."

Russell held up her hand. "Take a moment to catch your breath. We're not quite done here. I have a few questions to ask you regarding the investigation."

"Okay," Veronica squeaked, but in her mind she was screaming–Oh God! Not now. Please not now.

"These are very important question, but you should have no problem answering them. First, do you know what the plant Wisteria is?"

"Yes." Veronica felt the anxiety that built so quickly, begin to ease. This was a question she could answer.

"Could you describe it?"

"It's a fast growing, flowering vine. The flowers are purple and hang down in clusters. When the vine is in bloom it's really very beautiful."

Russell handed her a picture of wisteria in bloom. "Could you identify this plant?"

"That's wisteria. This is beautiful, wherever this is."

"When does it bloom?"

"As a matter of fact, in this area, right now."

"Is there any wisteria on the property of the Mason House?"

"No. Papa considered it invasive and hard to control. As far as I know, there never has been any wisteria there."

"Do you know of any wisteria growing anywhere nearby?"

Veronica only had to think for a second about where she'd seen some. "Yes. At Addie Sweet's, who is really Doris Norris. Her house is covered in it. Salvador and I were there last Sunday when we were looking for Papa's dog, Brandy."

"What were you wearing when you went there?"

"What was I wearing? Umm, jeans and a T-shirt. I had a hoodie in the truck, but I wasn't wearing it. That's when Sal petted the cat I told you about, but I've never touched it."

"Thank you. I have all I need for today. Go home and relax, and celebrate having a home."

Veronica walked to her truck in a daze. She had to concentrate hard on driving the short distance to the lawyer's office on Main Street. With time to spare before she had to be at the lawyer's office, she walked along the historic Main Street, easing the tension out of her muscles.

When she got to the office, Marcia Waters' secretary had all the papers ready to be signed. Sticky tabs pointed to the places that needed a signature. Once she was done the lawyer met with her to check each of the papers. Before she left, Ms. Waters suggested Veronica go to the bank right away and have the accounts changed into her name and change all the passwords and pin numbers.

She sat at a desk with the bank manager to finish the paperwork she couldn't do at the teller's window. She was now the executor of the trust. As such, she was able to get the information that as of that day none of the other accounts had been drawn on or closed, so Veronica had to wonder if anyone else had been called by Marcia Waters.

On the way home, Veronica stopped at Raley's before picking up Salvador. She made her way along each aisle, checking her list as she went. She stopped when she got to the Latino food section. She visualized the dinners Jessica was going to make with the items she had on the list. She felt herself tense with joy, but also a sense of disbelief. It's real, she thought to herself. Nothing has to change. Arturo and Jesus will still be the gardeners and Jessica can still be my housekeeper and my sister. I don't know what Tyler will do, but I'll welcome him if he wants to stay and work. The big question was Lydia. Veronica took a deep breath and ran her fingertips over the zipper on her purse as a distraction. I have to be honest, I hope she decides to leave.

Sitting in her truck in front of Sarah's, Veronica's entire body tingled with giddiness. She imagined the conversation she'd have with Sarah about the Gardens. She stopped herself with a sudden whole-body twitch. *No wait. I'm not going to say anything just yet. I need time to let things settle.*

Sarah greeted her at the door with a hug. "How are you doing? What happened with the police?"

Thank you, God. I only have to talk about meeting with Detective Russell. "I'm fine. The detective only asked me about things that had nothing to do with me, but must have been important to the case, and ... I need to know how much you spent on lawyer fees for our agreement. I have to pay you back."

"Absolutely not! Dale and I are doing fine, and the cost wasn't that much. Consider it my gift to you in your time of need."

Veronica sent a silent plea. *Help me Papa, I don't know what to say.* A thought came to her that she was sure was from her Papa. She would call the lawyer and ask what the cost was for his services. "All right, I'll accept you gift for right now."

57

Sarah gave her a knowing smile. "We'll worry about it in the future." She called out for the boys.

Salvador came running. "Hi Mom. Is it time to go home already?"

"It is. Get your school pack. We have groceries in the truck, so we need to get home and help Jessica put everything away."

Veronica stopped at the top of the drive to get the mail, and instead of tossing it on the other front seat as she usually did, she took a moment to look through it. Along with the usual junk mail and letters from rose breeders, there were some of the monthly utility bills and credit card bills in her grandfather's name.

Her papa considered credit cards a necessary evil and only used them when he ordered supplies online. She knew Lydia was also on the account of the two cards. Veronica wanted to know if Lydia was using the cards and what she might be using them for, but felt it wouldn't be right for her to open the bills. Because she had all her Papa's usernames and passwords, she would get into the accounts on line and check.

Because the utility bills were paid automatically she made a mental note to contact each of the utilities to make sure the bills were put in her name. Veronica set the mail on the other seat, closed her eyes for a moment and took a long deep breath. There was so much to do. I need to make a list, she thought. She made a mental plan of categories on that list, so she didn't forget anything.

Veronica eased her truck down the drive and parked in her usual spot. She went around to open the back door for Salvador. "Would you help me bring in the groceries?"

"Okay." his voice meek as he looked in the direction of his dirt pile.

"How about taking in just two bags for me, then you can change into your work clothes and head out to your construction site. What are you going to work on today?"

Salvador jumped down to the ground and wiggled in anticipation for his mom to hand him two of the lighter bags. "Tyler said he was going to let me help him build a bridge!"

"That sounds awesome. Be sure to thank Tyler and Lee when they build something for you. And ... Make sure you don't cross into the area marked off by the police tape."

"*Si, Mama!*" He grabbed the bags and rushed through the gate to the kitchen door.

Veronica smiled at her son's enthusiasm, then a pang of worry washed over her. She had only been a little older than Salvador when she learned not to trust being alone with men.

Even though she had instructed him about keeping himself safe and not being afraid to get away if someone tried to touch him in places he shouldn't be touched–until he was much older, she would keep an eye on the camera apps for that area. There was a camera on a tree, aimed into the shop, and one focused on the walkway to the basement and front door. Each would allow her to keep an eye out for her son's safety. Because of her experience as a girl, she couldn't tell herself that Salvador was safe and that Tyler could be trusted. She still wasn't sure if Tyler had not harmed her papa.

Jessica stopped mopping the floors to help Veronica put the groceries away. They were in the privacy of the pantry down in the stairway when Veronica noticed Jessica seemed distracted. "*Que es, hermana?*"

Jessica sighed and looked away. "I have begun putting in my application for other jobs. Jesus and I so much want to have a home of our own, but we both need to work. With your mother and uncle going to sell, we are both worried."

Veronica put her hands together as if in prayer and placed them against her lips. *So much for not saying anything to anyone yet.* "Put those applications in the garbage. Neither my uncle nor my mother are going to do anything with the Mason House or the Gardens. Your jobs will be here for as long as you want them."

"But …."

She grabbed Jessica by the hand and pulled her up the stairs. "We need to include Arturo and Jesus in this conversation."

They found Arturo and Jesus in the Formal Rose Garden. Jesus was pulling weeds from around the fountain and Arturo was dead heading the teas roses–cutting off the faded blooms. They both stopped what they were doing when Jessica and Veronica came through the gate. "*Hola.* Do you two have a moment?" Veronica called out.

"*Si, Chiquita,*" said Arturo, *Que es?*"

"We need to talk." Veronica glanced over at the fence. She didn't think anyone was hiding just outside the garden, but she felt the need to ensure the privacy of this conversation. She spoke in Spanish and pointed to an area of lawn on the other side of the fountain. "Over there." She wondered if there was a way to say what she needed to say without telling all. Of all the people in the world, she knew she could trust these three.

"I know you have been as worried about what was going to happen to the Gardens and the "house" as I have been. This has been my home for almost eight years. I love these gardens and the roses. You three have worked here for almost as long. I hope I'm not wrong is thinking you care about this place as deeply as I do, and you take pride in the work you do.

"I know the Gardens and the house wouldn't be as beautiful without you, that's why I want to ask you to stay. My mom and uncle are not getting all this." She paused trying to think of the best way to say it. "I found out today that Papa Al left it all to me. When he began to teach me all I needed to know to take over the gardens, I promised him I'd take care of it with the same love and devotion he did. I'm going to keep that promise and I want to ask you to stay and continue to work here–if you want to."

"All this is yours?" Jessica threw her arms around Veronica.

"*Si.*" Veronica returned Jessica's hug.

Arturo and Jesus threw their battered cowboy hats into the air and let out a celebratory "Yee Ha!" Jesus hugged Jessica and Veronica and kissed them both. Arturo wrapped Veronica in his arms and kissed her on the cheek. *used for each hug*

Once the laughter quieted, Veronica said, "Wait, I have a big favor to ask. For right now, please don't say anything to anyone. I just found out from the lawyer. I'm not sure Lydia or Mom or Uncle Jerold know. They certainly haven't said anything. So, until everything is worked out with them, I'm going to ask you to pretend you know nothing. If any of them ask you what your plans are, just say you're putting in applications."

"*Si, si.*" Arturo nodded his head, "*No dire nada.*" He gave Jesus and Jessica the look of–and the two of you will also say nothing.

Jesus spread his hands and shrugged his shoulders. "*No se nada.*"

58

Veronica laughed and put her arm around his waist with a hug. *"Gracias, hermano mayor."*

After more quiet congratulations, Veronica and Jessica headed back to the house.

Instead of going through the front entrance with Jessica, Veronica walked along the sidewalk to the basement. The door was wide open. She found Tyler in the bathroom polishing the newly installed stone tile floor. "Tyler, the bathroom is beautiful. Thank you for doing such a great job on all this."

A wide grin split his face. "You're welcome, and thank you. The bridal lounge and apartment are finished now. If I'm going to be here for a little while longer, what would you like me to start on next? It can't be a big project but something I can get done in the time I have left here."

"You sure you don't mind? I know you mentioned getting some other jobs."

"Those other jobs are little things. They're getting me back out in the world and getting my name out there again, but I still plan to continue doing what you need here–if you still want to put the time and effort into this place before your uncle and mom put it up for sale. I have to admit I'm going to hate to see that happen. Bringing this old mansion back to life has been satisfying. It almost feels like I'm coming back to life with it."

"I plan to continue bringing the Mason House back to life, and I would like very much for you and Lee to be part of that.

Could you start on the empty bedrooms upstairs? Paint the rooms and maybe refinish the wood floors? That shouldn't take too long."

"I'll get started on one tomorrow. You'll have to give me your ideas for colors, maybe redecorate them as a guest rooms."

"Oh, I like that idea." Veronica's thoughts went to how she could continue making the historic Inn her home. New beds, matching bedspreads and curtains to go with the dressers and wardrobes already in the rooms. New area rugs. This could be fun.

Veronica left the basement with a light heart. Her imagination blossomed with decorating ideas for the other rooms and whirled in delight at the thought of redoing her own bedroom and bathroom. The thought of a large walk-in shower so she didn't have to climb in and out of that little claw-footed tub, more cupboard space, and a sink with a real countertop felt almost decedent.

She walked around the corner of the shop and looked for Salvador but didn't see him. When she got closer to the dirt pile, she noticed him sitting quietly with his back against the bank. She had a moment of concern until she saw he held the cat in his arms. He had his face buried in the cat's fur, and Veronica was almost sure she heard the cat purring from where she stood. *"Mijo,* you found your kitty."

Salvador looked up at his mother with tears in his eyes. "She found me. I think she's happy."

"I'm not sure who's happier, her or you." Veronica took a step closer. "Do you think she'd let me pet her?"

"Si, It's okay now."

Veronica knelt and reached out to the cat. The cat sniffed her fingers then pressed her head against Veronica's hand. "Hello, pretty kitty. Salvador would like it very much if you came to live here." She petted the cat in all the places cats like to be petted. *And here I am, sitting in a pile of dirt with my son, petting a stray cat. After everything that has happened, what more could I ask for?*

"She'd not scared of us anymore, but she's scared of something."

"What is she scared of?" Veronica asked.

Before Salvador could answer, the sound of car tires crunching over the gravel drive drew her attention away from the cat. She touched Salvador on the shoulder and said, "Someone just pulled into the parking area. I'll be right back." She stepped around the corner of the shop and watched the car come up the paved section of the drive to the house. A beautiful, brand new Mercedes Benz sports coupe, top down, still with paper plates advertising the dealership in El Dorado Hills.

Veronica felt her shoulders do a quick drop of dismay when she recognized her uncle in the driver's seat. Before she could even acknowledge her anxiety her whole body tensed in fury. *What's he want?*

Veronica surprised herself by standing her ground instead of slinking away to hide like a feral cat. The compulsion to stand and fight, with wit and words, was so strong it frightened her. An idea came to her just as quickly. She turned and walked into the shop, out of sight of her uncle. She quickly undid the top two buttons on her shirt to expose more cleavage than she'd normally show. She took her phone out of her pocket, put it on video, and tucked it into her bra so the camera lens was exposed. She'd seen several women in church keep their phone in their bras resting against a breast.

As she left the shop she planned how far to stay from him. Her uncle walked up to her, his stance aggressive. "We need to talk." He glanced at the gardens. Veronica followed his gaze. Arturo and Jesus had just turned the corner to go behind the house into the back yard.

"What do you want?"

"Let's go in the house." He took a step toward her.

Veronica took two steps back. "We can talk right here."

"This is a private conversation."

"Whatever you have to say will be in front of God no matter where we are, so here is fine."

Jerold's color deepened. "Fine, if that's the way you want it. I want you out of the house now."

Veronica decided to play along. "You said I could have 30 days and Papa's will hasn't been read yet."

"I met with the lawyer yesterday morning. Just like the will said, this place is now mine, and I've changed my mind about the 30 days. I have a buyer right now. I want you out today. Pack up your clothes and personal belongings and get out."

"I don't have any place to go."

"Get a motel, camp–whatever. I don't care if you have to live in your truck. I want you out, now."

"You can't do this to me. You're my uncle, not some slumlord."

Veronica heard the rattle of tools and footsteps behind her. Even though her uncle looked past her to see who was there, she wasn't willing to take her eyes off him. A second later she was thankful for her caution.

"We're going inside," Jerold growled. He reached out to grab her. "Now."

Veronica slapped his hand away. She raised her voice. "Don't touch me!"

He lunged at her and grabbed her arm. "I'll touch you whenever and wherever I want."

When she tried to jerk away from him, she caught a flash of red and blue coming toward her. Bee Bop was in full flight. The macaw dove for them with folded wings.

59

Bee Bop tipped her wings at the last second, extended her claws as if for a landing, screamed, and raked Jerold's cheek as she flew by. Jerold yelled out and swore as he punched in the direction of the macaw, hitting Veronica in the face.

Only Jerold's hold on Veronica's arm kept her on her feet. He let go and backed away from her when Bee Bop swooped over his new Mercedes and unloaded a large, well-aimed bomb of droppings across the dashboard. She circled around toward them.

Veronica staggered back a few steps. She stretched out her hand for Bee Bop to land on and noticed Tyler, Jesus, and Arturo came out of the shop, tools in their hands.

Jerold dabbed at the blood that dripped down his cheek, then raised a fist and went for Bee Bop. Bee Bop screamed, spread her wings and lunged at him beak open. Her pupils constricted to mere pinpoints.

Jerold glanced went between Bee Bop and the men behind her. He dropped his hand and took a step back. His eyes opened wide in fear and surprise. From very close behind her, Veronica heard the whirr of an electric motor and the deep voice of Tyler Arnold. "Touch the woman or the bird and it will be the last thing you ever touch with those hands."

Veronica stepped far enough to the side so she could see behind her and opening up the space between Tyler and her uncle.

Tyler held the battery powered chain saw. He hit the trigger, sending the chain spinning on the bar. It wasn't a huge chain saw, the bar was only about 15 inches long, but the threat was serious. A swipe of the sharp blades would take off a hand as easily as a wayward tree limb. On either side of him, Arturo and Jesus stood with tools of their own. Arturo had a pry bar. Five feet long and made of solid steel he held it like a baseball bat, ready to swing. Jesus held an ax the same way.

"Veronica," said Tyler without taking his eyes off Jerold. "Get into the house and lock the doors." He hit the trigger of the saw a couple of times to make his point. "This scum bag is just leaving, but I don't want to take any chances. And feel free to call 911 to report his assault on you. I saw the whole thing and will tell the police exactly what I witnessed."

Jerold backed up a few steps. "Go ahead and try to press charges. I own this place. I have every right to throw out an unwanted occupant and defend myself when she encouraged that bird to attack me.

"Who do you think the police will believe? I'm a successful plastic surgeon with a million-dollar medical practice in El Dorado Hills. Are they going to believe me or a murder suspect?" Jerold glared at Tyler. "Or a drunk? I suggest all you keep your mouths shut and get out before I press charges."

Bee Bop climbed up Veronica's arm to her sit on her shoulder. "Pretty bird," whispered Veronica as she stroked Bee Bop's head. She took her phone out of her bra and aimed it at her uncle to make sure she was getting a good recording.

Jerold went back to his car and saw the mess on the dashboard. He swore and yelled, "I'm going to kill that bird."

Bee Bop let out a loud F bomb with a 'you' at the end.

Tyler let out a mighty roar of laughter. "Well said Bee Bop!"

The four of them watched Jerold get in his car. He grabbed his coat out of the back seat and wiped the dashboard, then backed his car all the way to the gravel parking area. Once he was in the public parking area he stomped on the gas, throwing gravel behind him and leaving ruts where the tires spun as he sped away.

Tyler turned off the saw and set it down on the pavement, then turned toward Veronica, careful not to get to close too Bee Bop. "Are you okay?"

"Yeah. Just sort of freaked out." She made eye contact with each of the men, then made kissing sounds at Bee Bop.

Bee Bop repeated the sounds, and said, "Give me kiss." She pressed her thick tongue against Veronica's cheek. She bobbed her head and said, "Pretty bird" then launched herself off Veronica's shoulder and flew into the shop to land on the tail gate of Tyler's truck where she let out a wolf whistle, and a series of loud screams.

Veronica reached out to Tyler, Arturo, and Jesus. "My heroes." A second later she was wrapped in strong loving arms. She felt safe, even when Tyler joined the hug. Tyler backed away but continued to hold Veronica's hand, and said. "Call the police and report the assault. Don't let him get away with what he did. And if he gave you 30 days, he can't make you leave sooner."

Veronica sighed. So much for the plans of mice and men, she thought to herself. "I'm not going anywhere, Tyler. Not now, not in 30 days and not in 30 years."

Tyler's eyebrows arched in question.

"There was no will. Papa Al put everything in irrevocable trusts. The Mason House and gardens are now mine. And you better believe I'm calling the police to report the assault." She started the video from her camera app to see what was recorded. Tyler moved to her side to watch. The aim was perfect. It caught the entire interaction.

"Son of a–" He stopped himself from saying more.

"It got everything. I am going to report this, but I need to check on Sal."

"I'm sure he's fine," said Tyler. "I had Lee take him and his cat to his room when I saw that idiot come up the drive. I knew you'd want Sal safely out of the way."

"Thank you, Tyler." Veronica felt as if someone just opened a balloon to release air and the tension.

"So, You're now the grand dame of The Mason House?"

Veronica took a breath and her jaw clenched on its own. "Yeah. I'm hoping I can talk you into continuing your work here. There's so much to be done and you've done such a beautiful job on everything."

"It will be my pleasure to sit down and plan what you want."

"Cool. But please don't say anything to anyone just yet. I'd like all the inheritance stuff done and over with before I announce the change."

Arturo and Jesus stood back, wide grins on their faces.

"My lips are sealed." Tyler made a show of dragging his fingers across his lips as if he was closing a zipper. "Now, go make that call and check on your son. Also, get a good photo of your face and put an ice pack on it. I think you're going to end up with a real shiner."

"Oh great." Veronica's comment dripped in sarcasm. She held the phone up to her face and filmed it as a video. She turned her head from side to side and moved her phone to get the injury from all angles. She also described how she got the injury and that Tyler, Arturo, and Jesus were there with her. She felt safe for the time being.

60

Bee Bop suddenly flew onto her shoulder and photo bombed the recording. She said hello and announced that she was a pretty bird.

"I'm going to get that ice pack now." She turned to Tyler. "We'll talk later and I'm sure the police will want to talk to you."

"This will be one time in my life when talking to the police will be a pleasure," said Tyler. "Now, go take care of yourself and your son." Tyler picked up the saw and walked into the shop.

Arturo and Jesus faced Veronica.

"When we saw Jerold come up the drive, we thought we'd better be nearby, just in case," said Arturo.

"When we head Jerold yelling, we went into the shop to get tools. Tyler was there and suggested what to grab," said Jesus,

"Thank you, both of you." She gingerly touched her cheek. "I need to get an ice pack." She headed for the kitchen. When she got into the house, Bee Bop looked up at her and said, "Cracker?"

"Yes, Bee Bop, you can have a cracker." Tears pressed at the back of Veronica's eyes. "For what you did you can have as many crackers as you like for the next year." She picked up the container of organic almonds. She set Bee Bop on the floor and held the container out to her. "Take as many as you want. You've earned them." Bee Bop dug into the container.

"Thank you, Bee Bop," said Veronica, then she added, "Thank you Papa. Thank you, God."

As Bee Bop started whistling and went inside her closet letting the door close behind her, Veronica got a small, flexible first aid ice pack out of the freezer and wrapped it in a damp paper towel. She went upstairs to check on Salvador. Lee met her at the top of the stairs. His complexion paled. "Ronnie, are you okay? What happened?"

She moved the ice pack for him to see. "Your father tried to hit Bee Bop, but nailed me instead."

"Oh God, he's done it again." Lee sat down hard on the top stair.

"Did what again?" Veronica sat next to him.

"Hit someone. Last month he punched Marcus. I was there when he did it. It really scared me. I even thought of hitting him back."

"I'm glad you didn't. Was Marcus hurt?"

"A bloody nose, but nothing more."

Veronica focused on her cousin. "Are you okay? You looked like you were going to pass out for a moment."

"I'm fine. You'd better check on Sal. He's pretty stressed."

Veronica found her son on his bed with the cat curled up in his lap. They both looked up at her when she opened the door. "May I come in?" She asked.

"Mom! Tyler said Uncle Jerold was going to cause trouble. What happened?"

Veronica sat down next to Salvador and reached out to pet the cat. She would be honest. She could be nothing else. "Uncle Jerold hit me. It hurts a little but it's going to be fine."

Salvador began to cry. "I hate Uncle Jerold! I wish he would die."

Right now, I do, too. "I'm going to call Detective Russell and tell her what he did." She wiped the tears off his cheeks. "But first, I need to take care of you. Are you going to be okay?" When he didn't answer she drew him to her side and focused his attention to the cat. "Have you been talking to your kitty?"

He nodded and sniffed.

"You said she was scared. Do you know what she was scared about?"

"I get the feeling it was a smell."

"A smell. Do you know what she smelled?"

"Only sort of. But the pictures I got was behind the shop where the police were and Miss Sweet's house. The smell scared her."

"Did she know what the smell was?"

"I think she did, but I couldn't understand what she was trying to tell me."

"Maybe she's not used to talking to people and she just needs time to learn." Veronica could feel Salvador tension ease. "Has she told you her name?"

"She thinks Kitty is fine. She likes it when I call, here Kitty, Kitty. She also likes being told she's a pretty kitty, and she likes it here."

"I guess she has to decide if she's willing to live in the house with Bee Bop and Brandy. If she wants to stay, we'll have to get all the things cats need, like a litter box, and she'll need to get her shots so she can be healthy."

"Thanks Mom. I know she'll understand."

"I'm going to let you two visit and talk." Veronica saw the life coming back to her son's eyes. "I need to go call Detective Russell."

"Okay, Mom. I love you."

"I love you." She kissed him on the top of his head as she stood up and went to her room.

Veronica speed dialed Detective Russell. Her call went right to voice mail. She gave a brief explanation of why she called and mentioned she'd call Detective Norton next.

He answered with a business like, "Detective Norton."

"Detective Norton, this is Veronica Vallejo."

"How can I help you, Veronica?"

"There was a problem here at the house with my uncle." She described what happened.

"Were you injured? Were there any witnesses?" he asked.

"Yes, and yes. Tyler, Arturo, and Jesus were all there and saw everything. Tyler was the one who made my uncle leave. And I videoed the entire incident on my phone. It shows everything."

"Do you need medical care?"

"I don't think so. I've got an ice pack on my face where he hit me."

"Have you called Detective Russell?"

"I called her first, but my call went right to her voice mail. I didn't know when she might get back to me, so I called you."

"I'll be there in about ten minutes."

"All right. Thank you."

Twelve minutes later, Veronica's phone notified her that someone was coming up the drive. She was surprised to see Russell's SUV right behind Detective Norton's muscle car. Veronica went out the back gate when they didn't come to the door. She found them in the shop talking to Tyler.

61

Russell had her phone out recording the conversation.

"You saw Mason strike Veronica?" Norton asked Tyler.

"Yes sir."

"Can you show us the chain saw?" asked Russell.

"It's right here." Tyler moved to where the saw sat on the work bench. "I didn't get too close to him. I have to say that the man is smart enough to know when to back down."

Norton photographed the chain from several angles. "Looks clean." He turned to Tyler. "All right, thank you for your willingness to step in and help a person in need."

Norton then spoke to Veronica. "We're almost done here. Go back into the house. We'll be there as soon as we're done talking to Mr. Arnold."

Veronica went back inside and asked Jessica to make some coffee and put some of her homemade chocolate chip cookies on a plate. While Jessica was busy, Veronica knocked softly on Bee Bop's closet door and got a reassuring, "Hello," in response. Veronica knelt to the floor and opened the door to offer Bee Bop scritches and banana chips.

A short time later there was a knock on the kitchen door. Veronica opened the door, still holding the ice pack to her cheek. "Thanks so much for coming." She stepped back to open the door wider. "Please come in." Bee Bop burst out of her closet to say hello. Veronica picked her up to say hello to the Detectives.

Bee Bop bobbed up and down, said, "Pretty girl," and "Give me a kiss," then made loud kissing sounds.

Russell laughed, "Hello pretty bird. Can I pet you?" She reached out her hand and Bee Bop let Russell stroke her head.

"Let's go into the library." Veronica set Bee Bop in her cage. "I've asked Jessica to bring us some coffee."

In the library, Norton set his phone on the table, "I'm going to use my phone to record this conversation. I'd like you to tell us what happened today."

"But I recorded the whole thing." Veronica's anxiety notched up a level.

"We'll get to that in a few minutes," said Russell. "We have to do this by the book."

Veronica told about hearing her uncle's car come up the drive, confronting him in the driveway, refusing to go into the house, and him telling her to leave the property immediately. She paused when Jessica brought in three cups of coffee and cookies, then continued after Jessica left. When she was done, she played the video she'd recorded.

At the end, Russell said. "It appears that your hero flies and wears a blue cape. I'm glad she wasn't hurt."

Norton replayed the end where Bee Bop flew into the scene. He shook his head, the look in his eyes was one of amazement. "Do you think she knew what she was doing? I mean, she's just a bird."

Veronica clamped her lips for a moment then said, "The term 'birdbrain' is a complete misnomer. Birds are smarter than most people think, and parrots are the most intelligent and sensitive."

"My apology for underestimating her," said Norton.

"What's going to happen now?" asked Veronica. "What if Uncle Jerold comes back to carry out his threat against Bee Bop or decides to go after my son or me?"

"Where was Salvador when all this was happening?" asked Russell. "And was your cousin here?"

"Tyler and Lee were working in the shop when Jerold drove up. Tyler told Lee to take Sal inside to get both of them out of harm's way."

"I have to give Mr. Arnold credit for that. Has your uncle ever threatened or hurt you before?" asked Russell.

I don't know what to say. The physical and emotional pain of her trauma when she was nine screamed through her brain. Lost in thought, it was a moment before she realized Detective Russell was saying her name. "I ... I'm sorry. I just ...."

"He's done something before," said Detective Norton. "What happened?"

"It happened when I was nine." She wasn't sure if she could or should continue even thought there was an eagerness to tell what happened, To let that skeleton out of the closet. To stop keeping it hidden inside. She took a sip of coffee and swallowed hard. "He molested me when I was nine. I never told anyone because he said something bad would happen to my dog if I said anything. I loved my Sammy and stressed for months that something might happen to him."

Russell swore under her breath. It was Detective Norton who asked, "Did it happen again?"

Veronica nodded. Tears slid down her cheeks. "It happened again and again for the next two years, then I started taking Sammy and running away and hiding when he came. That's when my new stepfather started beating me. He never missed a chance to tell me how worthless and useless I was."

"Did Jerold threaten to hurt you?"

"He never threatened me, just my dog, but I now know I'm as much a target as the pets I love."

"This opens up a whole new can of worms," said Russell under her breath. "Pedophiles don't stop because a victim gets older, they move on to other children."

"We'll do what we can to keep you safe," said Norton. "Because what he did today was simple battery, not assault, we can't arrest him or file for a restraining order, but we can ask for a 'stay away' order. You'll have to sign it and we'll serve him today, but you'll have to go and file a request for a restraining order tomorrow. The clerk will put in your request then you'll go before the judge or the commissioner to decide if there needs to be a restraining order."

"So he's not going to be arrested?" asked Veronica.

"Not at this point, but if he comes back after the stay away or restraining order has been served we can take it to the DA to issue a warrant," said Russell. "Now, I want you to call me when you go into court so I can offer testimony that your uncle could be a danger to you and this whole thing is wrapped around a murder investigation. That will almost ensure that they will issue a restraining order."

"What I don't understand is why he said what he did," said Veronica.

"I don't know that much about inheritance," said Russell, "but we have to believe that since the lawyer called you about the trust, she has also called everyone else."

"Uncle Jerold said he went to the lawyer's yesterday. That means she probably told him she hadn't talked to me yet, so he was probably thinking I didn't know about the trusts."

"It's possible that your uncle was thinking, that if you abandon the property and left the area, the property would go to him."

"My mom and my uncle. That's why he wanted me to leave today. To just get lost." A new fear washed over Veronica. "What happens if something happens to me? Like I just happen to die ... or disappear never to be found again?"

62

"That's a very good question and probably a valid concern right now," said Russell.

"With a simple battery and with the lack of an actual threat against you, we can't assign police protection, but I do have the names of people who do private protection which I think would be a very good idea for a few days," said Norton. "I also think it would be a good idea to change the locks on all the doors." Norton got into his phone and wrote down several names and phone numbers on a piece of paper and handed it to Veronica.

"Do you think …." Veronica scrunched up her nose as she looked at the paper Norton had given her.

"Veronica," Russell reached over and put her hand on Veronica's arm. "You have your son to think of."

"All right. I'll call them." Veronica put the paper under her phone.

"I think we have all we need here. Let's go talk to the gardeners," said Norton.

Veronica headed upstairs to check on Salvador as soon as the detectives left the house to talk to Arturo, Jesus, and Jessica.

Lee stepped out of the bathroom as she reached the top of the stairs. For a second she was shocked by his appearance. He had been crying. She knew exactly what happened. There had been many times when they listened in on adult conversations when they were young. "How much did you hear?"

"Enough." He inhaled a sobbing gasp and wrapped his arms around her in a hug that offered as much comfort as it asked for. "Oh God, I'm so sorry about what he did, Ronnie."

"Thank you, but it's over now," she said.

"I don't think it is."

"What do you mean?"

Lee staggered a step and sat down on the top stair. He rested his elbows on his knees and buried his face in his hands. Veronica sat next to him "Did he do it to you too?"

"No." He shook his head but kept his face buried. "But now I realize why he spent every Saturday at the tennis club teaching when Marcus and I begged him to do stuff with us. I always felt he liked little girls better than us." Lee balled his hands into fists and pummeled the sides of his head. "I should have known."

"Lee, stop!" Veronica wrapped her arms around his head.

"He's still doing it. He still spends every Saturday at the club teaching little girls. How could I be so stupid to not have seen it?" He looked up, tears streaming down his cheeks. "I don't know what to do. He has to be stopped."

"We'll do what we can to stop him. But we're going to do it right."

"How?"

"Detectives Russell and Norton are still here. We're going to explain our suspicions and give them the information they need."

"If he's still victimizing little girls, why haven't they said anything," Lee sounded defeated. "Maybe he's not doing anything wrong. It all in my mind."

Veronica felt herself go into that mom/friend/mentor mode she discovered in herself when she was taking her early childhood education classes at the Junior College. She loved Lee. They'd always been close. As close as she had been to Jesus when they were growing up. "Lee, think back to the sexual abuse scandal of the girls' gymnastics Olympic team. That had been going on for years. The code of silence has as much to do with the perpetrator's power over his or her victims as it has to do with the survivors feelings of shame, guilt, and fear. Fear that no one will listen or believe them and that they will be blamed if they say anything."

Lee stiffened. "I hate him."

"So do I, that's why we're going to do this right. When we've done what we can we're going to walk away with our heads held high, knowing we did the right thing."

"Will it ever be over?"

"He can be stopped, but it's never over for the victims." Veronica clenched her fists. "I've been determined to move on, but I'll never forgive him, or forget what he did. It's never over for the girls and boys who experience that kind of abuse. That kind of trauma can never be fully healed, just coped with."

When Lee looked at her again she could see a new strength in his expression. Maybe it came with determination or self-confidence, but it was there. "I don't know what I'm going to do, but I'm not going home again."

Veronica reached for her cousin's hand. "We can't do anything to change what happened, but now we can begin our new lives for a better future."

"What do you mean?"

"Your dad didn't tell you about your inheritance?"

"No. He said the lawyer hasn't set a time to read the will yet.'

"What a mother–" Veronica almost used the kind of words she normally wouldn't have used in front of others. "He's lying Lee, there is no will. Papa Al put everything into trust accounts. The lawyer told me you and Marcus are getting a pretty good amount. All you have to do is go to the lawyer's and sign the papers."

"He never said anything to us." Lee's face turned scarlet and his body tensed in anger instead of the hopelessness of defeat. "I'm sure he's hoping to keep it all for himself. But what about you? I'm worried about if you have to leave."

"I'm sure his coming here to tell me to leaves is all about him wanting everything for himself, but I went to the lawyer's today and found out the Mason House and the gardens are now mine. So I'd like to offer both you and Marcus to come live here."

"You'd let us come live here?"

Veronica's mind lit up at her next thought. "Yes. Do it tomorrow while your dad's at his practice. Use Papa's Escalade and get all your personal stuff. Don't bother boxing anything, just stuff it in the car and get out. I'll help you unload everything when you get back.

"I've asked Tyler to start redoing the rooms upstairs, so you can each chose the ones you want and you and Tyler can start there." Veronica paused. Wondering why Lee wasn't thinking about using his money to get a new start in life. "However, with the money you and Marcus are getting from Papa's trust funds you could both rent or buy your own places if you were working."

Lee reached over and hugged her so hard it almost hurt. "Oh God, Ronnie. You are the best cousin ever. If Dad comes anywhere near you again, I swear, I'll kill him."

She almost laughed. "I almost like Tyler's idea of taking a chain saw to his hands better, but right now we need to talk to the police."

"Ronnie, do you think Dad could have killed Gramps?"

63

"I don't know. He said he was at the tennis club all day ... but that doesn't mean he didn't have something to do with it. I'm trusting the police will find out." She pulled her phone out of her pocket and texted Russell. The beep of a reply came back quickly. "They're on their way back into the house. Let's go downstairs."

A loud meow, the kind of yowl only a Siamese can make, came from Salvador's room. "You go check on Sal, I'll go down and talk to the detectives," said Lee. "If I'm going to man-up against my father, I need to start now."

Lee headed downstairs and Veronica went to Salvador's room. She found him sitting at his art table, markers spread out around the paper he was working on. The cat was sitting on the table watching his every move. Salvador looked up. "Mom! Kitty is telling me about the scary stuff she smelled. It was blood!"

Veronica rushed over to the table and looked down at what Salvador was drawing. There were three papers. One was covered in red dots and slashes. Another drawing was of Papa Al, red covering his torso. The last paper, the one Salvador was working on, was of two sets of hands and arms covered in red. Veronica's knees went weak and she had to sit down. Kitty walked across the table and stared her in the face.

The sound that developed in her head was like listening to a radio between stations. She concentrated on trying to understand but the best she got was a few individual words.

She reached up to pet the cat. "I don't know what you're trying to tell me Kitty, but I have a feeling it's important."

Salvador leaned over the table and hugged the cat. "She says she really likes it here and is glad she doesn't have to live at that other place anymore." He pointed to his paper. "Kitty remembers smelling blood all over the people's hands."

Veronica stomach roiled like an overactive volcano. "Do you know who the people are?"

"Kitty doesn't know names and I didn't get a picture of them in my mind the way I see things from Bee Bop."

Veronica looked down at the drawings Salvador had made. Even as advanced in art as he was, there was nothing to identify a gender or age. There were just hands and arms. She fought the shiver coursing up and down her body, from deep in her gut to the top of her head when she looked at the drawing again. *I should go down and see how Lee is doing with the detectives and ask if they need me for anything.* She focused her attention on her son. "How would you like to go to the store with me to pick up some kitty litter and a box? If she's going to be inside that's something she'll need."

"What about Kitty?" Worry leaked around the edges of his voice. "She's still upset."

"We'll put her out front and you can tell her that if she stays in the yard she'll be safe. There's lots of places for a cat to hide and we'll let Arturo and Jesus know she can be here. Or we can leave her in your room and you can stay with her. I'll only be gone a short time. There are lots of adults here and you can go to any of them if you need to."

Salvador picked up the cat and buried his face in her fur. "It's okay to put her outside. She feels safe here, but I'm going to stay with her."

"Okay. Problem solved." Veronica stood up. "I'm going to get my purse and let everyone know you're going to be here while I'm gone. You take Kitty outside."

When she returned from the feed store with the necessary cat items, including a couple of toys, Salvador was still sitting on the front porch with Kitty. He was using a long green stem

w/a black cage?

from a wild oat, seed heads still firmly attached to the end, as a toy for Kitty to chase and bat around with her delicate paws. The expression of joy on Salvador's face was similar to when the dump truck delivered his pile of dirt, but there was an added serenity in his eyes that melted Veronica's heart.

She sat on the porch floor and put the bag down. In an instant, Salvador was at her side. "Kitty is so happy! She likes to play."

"I see that. If you look in the bag you'll find some toys I bought for her." She laughed when Salvador almost dove head first into the large bag.

He pulled out the toys, his face lit up with excitement. "Kitty will love these. Brandy will like this one." He held up a mouse like creature with a squeaky noise maker inside.

"Brandy?"

"Papa came to visit me and Kitty while you were gone. He said Brandy will like having a new friend. I saw Papa sitting there," Salvador pointed to the porch swing at the other side of the large, covered porch. "I sat down next to him. I couldn't feel him, except it was warm when he touched my shoulder. He said the lady vet will call and it will all be over, then we can bring Brandy home."

Veronica's head spun with such intensity she put both hands on the porch floor to keep her balance. Her equilibrium regained, she put her hand to her heart and said, "Thank you Papa. And thank you, Sal, for having the ability and willingness to hear and see beyond what most people can. I'm going to take these things to the upstairs bathroom. Do you want to bring Kitty, so she'll know where to find her box? And I think you might want to keep her new toys in your room, so they don't get lost."

"Okay." Salvador opened the front door and called the cat. Veronica was amazed to see Kitty follow him in and up the stairs like a well-trained dog.

They had just finished filling the litter box and setting out food and water bowls in Salvador's room when Lee came in.

"Dinner's ready. Jessica asked me to come up and get you."

"Awesome, I'm starved." Veronica ran her fingers through Salvador's hair. "Let's go eat, *Mijo*."

"What about Kitty?" There was a whine of concern in his voice.

Lee directed Salvador's attention to his bed where Kitty was settled on his pillow, bathing herself. "I'd say she was fine. She has everything she needs, so why don't you shut the door so you know she's safe?"

Downstairs, the smell was heavenly. Tyler and Lydia sat quietly at the table while Jesus and Jessica said goodbye to Arturo as he headed for home to have dinner with his wife. After their ritual goodbyes they began bringing dinner to the table.

Veronica placed Salvador's napkin in his lap when he sat down next to her, then she offered her usual thanks for such a fine meal once Jesus and Jessica joined them. What surprised her was that dinner was almost normal. There was talk about the area of high pressure predicted to bring the spring's first heat wave, and what needed to be done to protect the gardens. Lydia mentioned the new shopping center going up off Broadway and Lee talked about the summer symphony concert series at the fairgrounds.

"I read about the selection of music to be played during the series," said Lydia, "But I don't think I'm still going to be here."

"Did you find a new home, Lydia?" asked Salvador.

"I think I'm just going to travel and enjoy the world," Lydia smiled at him. "Have you and your mom decided on a new home, Sal?"

"No, Mom said we're going to go visit some pretty gardens first," Salvador repeated what Veronica had told him earlier in the week.

"That's a good idea," said Lydia. "Jerold is right. You two should leave now before the place is put up for sale so you won't have to deal with all that chaos. Just pack your bags and go."

64

Lee pushed back his chair with a loud scraping noise. "Thank you for the fine meal, Jessica. Can I help you clear the table?"

Veronica thanked her cousin in her mind for his awareness and understanding of the situation. She stood also. "I'll help clean up, too." She put a hand on Salvador's shoulder. "*Mijo*, why don't you go check on Kitty. Then we'll leave to go to Bible Study."

Feeling blessed that her prayer group and Salvador's study group seemed to be as soothing as normal they went home to end the day together in Salvador's room reading a story. After closing up the house for the night and making sure all the doors were locked, she went into the office to close out her computer.

***

The next morning Veronica woke early, surprised she'd slept so well. As had become her morning routine, she sat in bed and checked the videos from the security cameras overnight. Once again, the hooded nighttime visitor walked up the trail from the creek and sat on the bench near the gift shop. Her thoughts went right to her brother. "Is that you CJ? If it is, please come to the house."

At breakfast Lee set the newspaper next to her that he'd just gone up the road to get.

Veronica opened The Mountain Democrat, the oldest newspapers in the west.

A sudden surge of excitement washed over her. "Oh my God, I totally forgot about the add coming out today." She began going through the paper page by page. Once she found the half-page add she smoothed it out to allow herself to melt into its beauty. Even thought she'd created it, seeing it so large and in the paper was thrilling. Photos of the roses and gardens took center stage in the advertisement, under the large headline – "Serenity Valley Rose Gardens of Placerville." She silently thanked her Papa Al for paying for the extra classes in advertising and promotion.

After celebratory comments about Veronica's add and the opening of the gardens on Saturday, Lee offered to help with anything she needed done in the garden and to go to the courthouse with her for support.

"Aren't you going to your dad's today to get your stuff?" asked Veronica.

"I'm going to try to get to the lawyer's today to sign papers from the trust. I thought I'd hang around and help you in the meantime."

"That would be awesome." Veronica welcomed his help as well as his companionship and felt a warm infusion, like the first sip of coffee in the morning, at the idea of sharing her knowledge of their grandfather's roses.

But first things first. "I have to meet Detective Russell at the courthouse this morning to see about the restraining order. I'd appreciate it if you could be there. Russell thinks your knowledge of you father could be helpful."

"I'll be there."

After taking Salvador to school, she met Lee at the courthouse to ask for the restraining order. Detective Russell met them at the clerk's office.

They were sent into the judge's chambers. When Lee told the judge of his father's aggression toward Marcus and that his mother had left because she feared for her life, the judge picked up a pen and signed his name with a flourish. "I'm issuing a temporary restraining order against Jerold Mason with a court date in two weeks. At that time it will either be allowed to lapse or a permanent order will be issued against him."

"Thank you, Your Honor," said Veronica. "This makes me feel so much safer."

Veronica and Lee walked side by side out of the courthouse to their cars. "I feel so much better knowing you might be safer now." Lee put his arm around his cousin. "So much has happened in the past two weeks I've even begun to wonder what's going to happen next."

They stopped at their cars. "Speaking of what's going to happen next," said Veronica. "Are you going to go to the lawyer's now?"

"Yeah, I already texted her office to let them know I'm on my way. She's just down the street, so I'll leave my car here. I'll be back at the house as soon as I'm done."

When she returned home, Veronica walked along the paths in the gardens and allowed her mind to wander. While she thought about everything that had happened over the past 10 days, it was when she thought about the future that she felt a new kind of serenity.

When Lee returned from the lawyer's office, Jesus, and Arturo joined him in washing benches, picnic tables, and the outside of the little red barn. After picking up Salvador from school, Veronica took him and Lee out to the shop. "Papa Al painted the miniature rose tables in the sales yard every three years. We're going to keep with his routine."

She pulled a can of Forest Service Green paint out of the cupboard and handed it to Lee. "Here is the paint, your paint brushes, and the canvas drop cloths to put under the tables."

In the sales garden she helped move all the small roses so they were out of the way. She and Lee turned the tables upside down on the drop cloth to paint the legs and underside first. "By the time you're finished with this last table, the first one will be dry and ready to turn over so you can paint the top."

Once the guys got started painting, she headed for the greenhouse. There were always things to do in there. She sat on the tall stool at the work bench and let out a sigh. "Things might just work out Papa. It's going to be tough going for a while, but you've given me the courage to see it through. I just wish I knew more about what you told Sal about finding Brandy. I really do miss her."

She began setting aside the roses that were ready to go out to the sales yard, making sure each one had its name and species tag. She filled one of the fat-tired wagons with pots of roses and headed for the sales yard. Once she set the roses in their proper places, she went to see how the painting was going. The beautiful Forest Service Green glistened in the late afternoon sun. The tables were still upside down. She wasn't sure what had the most complete coat of paint. The tables, the drop cloth, or Salvador. "These tables look great. You guys are doing such a good job. Thank you, both of you." Knowing both the tables and her son were in good hands she said, "I have some things I have to do in the office. I'll be there if you need me."

Going online, she put in a new order for organic fertilizer, formulated for flowering plants, then she began going through her email. Her heart raced when her phone rang and she saw the caller was one of the Veterinarians from Auburn that she'd contacted.

Her hands shook as she answered. "Hello. This is Veronica Vallejo."

"Hello Veronica, this is Doctor Marta Lestermann at Auburn Creek Animal Hospital. I'm calling about your dog Brandy. She's been found."

65

Veronica jumped to her feet and paced across the room. "Do you have her?"

"No, the gentleman who found her still has her. I do have to tell you that Brandy had been brought to the office over a week ago. Her microchip was scanned, and the number associated with the chip was called, but the lady who answered the call stated the owner had died and the dog had been given away a few months ago. It wasn't until you called that I remembered her and contacted the man who found her."

Veronica thought she was going to be sick. "Brandy's owner died just a week ago, and she disappeared at the same time. I don't know who told you she was given away months ago, but that isn't true. Is there any way to get her back?"

"I'm sure there is," said Dr. Lestermann. "The man who found her is Zachary Alder. He has several rescue dogs, but I'm sure he'll be delighted to see Brandy go home. Let me give you his number."

Veronica called Mr. Alder right way. There was no answer so she left a message. She called again and again until Jessica announced dinner was ready. She didn't say anything about getting the call. She wanted to wait until she knew for sure.

After dinner she called again. The man answered with a simple, "Hello?"

"Mr. Alder? My name is Veronica Vallejo. Dr. Lestermann gave me you name and number because of the possibility that you may have Brandy, our Golden Retriever."

"The Golden Retriever? Her name is Brandy? Yes, I still have her. Dr. Lestermann told me she was given away, so we thought she must have gotten lost from her new home."

"Brandy wasn't given away. Her owner was murdered and she was stolen away just over a week ago. Brandy is a beloved member of the family, and I've been looking all over for her. You can't believe how worried my son has been, and knowing she's safe is the answer to our prayers. Could I ask how you found her?"

"I was down at the river with my other rescue dogs. We were just leaving when I saw a car pull up. The driver got out with the dog on a leash. The driver took the dog's collar and leash off, then threw a stick over the bank toward the river. When the dog, uh Brandy, went for the stick, the driver got back in the car and drove away."

"Were you close enough to see the car and the driver?"

He described the vehicle and the person driving.

Veronica collapsed back into her chair. For a moment she thought she was going to be sick. "Can I come pick Brandy up this evening? I'm Placerville. I can be there in about an hour."

"That sounds fine. I'll be happy to know Brandy's home where she belongs. Let me give you my address. It's just off Highway 49. It's easy to find."

"Thank you so much, I'll call you right before I leave Placerville." A mental image of Brandy being abandoned and how she must have felt lost and alone whirred through Veronica's mind–as her anger turned to rage. She sent a quick text to Lee and rushed out of the office.

Veronica flew across the hall and threw the door open, letting it smash against the wall. Instead of screaming like she wanted to, her voice came out as a pressured growl. "Why'd you do it?"

Dressed in her nightgown, Lydia sat at her computer desk. Veronica saw her close out the window she had open. Her expression was one of innocent confusion. "What are you talking about?"

"You were seen! Someone saw what you did!" Veronica's voice rose as she crossed the room to face Lydia. What she didn't say out loud was, you're a liar and a murderer.

Lydia opened a desk drawer and stood up. "You're confused. You've experienced a horrible shock recently and need professional help."

"What I need is for you to stop lying. I know what you did!"

Lydia came toward her, her voice calm. "That's unfortunate. I can't have you telling others." In a quick move, she rushed at Veronica and raised the hand that had been hidden in the folds of her nightgown. She had the knife that was missing from the kitchen. She lunged at Veronica, aiming at her chest. "Now I'm going to have to kill you, too."

Instead of trying to run away, Veronica rushed into Lydia's lunge and grabbed her arm with both hands.

Lydia was larger than Veronica, but they were a match in strength. During that momentary skirmish between life and death neither said anything. Finally, Veronica pushed Lydia backward against the foot of the bed. Lydia held on and they both fell. They bounced off the mattress and rolled to the floor into the narrow space between the wall and the bed. Trapped under the larger woman, Veronica attempted to roll under the bed, but Lydia's weight was too much and the space she was too cramped. Lydia pinned Veronica's arms to the floor and against the wall with her knees. In a flash she had the knife against Veronica's throat.

Lydia glanced at a small cut on her arm and smiled. "Oh look. You cut me during the struggle when you came at me with the knife you used to kill your grandfather. Now I'm going to have to kill you in self-defense."

Veronica wanted to scream, but she knew if she did Lydia would silence her in an instant. She tried to get Lydia talking, to stall for time in hopes Lee would find them. "Why'd you kill Papa?"

"For the Blue Moon, of course. That blue rose is worth a fortune. It's going to make me rich. I knew Al had the brains to create it. It took longer than I thought it would, but I'm a very patient person. I just had to wait."

"You have it!"

"No, I don't, but I'll find it. It's on this property some-where. I'm sure it is. I'll just have to continue looking for it."

"That's why you've been spending so much time in the yard. You're not going to get away with this."

"Oh, it's all set up." Lydia's smile was cruel and mocking. "I left enough evidence for the police to be sure you did it. That stupid blue coat you wear around the house all winter. I found it in the garbage can with blood on it. The police were very pleased to get it.

"And then you killed Daniel Benson. He knew about the Blue Moon and came here to buy it. You couldn't take the chance that he'd tell me and he wouldn't tell you, so you killed him."

66

"He never suspected I'd kill him. I left enough evidence to lead the police right to you. I'm surprised they haven't arrested you already." Lydia pressed the tip of the knife hard enough into Veronica's throat that she could feel the sting. A second later she felt blood trickling across her throat. "In three minutes this dump and all the property will be Jerold's and the rose will be mine."

"He was in on this with you!"

"No, your uncle's too wrapped up in his own desires to care about what I do."

Too afraid to move, Veronica focused on keeping Lydia talking. She barely saw the flash of red and blue hit the back of Lydia's head. Lydia screamed, dropped the knife, and leaned back to reach back behind her head.

She attempted to grab Lydia's hands but two strong arms reached down from the bed, grabbed Lydia's wrists and twisted her arms to hold them behind her back, away from the screaming macaw.

Lydia collapsed, her face smashing into Veronica's. She saw stars and the lights started to go out in her brain until she noticed Lee's face hovering above Lydia.

Bee Bop's voice, "Bad girl. Bad!" reached Veronica's brain and gave her a surge of energy. She saw that Bee Bop was on Lydia's neck. What she couldn't see was that she had her sharp and powerful hook beak buried deep in the back of Lydia's neck, but she heard a sickening crunch of tissue being dug into.

"It's over now, Beep." Lee's voice was soft.

"Get that bird away from me." Lydia screamed. Bee Bop let go of her hold, climbed up the bedspread, and onto the bed.

"Get me off of this–" Lydia swore, called Veronica names and demanded to be moved.

"Lee, do as she asked," said Veronica.

Tyler rushed into the room and threw himself to the floor at Veronica's feet. "I'm here. How can I help?"

"Help me get Lydia off Veronica," said Lee. "I don't want to let go of her hands."

Tyler grabbed Lydia by her feet and pulled her out of the narrow space between the wall and the bed.

"Don't let her go!" cried Veronica.

"She's not going anywhere," said Lee his voice firm. "Tyler, grab the belt off Lydia's robe. I'm going to tie her hands."

A loud, panicked scream erupted from behind Lee. "Mama!" Salvador flew onto the bed, his arms reaching for his mother.

"Sal, stay on the bed," said Lee "We don't want to hurt your mom."

Salvador's nose ran and tears streamed down his face. "Mama."

"*Estoy Bien, Mijo,*" said Veronica. She lightly touched the wound in her throat. "I need something to put on this cut."

"Okay, Super Sal," said Lee, "Run into the bathroom and get two clean towels from the cabinet." Lee finished tying Lydia's hands behind her back. By then Salvador was back with the towels. When Lydia remained still and quiet, Lee took one of the towels and pressed it against the bite on the back of her neck while Salvador crawled back on the bed and handed Veronica the other towel.

"How bad are you hurt?" asked Tyler.

"I don't think it's that bad," she said. When she struggled to sit up, Lee offered her his hand to help her.

Bee Bop stepped onto Veronica's shoulder when she leaned against the bed. "Good girl. I'm here." Once again the voice was her grandfather's, even though it came from Bee Bop.

"Whoa. Did you hear that?" Lee looked up from his phone and stared at Bee Bop, wide eyed.

"Yeah." Veronica put her hand near her shoulder for Bee Bop to step onto, then set her on the bed. "Thank you, Bee Bop, and thank you Papa. I need to check Lydia." She scooted to where Lydia lay, her hands tied behind her back. Veronica laid a fingertip against Lydia's throat. Her pulse was weak, but it was there. *Good, she's alive. I want her to live to pay for what she did.*

Lee had dialed 911. His voice had an urgency to it, but it was strong.

Bee Bop walked to the end of the bed and hopped onto Salvador's lap. "Cracker?"

"I wish we could all just think about having a cracker at a time like this," said Veronica. "Yes, Pretty Bird. You can have all the crackers you want."

"The ambulances are on their way," said Lee. "I asked for two. You need care too."

"Call Detective Russell and Detective Norton. They need to be here. I have their numbers in my phone." Veronica pulled her phone out of her back pocket. Even though the screen was shattered from where she fell off the bed on it, it opened up. Her phone chirped to tell her someone had come up the drive. A moment later there was a loud pounding on the kitchen door.

"I'll get it." Tyler got to his feet and rushed out of the bedroom.

In the quiet of the moment, Salvador crawled off the bed and snuggled against his mother's side. Lydia moaned as she struggled to move her head. "Don't try to move Lydia. The ambulance is on its way."

There was the sound of footsteps coming down the hall. Detectives Russell and Norton, and two sheriff deputies came into Veronica's view. "Veronica, the ambulance will be here in a few minutes. Sal, could you to take Bee Bop and sit over there in that chair?" Detective Russell pointed to the lounge chair near the window. "I need to check your mom and Lydia."

"I'm fine," said Veronica. "Lydia's breathing but not moving."

Russell carefully lifted the corner of the towel over Lydia's neck. "What happened? This almost looks like a knife wound."

Bee Bop, now in Salvador's lap, bobbed her head up and down and said, "Hello, pretty girl."

"It's a parrot bite. Bee Bop flew into the room and bit Lydia as she was stabbing me and saying how she was going to kill me and make it look like self-defense. How did you get here so quickly?"

"We were at your neighbors. Doris Norris has been arrested as an accomplice to your grandfather's murder. She confessed that Lydia killed him as part of their plan to steal the blue rose."

67

"Doris and Lydia are related, aren't they."

"Doris is Lydia's daughter."

Veronica's phone beeped again. "Someone else is here."

"I'll go check," said Lee.

"I need to get Bee Bop safely away from all this," Veronica struggled to get to her feet.

"Stay where you are. You're injured and have lost a good deal of blood. Can anyone else take her?" asked Russell. "Do you think Bee Bop will let me take her out of the way?" Bee Bop, still on Salvador's lap, made a slight lunge with open beak when Russell put her hand out. "Okay, I guess not. What do we do?"

Bee Bop started screaming when Lee came in with several people carrying what appeared to be luggage.

"Lee, do you remember how I showed you to wrap Bee Bop in a large towel?" asked Veronica.

"Yeah, I'll try that," said Lee. "I don't want anyone to get bit. Not after seeing what she did to Lydia. She'd take a finger off, in the mood she's in." Lee pulled the blanket off the foot of the bed, folded it into several thicknesses and quickly had Bee Bop safely wrapped and secured. Bee Bop announced her thoughts with a series of screams loud enough for the EMTs to put their hands over their ears. "I'll put her in her cage so everyone is safe, including her," said Lee.

"Put lots of treats in her treat cup," said Veronica. "Sal, could you help your cousin?"

Salvador shook his head. Tears streamed down his face. Veronica understood. He wasn't going to let her out of his sight. She worried about how much more trauma a child could endure.

By the time Lydia was taken to the ambulance, Salvador began to calm down.

Detective Russell knelt next to Salvador and put her hand on his. "Your mom is going to be fine, Sal. It's all over now. Bee Bop stopped the bad person who hurt your papa and your mom, and the police have taken that bad person away. Now we're going to take your mom to the doctor to make sure she's okay."

"No ... Brandy, I have to go get Brandy." Veronica couldn't catch her breath, but a questioning look from Russell helped her gather her wits and her thoughts. "That's how all this started. The man who has her described Lydia's car and Lydia when she abandoned her at the river. I have to go get her. I said I'd be there this evening."

Russell pressed her lips together in thought, then said, "It's going to be a few hours before you're done at the hospital, and with the police investigation that has to be done tonight. I don't think it would be safe for you to drive all the way to Auburn. It would be after midnight before you get there.

"So, I have an idea. I have a friend who has an animal rescue. I'm sure I can talk her into getting Brandy for you. Give me the name and number of the person who has her. I'll call them, explain why you can't make it and let them know someone will be there. You'll have a very happy and excited dog greeting you at the door when you get home."

"Would your friend do that? I can't leave her there, not now." said Veronica.

"I'm sure she would. We're going to get Brandy and bring her home." The expression on Russell's face was one of a friend, not a police officer.

By the time Veronica got to the ER, everything had been worked out. Detective Russell's friend was on her way to

Auburn. Lee drove Veronica's truck to the hospital because it had Salvador's booster seat in it. He was able to talk Salvador into going to the cafeteria with him while the doctors took care of his mom. Detective Russell never left her side.

After her vital stats were checked and rechecked and the wound on her throat cleaned and stitched, it was time to answer questions.

Russell and Norton recorded everything on their phones while Veronica answered their questions as carefully as she could. The interesting part of the evening was how the detectives used the information she gave them to solve the case even though they were well on their way to finding the answers on their own. She was getting ready to be released when Russell got a call. She walked down the hall away from everyone then returned a short time later. "Lydia has been transferred to the trauma center in Sacramento. She is awake and alert, but has no movement below her neck. They talked to a veterinarian who specializes in macaws who said that while a greenwing's bite can be severe, they're shocked that Bee Bop could have done that damage to Lydia's spine. I talked to the physician in charge of Lydia's case and he said in all his years of practice, he's never seen that kind of injury before."

"I think Bee Bop had help. Both Lee and I heard Papa Al's voice come from Bee Bop the way you and I heard his voice. He said, "Good girl, I'm here.""

"Officially, it will still be a parrot bite. Something your little hero did to protect you." Russell took a deep breath and smiled at Veronica. "Case solved, and case closed. No matter what her medical condition is, Lydia will be charged with first degree murder of your grandfather and Daniel Benson."

It's over. It's really over. Veronica felt a tingle each time Russell's phone rang or beeped with a text. One of the calls was from her friend Emily, she was in Auburn. She used facetime to show a picture of the Golden Retriever she was picking up. "Brandy! Yes, that's her," said Veronica when Russell held the phone for her to see. "Hello puppy. Are you ready to come home?" At the sound of Veronica's voice, Brandy danced in circles and barked, her tail wagging.

Emily introduced Zackery Alder, the man who'd found Brandy. An older man with a baritone voice, he said he'd miss having Brandy around the house as she was playful and well trained, but he couldn't think of a better ending to such a tragic tale. Emily then announced that she'd head back to Placerville and would text when she got to the house.

"Someone needs to be at the house when she gets there," said Veronica. "I mean, Tyler might still be there, but he was pretty stressed by the time we left. If he's still there he could probably use some support."

Veronica called Jessica and Jesus. She explained what had happened and asked them to go to the house to be there when Emily arrived. An hour later, both Emily and Jesus texted that Brandy was home. Emily also sent a video of an overwhelming fur and feather greeting that started with ear shattering screams and whines that quickly evolved into soft whines from Brandy and a litany of hellos, pretty girls, and Bee Bop's soft calls for Brandy to come. Within minutes Brandy lay belly to the floor rubbing faces with Bee Bop. The video ended with Bee Bop standing next to Brandy, petting her ear with her foot, repeating, "Good girl."

68

Eventually Detective Norton announced he had all the information he needed and left. When they were alone, Russell admitted that it was the evidence from Bee Bop and Salvador's conversations with his Papa and Kitty, as well as the information Veronica was willing to share. that helped them solve the murder.

It was after midnight when they left the hospital. Veronica walked between Detective Russell and Lee, with Salvador draped over his shoulder, asleep. "Detective Russell, I know it's late, but I'd like to invite you over to meet Brandy and be part of the celebration that the investigation is over and our ragamuffin dog is finally home."

Russell gave Veronica a warm smile. "I'd be honored to be part of that celebration. I love dogs." She set a hand on Veronica's arm. "You can call by my first name now. If you don't mind, I'd like to be considered your friend rather than the detective in charge of your case." She must have read Veronica's thoughts. "It's Jillian."

"Cool, Jillian." Veronica smiled. "Friends call me Ronnie."

At the house, the joyful greetings from Jesus, Jessica, Arturo, and his wife Maria, and Tyler, were eclipsed by the cries, tears and laughter from Salvador, Bee Bop, and Brandy. Veronica ended up on the floor with Salvador, Lee and the animals. She hugged and petted Brandy and cried as much as Salvador. She was just glad she didn't wet all over the floor the way Brandy did in her excitement.

Jessica offered an old towel from the mud room for a quick cleanup, then from the still intact wine room in the cellar, she brought out a bottle of sparkling wine. The bottle was just enough for one glass for the adults. For Salvador, Jessica made cocoa with marshmallows, and pulled out the rest of the sugar cookies, which everyone shared.

Goodbyes were accompanied by hugs and kisses. "Tomorrow," said Jesus, "life at the Mason House Gardens starts anew."

Arturo ruffed his son's hair. "But the work will continue as always."

"Come in late." Veronica looked at her watch, "I can't believe it's almost 2AM. We could all use some sleep."

On her way out, Detective Russell asked. "So where did the name Brandy come from? Your grandfather's favorite spirit?"

Veronica ran her fingers through the hair of the dog by her side. "A rose. Introduced in 1981, it won the All American Rose Selection Award in 1982. The flower and the pup are the exact same color. There's one growing just outside the front porch."

Jillian laughed. "A rose. I should have known."

"I'll show it to you the next time you're here."

The detective rubbed her chin to hide a bashful smile "Hmm, the next time I'm here. Is that an invitation?"

Veronica's smile was full and open. "Yes, it most definitely is."

"Invitation accepted. Just let me know when and I'll hope I'm not called on a case."

"From what I experienced these last two weeks, it seems that's part of the life of a detective. If something happens you have to go to be there."

"Yeah, that's why being married to a cop can be hard on spouses. Too many wives or husbands feel like family comes second to their partner's job."

"Is that why you're not–I'm sorry." Veronica caught herself and fiddled with the latch to the gate. "I shouldn't ask such a personal question."

Jillian reached around Veronica and opened the gate. "That is pretty personal, but I don't mind telling you that I've just never found the right ... uh, person ... to share my life with–yet."

Veronica walked with the detective to her car. "I hope I get to see you again, and I want to thank you for all you've done for me, being patient and trusting me, and not thinking I'm a total nutcase for believing in ghosts and believing in a child who talks to animals." She stepped back from the car. "Call me any day of the week for dinner. With Jessica cooking, meals are always special."

Unable to sleep, it was nearly four in the morning when Veronica finally gave up staring at the ceiling and took the pain pill the ER doctor had given her. It was after nine in the morning when she woke up, still aching and feeling like she had cotton candy for a brain.

The memory of the night before churning through her mind was enough to get her out of bed and across the hall to check on Salvador. He wasn't in his room. His bed was made and his pajama were folded neatly on his dresser. There was a short note on his bed.

Ronnie, I called Sal's school and let Sarah know that after last night he wouldn't be there today. I'm heading to Dad's house this morning.

Lee.

Still in her pajamas, Veronica wandered to the end of the hall and leaned over the banister to peer into the great room. Bee Bop worked on chewing up a piece of wood hanging on her play stand. Salvador sat on the floor with Kitty curled up on his lap and Brandy stretched out next to him. On the TV, the roadrunner was doing his usual best to outwit Wiley E. Coyote. There were also sounds coming from the kitchen.

When she walked down the stairs Bee Bop announced her presence with a loud scream. Brandy let out a small bark and ran to her, tail wagging. Salvador, with Kitty following at his heels, was right behind her. Veronica sat on the bottom stair to be greeted with hugs from Salvador and a wet dog kisses from Brandy. Bee Bop flew over to land on the stair banister. Kitty sat on the area rug at the foot of the stairs, observing the entire ritual.

"Brandy and Kitty are getting along?" Veronica looked between the dog and the cat.

"I talked to them and said we can all be friends. Bee Bop's not sure about Kitty, but I think it'll be okay."

Jessica came from the kitchen. "Would you like something to eat?"

"Jessica! What ... Why... it's early!?" Veronica couldn't get her brain to function.

"Lee called this morning and asked if I could come in early to watch Sal and help you while he was gone. You do not have to pay me for the hours. It is my gift to you. Jesus said he would help Lee unload his things when he got back."

"*Gracias, hermana.*" Veronica got up and hugged her friend. "*Gracias* for being such a good friend."

After breakfast, Veronica summoned her courage to go into her Papa's and Lydia's room. Beyond the messed up bed and the blood still on the floor, everything looked normal, but she understood that things were anything but normal. Her Papa would never again use or need his things, and she would never again let Lydia into the Mason House.

The phone ringing in the office drew her attention away from the bedroom. It went to voice mail before she got there. She gently eased herself into her chair and pressed the button for voice mail. *Hey Veronica, this is Will. Nolan and I saw you were admitted to the ER last night, but we were both assigned to a possible contagion and couldn't come see you. I sneaked a peek at your chart after you left. If you need anything, please let us know. We were both able to get Saturday and Sunday off, so we'll be there for opening day and Mother's Day. Love you, sister.*

69

Veronica smiled at the caring offer of help from her two friends. She sat at her desk and began to return emails offering days and times for buyers to come view her papa's roses. Next she returned calls from people who had seen the advertisement in the paper and wanted to know about rose sales and the Garden's set up for weddings.

She was dialing the third call when Salvador peeked around the corner. "Mom, can I come in and play my game?"

Veronica put the phone down. "I thought you were watching cartoons."

Salvador shrugged, then sat on the small couch across from where Veronica worked. Brandy came in with him and jumped up on the couch next to him. Kitty followed right behind. She settled on the other side of Salvador. Veronica could hear her purr from across the room.

She turned off her computer and pulled her chair around to sit in front of her son. "How are you doing, *Mijo?*"

"I'm worried about you, Mom. Lydia hurt you. I wish she was dead."

She didn't know what to say. *I don't wish she was dead. The Hell she's going to be in while she lives is better than anything she will experience after she dies.* "It's over now *Mijo.* The police know who killed Papa Al, and I'm going to be fine.

"The most important part is that you and I have a home, Brandy is home safe, and even Kitty has a home with a little boy who loves her." She watched the expression on her son's face change from worried and desolate to a smile that shined more from his eyes than his mouth.

"It's almost lunch time. What do you say we go have something to eat?"

It was nearly two when Lee returned with the Escalade full of stuff. He flopped down on the small couch opposite where Veronica worked on her computer and closed his eyes.

"How'd it go?" She asked.

"Ugly." The word sounded more like an exhausted exhale. "Marcus wasn't there but Dad was still home when I got there. He started cussing about the police coming and threatening to arrest him if he hit anyone or came here again. He yelled at me when I asked him why he wasn't at work. He accused you of making up lies about him. He ranted about two of his technicians at his practice quitting and the club closing down his program." Lee took a deep breath. "It got even uglier when I told him I was moving out. The only thing I can hope for is that when they start questioning the girls in his tennis program, someone will be brave enough to tell the truth."

"You were able to get your stuff?"

"All the important stuff. Gramp's Escalade holds a lot."

"Which room do you want? Jesus will be here in a few minutes to help you carry your stuff upstairs."

"The one I've been sleeping in, is just fine." Lee stood and shook his head.

The way he looked at Veronica got her attention. "What?"

"Cuz, you will always be my role model. You are so together. If I just went through what you did last night and over the last week and a half, I'd be a mess, in pieces on the floor."

Veronica said, "Don't think for a minute that it hasn't been hard and that I wasn't falling apart at times. I got through it for Salvador and Papa. Right now, whatever you need to get through, you need to do for you. To be okay with being happy and creating your own peace and future."

"Isn't that kind of selfish?"

"Lee, taking care of yourself and being happy isn't selfish. It's an act of love and personal responsibility.

"Okay. Time for me to care about myself and be responsible. Can I admit to you that I'm really worried about Marcus?"

"Yeah, I'm worried about him, too. I just hope we're able to be there for him." Veronica looked up as Jesus came through the door. *"Hola, amigo."* She grabbed Lee's hand and started for the door. "Let's get you moved in."

After two trips, Veronica sat and watched.

Lee stopped to check on her. "Are you okay?"

"I thought I was in pretty good shape," she said, "But I think last night did me in. Sorry, I'm not more help."

Lee sat next to her. "You've already helped me more than I could ever imagine. Thanks again for letting me stay here. Whatever you need done around here just let me know. I'm not going to take advantage of your kindness and act like this is a free ride. I've learned so much from Tyler, I honestly think I could redo the bedrooms upstairs by myself. I might even go into remodeling as a profession. I enjoy seeing the change happen."

Veronica leaned her head against her cousin's shoulder. "It's been great having you here. At times it feels like when we were kids. Building dirt forts and defending them from space aliens."

"Do you remember that time we dug a fort over the leach line from the septic tank? We smelled so bad our parents wouldn't let us in the house."

Veronica and Lee laughed together. Lee added, "I'm glad it was summer, and we were as young as we were. Standing naked in the back yard and getting hosed down could have been embarrassing. As it was, it was fun."

70

In some ways, Friday morning felt like any other morning. Veronica woke, got on her phone to check her email and the security cameras, did her morning exercise routine, made breakfast, then took Salvador to school. In other ways she wondered if life would ever feel normal again. She and Lee began boxing up her Papa's and Lydia's things. "You know, you can move down here if you like. These rooms make a beautiful little apartment."

"Hmm, I'll think about it." Lee looked around, "A bedroom and sitting room and a private bathroom. That's pretty deluxe."

"The beauty of having this as an apartment is that you could come in late without having to worry about waking Sal or me when you come down the hall." Veronica gave him a shy smile. "I'm assuming you'd like to have a friend over now and then."

"You think of everything."

Veronica glanced at her watch. "I have two appointments to show the wedding venue and have three appointments to show her papa's roses for potential sale this afternoon. So I need to get things ready."

The buyers who came, purchased every rose plant her Papa had wanted to sell. The highlight of the sales was, that due to her grandfather's success and the uniqueness of the colors he both bred and created, his roses were now going to be known as "Mason" roses. Just like David Austin or Meilland, just to name a couple. His name would not only be in catalogues but also on the tags of every one of his roses sold anywhere in the world. Her Papa's name would be known worldwide.

At noon, Sarah called and suggested she come get Salvador. Sarah explained that she didn't think Salvador was feeling well. He was restless and unable to focus on schoolwork.

As soon as she got home, Jillian Russell made an unannounced visit. "Part of this visit is official and part in friendship," she said.

Jillian and Veronica, followed by Salvador, Brandy and Kitty, meandered along a path in the Victorian garden. When Brandy headed for the goldfish pond, with Salvador right behind her, Jillian said, "I thought you might want to know about Lydia."

Veronica looked down at nothing. Did she really want to know? Part of her hoped for the worst and the other part of her never wanted to hear her name again. "I guess," she said.

"I can only guess how you're feeling right now, but this is something you should know. She's awake and talking, but at this point she still has no movement below her shoulders. The doctor at Sutter Trauma Center said some movement may return in time, but at her age it's not likely. She will probably never walk again and may never be able to feed herself. I would say the prison Bee Bop assigned her to is more secure than any cell with bars."

Thank you, Bee Bop. It doesn't bring Papa back, but in some ways he's not gone at all. Veronica stopped and stared at a large Joseph's Coat rose, just coming into bloom. It had taken over an old black oak snag, left standing after it died as a support for the rose. "Would I sound horrible if I said that's a fitting ending for a murderer? What about Addie–uh Doris? What's going to happen to her?"

Jillian paused for a second, then said, "She's singing like a canary. Because of her police record, she's being held without bail. The scratches you saw on her arm were from the blackberries. She wore your blue cover up to help frame you. She's admitting to everything, so she'll probably plea bargain for a lighter sentence."

"How did you link my cover up to her?"

"The wisteria pollen. It was covered in it. You said there was no wisteria here. Using pollen as evidence isn't new, but most people only think of hair and fingerprints, when they commit a crime. Tracking pollen to a specific plant has solved more than a few murders in recent years."

"What about all the cats at her house? Sal is worried about them. He said he can feel they're hungry. And there are kittens in the house. Would it be okay if we took them some food this evening?"

"It would be best if you didn't. Animal Outreach, the cat rescue, has already picked up the kittens, and several of the adult cats. They're trying to get as many of the outside cats as they can. Once they're caught, they'll be checked by a vet, socialized, and adopted out to new homes."

"I wish it'd be that easy to find Papa's Blue Moon."

The sound of Salvador giggling came from behind them. Veronica and Jillian turned at the same time. Salvador stood in the shadows of an ancient Ponderosa Pine. Veronica was almost positive she saw the shadowy image of someone standing there with him. "Okay. I'll tell her, Papa," said Salvador.

"Papa?" Veronica's voice wavered. The shape that appeared to be a person turned as if to walk away, then faded into the shadows.

Jillian took large gasps of air. "Did we just see ....?"

"Mama." Salvador ran up to them. "Papa was just here."

"I saw." Veronica reached a hand out for her son. "Did he talk to you?"

"Uh huh," "Salvador nodded. "He said, Take a walk back through time and you'll find my blue roses."

Veronica staggered a step "Did he tell you anything else? Do you know what he meant?"

Salvador shook his head.

Jillian took Veronica's arm and directed her to a nearby bench. "Sit down before you fall down." Jillian sounded like she was trying to catch her breath. "I think I just saw my very first apparition."

"Hang around and you'll see more." Veronica added with a soft laugh. "Now I need to figure out what Papa meant by taking a walk back through time."

"I have a feeling your grandfather either knows you'll figure it out or something will give you a clue," said Jillian. "Just like when he mentioned to look for Brandy at the end of the Western States 100."

***

Later that afternoon, Veronica showed the gardens and the new bridal lounge to a young woman, and her mother, who were in search for the perfect place to say the vows that would begin a new chapter in her life.

Veronica guided them along the smooth paths toward the gazebo covered in white Swan Lake rose blooms. The older woman stopped near a fountain and said, "I grew up in Philadelphia. There are so many historic gardens there and this Victorian garden is so lovely. It's like taking a walk back through time."

Veronica stumbled, catching herself from falling by grabbing a cupid statue. *A walk back through time. They're here somewhere. The Blue roses are here!*

She had to force herself to be a gracious hostess and sales rep to go through the contract, amenities offered, and event calendar, careful not to rush the soon-to-be bride in making her choices.

The second the mother and daughter drove away she rushed back to the Victorian garden. In her mind she visualized the blue rose and thought only of seeing blue. Within a few minutes she found herself in a shaded area near the fence above the creek. The first blue she saw was the brilliant blue blooms of several Porcelain Blue Corydalis backed by a large blue-green Hosta 'Abiqua Drinking Gourd.' In the back, near the fence were several blue, Summer Love Agapanthus. Directly in front of the Agapanthus, nestled among the Wedge-wood blue flowers of a Silver Heart Siberian Bugloss, was the single blue rose bloom. Behind it were two other blue tinted roses. One was blue with white stripes. The other was white with the outside edges of the petals nearly as blue as the sky.

Veronica dropped to her knees and caressed each of the blooms with her fingers to prove to herself they were real. She held her breath as she followed the stems to the ground to see that the roses had been set into the ground, still in their nursery pots. It was a simple task to grasp the pots by their rims and pull them out of the ground. She held the Blue Moon up against the sky. The blue rose nearly disappeared into the blue of the late afternoon sky.

She lifted the other two out of the ground and held all three of them in her arms. "I'm going to patent all of these." She caressed the white with a blue edges. "This one will be named Salvador's Whisper." She raised the blue and white striped higher. "This one will be Bee Bop." Tears blurred her vision. In that moment she felt sure her papa was near her. "Thank you Papa. Your gardens, Sal, and I are going to be fine thanks to your foresight. And you were right. Within a few years there will be blue Mason Roses in nearly every garden in the world."

ACKNOWLEDGMENTS

I would like to thank all those involved in my journey of writing this novel. The inspiration for this novel is my love of roses and the serenity I feel among my over 50 roses, including everything from Rosa Mundi, Peace, Mr. Lincoln, and Purple Tiger to name just a few. As a member of The American Rose Society, I have explored the history and modern world of growing and showing roses. As a volunteer foster parront for Mickaboo Pet Bird Rescue, I have been able to nurture my love for parrots with my three macaws. Two adopted-Sargent and Bambi, and one purchase/rescue-Susie Q a very verbal macaw with a large vocabulary who has chosen to live in my kitchen closet. I miss having a dog, but feel that rescue honor with Oliver Twist, an abandoned kitten who felt safe enough to show up after being dumped alongside the road to ask me for a home. As an author, I want to thank Kirk Colvin my editor and leader of El Dorado Writer's Guild, NYT bestselling author Marshall Karp, author, cover designer extraordinaire Karen Phillips, author Terry Shepherd, Jennifer Morita, Donna Del Oro and Dänna Wilberg members of Sisters In Crime and the Sacramento chapter Capitol Crimes for their support, encouragement, and shared knowledge of writing crime/mystery novels. I also want to thank my sister Cindy Carroll for her support and her husband, retired Placerville City Police Detective Tom Carroll for his willingness to explain police procedures and share the police officers' stories about the apparitions seen and encountered in and around Placerville over the years.

ABOUT THE AUTHOR

Ms. Sullivan's poetic writing style is poised at the event horizon of purple prose. She wrote her first novel at the age of 12 and nurtured her artistic talents through the visual arts until the flame to write ignited once again.

Ms. Sullivan is a Registered Art Therapist, and Mental Health Rehabilitation Specialist, who dedicated her life helping kids and teens in psychiatric treatment programs. Ms. Sullivan's passage into the life as an author started with her Si-Fi/Fantasy novel, *To Face the Rising Sun*. This novel has led to the creation of The Or'Dara Chronicles. Book two, *To Touch the Stone of Dreams* is nearly complete, and book three, *To Soothe a Savage Beast* is in the outline stage.

Ms. Sullivan's love of mysteries, roses, and parrots as well as living in the historic Gold Rush era town of Placerville California which is known for its multitude of ghostly apparitions and hauntings, led to her writing The *Parrot in the Closet* mystery series, *Murder Picks a Rose* with book two, *The Skeleton That Came Out of the Closet* in the early stages of its first draft. All of Ms. Sullivan's novels are multi-cultural, and gender and racial inclusive, with special inclusions that will be of interest to the LGBTQ community. Her novels are also without profanity, sex, or graphic violence.

Sandra's most recent project is an anthology celebrating the golden years of life. *Tales From the Golden State of Mind,* is a collection of poetry and short stories from some of the nation's top crime and mystery writers including the forward by New York Times bestselling author, Marshall Karp, co-author with James Patterson, Cowboy Poet Patrick Muldoon and other award winning authors.

Visit Sandra's website at sandraksullivan.com

Made in the USA
Monee, IL
27 June 2023

37659589R00166